A WALTZ WITH THE OUTSPOKEN GOVERNESS

Catherine Tinley

MILLS & BOON

First Published in Great Britain 2021
by Mills & Boon, an imprint of HarperCollins*Publishers*
1 London Bridge Street, London, SE1 9GF

© 2020 Catherine Tinley

ISBN: 978-0-263-28371-6

MIX
Paper from
responsible sources
FSC
www.fsc.org   **FSC C007454**

This book is produced from independently certified FSC™ paper
to ensure responsible forest management.
For more information visit www.harpercollins.co.uk/green.

Printed and bound in Spain
by CPI, Barcelona

For Lara, Janice, Harper, Laurie, Jenni,
Elisabeth, Virginia and Nicole.

Thank you for all the love, support and reassurance.

Thanks also to all the dedicated readers
in our Facebook club.

The Unlaced Historical Romance Group
is one of my favourite (virtual) places.

Chapter One

London—January 1810

'Miss Smith! Be seated this instant!'

Mary eyed her irate teacher with frustration. For a moment, she was tempted to be defiant, remain on her feet, give voice to what she truly believed. Instead, with great reluctance, she sank down into her seat, conscious that the shocked eyes of all of the other young ladies were on her.

'Plumpton Academy for Young Ladies is a place of learning, a place where young ladies acquire the skills they will need for marriage.' Miss Plumpton's steely grey eyes bored into Mary's blue ones. 'As I was saying, all women should be useful to their husbands. Useful and gentle, and *agreeable*. It is not seemly for a young lady such as yourself to offer your opinions in such a forceful, mannish way.'

The fire within Mary blazed into life again. 'I only said—'

'You will be silent!' Miss Plumpton's tone brooked no argument. Standing stiffly in a black bombazine gown, her ample bosom heaving with fury, she addressed Mary with barely concealed disdain. 'I heard what you said. You wished to express that a woman should be free to offer her opinions in mixed company? That is truly shocking! I do not wonder your poor father despaired of you and sent you to us that we might try to make a lady of you.'

'Do not speak of my father in such a way! He would *never* despair of me!' Mary bunched her hands into fists.

How dare she presume to speak for Papa, or imagine she knows why he sent me here?

Miss Plumpton's lip curled. 'It is unusual for a young lady of your advanced age to be placed in this academy. Most of the others—' her delicate hand indicated the eleven other young ladies, all of whom were listening with wide eyes and an air of horror '—are sixteen and seventeen years of age. At twenty, Miss Smith, you should have learned long ago how to behave in polite society. Instead, you are an unruly, opinionated hoyden. And—' she finished with an air of triumph '—no man will ever wish to marry you!'

Ignoring the gasps at this pronouncement, Mary simply smiled.

This seemed to anger her teacher even more. 'Are you *laughing* at what I have to say?' There were two spots of colour in her cheeks.

Mary raised an eyebrow. 'Not at all. I was simply reflecting that, as a woman with no plan to ever marry, your announcement comes as something of a relief. I have no desire to ever submit to a man—and nor should any female. Apart from a rare few like my own papa, men seem to wish only to quell us.'

'Miss Smith! I should declare myself to be shocked, except that, truly, I now expect you to say whatever makes you seem contrary.'

'Mistress Mary, quite contrary,' muttered one of the young ladies. A wave of unkind laughter rippled around the room. Mary flushed, unexpectedly pierced by hurt. She raised her chin. Never had she found another young lady she might call friend. She probably never would.

I have always known that Papa is my only friend.

Forcing herself to focus on the matter at hand, she refused to concede defeat. 'My aim is not to be contrary, only truthful. There is no harm in that.'

'Oh, but there is.' Miss Plumpton's temper was still high. 'For an unacceptable truth must always be hidden.'

Mary shook her head. 'I do not hide from honesty. I have been raised to honour truth and to speak plainly. I must continue to do so.'

'Not when your "truth" is hurtful to others. Or when it harms your reputation.'

'Reputation—pah! A notion constructed by society to control us.' Ignoring the gasps from young ladies on either side of her, Mary pressed on. 'Let me apply logic to your statement, Miss Plumpton. You have said that speaking plainly must be abhorred if one's utterances may hurt another. Is that correct?'

Miss Plumpton shrugged. 'Simple politeness dictates it.'

Mary tilted her head to one side, her mind working furiously. 'I do agree with you that we must temper the need for honesty with an understanding that harsh words may land like blows. Yet, there is something here that I do not understand. Why then did you not comment when one of my classmates said "Mistress Mary, quite contrary" just now?'

There was a pause. Miss Plumpton seemed momentarily lost for words. Mary waited, curiosity uppermost in her mind. These were exactly the kinds of debates she had used to enjoy with her papa. Logic. Morality. Human responsibilities and choices.

Everyone was awaiting Miss Plumpton's response. Her eyes flicked left and right, then, finally, inspiration came to her. 'I suggest, Miss Smith, that rather than trying to bring trouble on one of your classmates—not an endearing characteristic, you must agree—instead you should reflect on *why* you are held to be contrary by these other ladies.' Her expression grew victorious. 'You cannot change your behaviour until you understand it!'

'Well, I agree with you there.' Mary's tone was serene. 'Our actions are driven by our beliefs and our humours, and it is only by understanding oneself that one can hope to do better. And I should make clear that I did not wish to bring trouble to anyone. I merely wished to point out the lack of logic in your argument.'

Miss Plumpton's middle-aged face was now an interesting shade of purple. 'You would do well to remember, Miss Smith, that you are a student here and that I am your teacher.'

Mary's brow creased. 'Well, of course I remember that!'

The teacher tutted. 'I mean that you should not argue with your betters!'

'My betters? But no one is constitutionally or naturally "better" than anyone else. As human beings, we are all created by God.'

Miss Plumpton gave a most unladylike snort. 'Of course some are better than others. We are better than the poor creatures who live in the slums and the people who work in service to us, as well as those from other countries. In turn, we submit to our menfolk—husbands, fathers, priests and, ultimately, the King himself.'

Mary shook her head. 'That is evidently not the case. As women, we are more than ornaments or chattels, owned by men. I believe that we are human beings with the ability to think and to feel and to take our part in this society.'

Miss Plumpton's eyes widened. 'Utter nonsense! Who has been feeding your head with such shocking ideas?'

'Strangely, my head seems to fill itself, of its own accord. It is most interesting how it happens.'

'Well, from now on I forbid you to utter such absurdities in this school!'

'Forbid me? But—'

'I shall spend no further time on this foolishness!' Picking up her embroidery, Miss Plumpton held it aloft to show the students. 'Miss Ives, regard how neatly I have set this line of stitches. Now, let me see you do the same.'

Allowing the sewing lesson to waft over her, Mary was struck anew by the feeling of not belonging, of being the only poppy in a field of daisies—or, more accurately, an unwanted weed among the rose bushes. She glanced around the room. Oh, she *looked* similar to the other young ladies, with her dark curls and her blue eyes and her fashionable muslin gown. But she was not the same. Not inside. The sooner she could get through this year of schooling and return to Papa, the better.

Chapter Two

Stiffkey Hall, Norfolk

'And you are telling me that my sister intends to bring *all five* of her offspring to my house?'

Sir Nicholas Denny glared at his unfortunate secretary.

'That's it, sir. She has written to you to say so.' The man waved a paper in front of Nicholas. It contained the distinctive sprawling hand of Susan Denny, now Mrs Fenhurst. The lines were densely written and crossed, in a misguided effort to reduce the cost of postage, and Nicholas knew it would frustrate him to try to read it.

'I do not wish to see the details. That is why I pay you, Bramber,' he replied bluntly. 'Tell me the worst. For how long does she mean to remain?'

Bramber swallowed. 'Er…from early February until—until the beginning of the Season. A little longer than her usual spring visit, sir.'

'You wound me, Bramber! Am I to bear their company for more than two full months?' He shuddered.

His secretary had no response to this.

'Very well, it appears I have no choice. I know my duty to the family. My sister's visit must go ahead and I must endure it, however much it inconveniences me.' Nicholas frowned. 'Let me consider for a moment.' He tapped his long fingers on the mahogany desk. 'Ah! I have it! Bramber, do you remember the old folk tale of the hidden treasure and how the rightful owner forced the thief to reveal its location?'

Bramber looked startled at this seemingly unrelated conversation. 'Er…no, sir.'

'Well,' said Nicholas, 'the man marched the thief to the field where his treasure lay buried and forced the villain to point to the spot where it lay concealed. He then tied his handkerchief to a stick and placed it in the correct place, and made the thief promise not to remove it, on pain of arrest.'

'Yes, sir?' Bramber looked more than a little puzzled.

'The thief outwitted him. When the man came back with a shovel, the field was full of handkerchiefs on sticks! The *particular* handkerchief was lost in the throng, you see.'

'Ah. So, you intend to create a throng, sir?'

Nicholas smiled. 'Indeed I do! Draw me up a

list of friends and neighbours who might provide suitable diversion. Spring may be slow in arriving and people will be glad to come together. With my sister in residence we may invite females, too. Invite the usual families to evening entertainments—you know who I mean, Bramber. The Squire. Sir Harold. The Reeve family. Oh, and that new vicar over in Houghton St Giles. I met him recently and he seems a reasonable fellow.'

'Yes, sir. And—' Bramber's brow was creased '—I shall hire extra staff, as we usually do for your sister's visit. With all of the entertaining, we shall need footmen, maids, grooms… This year, perhaps I should add some nursemaids or a governess, since the children will also be visiting?'

'Capital idea, Bramber! No doubt my sister will bring that poor creature she uses as a governess. Best to have extra assistance with Susan's brood.' He grinned. 'Lord help the poor governess who will be forced to take on my nephews and nieces—as unpromising a clatter of children as I ever saw. Makes me glad that I have maintained my single state.' A sudden thought occurred to him and he eyed his secretary with curiosity. 'You are a young man, Bramber, only a few years younger than I am. Do you also intend to avoid the parson's mousetrap?'

Bramber gave a tight smile. 'I am not averse to

the notion of marriage, but I have not yet—that is to say, I—such things can be difficult...' His voice tailed off.

'Perhaps there will be a lady for you among the visitors, Bramber. Yet more reasons to create a throng this spring!' Nicholas grinned at him. 'Now, my studies are calling me.' He indicated the Greek text at his elbow. 'Go, then! Fill this house with people, so that I may hide from my own relatives!'

Bramber went.

'Miss Plumpton wants to see you, miss. In her parlour.'

Mary's heart gave a skip of alarm at the housemaid's words.

What have I done to earn her displeasure now?

Since the confrontation in the classroom last week, Mary had done her best to appear biddable. She had bitten her lip on numerous occasions and taken part without complaint in nonsense such as dancing lessons, deportment classes and Reading Aloud.

At least the latter had involved books. Actual books. For a school, Mary had discovered, the Plumpton Academy for Young Ladies contained surprisingly few books.

But then, she reflected, as she tripped downstairs towards Miss Plumpton's parlour, *they do not value book-learning here.*

Quite the contrary. Miss Plumpton actively dissuaded the young ladies from appearing in any way learned.

For Mary, having grown up surrounded by her father's books and his wonderful lively mind, this was a world quite unlike any other. But Papa had wanted her to come. So she had decided to stop dissenting with Miss Plumpton and accept this year as part of her journey of learning. It was only a year, after all. She had been here since September, so was now almost one-third done. And Papa was spending a lot of money to send her here. She paused, remembering their arguments over it. She had resisted to the end, but he had been resolute.

'I have been too selfish, keeping you with me,' he had declared. 'Your mama would have wanted you to enjoy your womanhood. Spending all your time with your old papa, discussing books, is not right for a young lady. You need to benefit from some time in London, dancing and laughing, and being young.'

'I miss you, Papa,' Mary whispered now. She had been home for Yuletide just a few weeks ago, but would not now see Papa again until after Lent. They wrote to each other every fortnight and Mary loved receiving his letters. He had now taken up residence in his new parish, in the district of Walsingham in Norfolk, and seemed to have settled well. This Hilary term already seemed endless and Mary was counting the days until Easter.

Reaching the parlour, she knocked, then entered on Miss Plumpton's call.

'Miss Smith.' Miss Plumpton looked even more stern than usual. 'Be seated.'

Mary slid wordlessly into a satin-trimmed chair, then, remembering who she was with, sat up straighter.

Miss Plumpton indicated a letter in front of her. 'I have just received some shocking news.' She looked directly at Mary. 'About your father.'

Mary felt the blood drain from her face. The room seemed suddenly to be spinning. 'What— what news?' She gripped the sides of the chair with both hands, as if doing so would anchor her to reality.

'This *letter*—' Miss Plumpton's tone dripped with disdain '—is from a Miss Sarah Lutton. Is the name familiar to you?'

'What? I—no. I do not recall anyone by that name.'

'The letter is confusingly written, filled with ink stains and on cheap paper, but I have deciphered it. It seems that this Miss Lutton is housekeeper at Houghton St Giles Vicarage, to which your papa has lately been assigned.'

'I see. What of Papa? Is he—is he unwell?' Mary could hear the tremor in her voice.

'Worse!'

Mary gasped. 'No!' *Papa!*

Miss Plumpton tutted. 'You may show me no airs and vapours, Miss Smith. He has not perished.' Her tone was clipped, her expression one of severe disapproval.

'But—you said worse than unwell. I—'

'Honestly, it would be better if he had simply been taken ill. Or even, might I suggest, if he had died. This is much, much worse!'

Mary had quite given up attempting to understand her teacher. Entirely bewildered, she simply begged, 'Please tell me what is in the letter.'

'Your papa—a seemingly respectable vicar— has been taken up by the constables!'

'Impossible!'

'And yet, here is the proof.' Miss Plumpton held up the letter. 'The housekeeper says they took him for nothing less than treason.'

'Treason! *Treason?* Let me see that letter!'

The teacher relinquished the paper and Mary quickly read through it, her mind racing. Papa had, it seemed, been caught in the possession of papers rightly belonging to the War Office and was even now being held in the local Bridewell, pending adjudication from the magistrate. As he was being taken away, he had begged Miss Lutton to write to the school, saying that all would surely be quickly resolved. Due to the magistrate's being only part time, Miss Lutton explained, she understood Mr Smith's case would likely not be heard until the next Quarter-Day session at Easter.

'But Easter is particularly late this year!' declared Mary aloud. 'There has been some muddle here. My papa is no more a spy than you or I!'

Miss Plumpton sniffed. 'As to that, considering your behaviour since you darkened my door, nothing would surprise me. I know your father to be somewhat eccentric. Such people are capable of anything!'

'Fustian! My papa is kind and gentle, and loves only to read his books and serve his parishioners.' Frowning, she muttered, 'I must go to his aid!'

She stood, as if she could instantly transport herself to Papa's side.

'You may go as soon as you wish,' said Miss Plumpton evenly. 'Your fees are paid monthly and I have no hope now of receiving the fee for February.'

Mary gaped at her. 'You surely do not mean to turn me out! You have read this letter, too. It may take until March to get this misunderstanding resolved and my father released. Until then I shall need a home!'

Miss Plumpton's lips tightened. 'Your fees are paid until the end of January, no more.'

'But it is nearly the end of January already.' She added, in a pleading tone. 'Please allow me to visit my papa and find out more details. I must try to secure some assistance for him. When I come back in a week or so, I shall keep to my room. You have no need to teach me.'

Miss Plumpton's expression grew shuttered. 'I do not intend to feed someone or put a roof over their head for nothing! This is a business, not a charity.' Her tone brooked no disagreement. 'Take the letter. You may go.'

'But—'

'Go to your room, Miss Smith!'

Angry fire blazed within Mary. She placed both hands on the desk and eyed her teacher directly. 'I shall not! You call yourself a God-fearing Christian? How can you? How dare you throw me out on the streets with no friends, no safety! Is this the true face of the Plumpton Academy for Young Ladies?'

Miss Plumpton's eyes narrowed. 'Never let it be said that I failed in my Christian duty.' She lifted a pen and wrote something on a piece of paper, holding it out to Mary. 'This is the direction of Mrs Gray's employment agency. There may be some family desperate enough to hire you as a companion—or, more likely, a scullery maid! I for one would not have you above-stairs!'

With a muffled exclamation, Mary took the paper. Whirling around, she left the parlour with neither a polite word of farewell, nor even closing the door behind her.

Such petty revenge was beneath her, she knew, but in this moment, overwhelmed with rage and fear and worry, she could do nothing more. Hurrying to her room, she donned her boots, cloak and bonnet, then, her coin purse concealed beneath her cloak, she hailed a hackney carriage.

Mrs Gray's agency was, it seemed, her only hope.

Chapter Three

Mrs Gray's agency was a popular place. Mary's heart sank when she saw the room filled with men and women, all seeking positions. On arrival she paid the fee and wrote her name in the book as directed. Almost twenty names were above hers in that day's list—including a female who had, it seemed, high levels of education, judging by her flowing handwriting. Glancing around, Mary thought she could work out who she was.

She knew her own talents in cleaning were limited. Her only skills were reading and writing, thinking and debating. Papa had raised her as a scholar, unfit for other work.

Her heart sank as she considered her situation. Miss Plumpton—her nails dug into her palms as she thought of the woman—was determined to throw her out on the first of February. Mary needed to secure a position—any position—in order to have safety, food and warmth while she endeavoured to assist Papa regain his freedom. Hot tears sprang into her eyes as she pictured her gentle, scholarly father captive in some dank, disease-ridden cell. He would not survive long in such conditions.

She had still some coins left, though not many. Papa had entrusted her safety and her security to Miss Plumpton, who had proven herself to be as perfidious as any villain! Mary urgently needed to earn enough money to travel to Papa in Norfolk and return safely.

Time passed slowly. As each name was called, the hopeful employee would disappear into the inner office, re-emerging some time later with expressions ranging from relieved to frustrated. Mary had noticed yet another genteel-looking young lady and engaged in an exchange of polite smiles with her. The first young lady went inside in response to a call for Miss Anne Bolton and, while she was closeted with Mrs Gray, Mary struck up conversation with the other young lady. When Miss Bolton emerged, twenty minutes later, she gave them both a small smile.

Finally, it was time. Mrs Gray called her name.

Heart pounding loudly, Mary stepped into Mrs Gray's inner office.

Afterwards, she could not have said much about the room itself, beyond a vague sense of

comfort and affluence. Mrs Gray herself dominated the room. She took her seat behind the rose-
wood desk, eyeing Mary as she walked towards
her. During their initial polite exchanges, Mary
was conscious of Mrs Gray's piercing gaze—dark
eyes assessing, reading, knowing her.

At any other time, Mary would have wanted
to pursue a deeper acquaintance with Mrs Gray.
She was clearly a woman of substance, a successful businesswoman with an air of confident inde-
pendence that quite fascinated Mary.

This is who I should like to be!

Here was evidence that a woman could have
an independent income and live an independent
life. Mary could only guess at the prejudice Mrs
Gray must have faced not only as a woman, but
as a black woman. She frowned. Had Mrs Gray's
husband ensured her success? She shook her head
slightly. Even silly Miss Plumpton had managed
to set up a school without a husband's patronage.
A man was not necessary for a woman to be truly
independent. Yet perhaps Mr Gray, whoever he
was, had assisted or at least enabled his wife to
achieve this success. Maybe, she reflected, there
were good men who saw their wives as more than
possessions.

Mrs Gray was watching her. She was advanced
in years, calm in demeanour and, it seemed, composed by nature. The woman was *wise*. Mary sim-

ply knew it. Her intelligent gaze pierced through all of Mary's carefully prepared half-truths—and she had not even asked a question yet.

'So, Miss Smith. What position are you seeking?'

'Anything!' The word erupted from Mary. 'I need a position—any position!'

'And why is that?'

Mary hesitated.

'You would do better to be truthful with me, Miss Smith. I have had quite enough of people lying to me today.'

Someone dared lie to her?

With a fleeting salute to the unknown deceiver, Mary sighed. 'Very well. I am a student at the Plumpton Academy for Young Ladies. My father has paid my fees up until the end of January, after which I shall need an income with which to support myself.'

Mrs Gray raised an eyebrow. 'Miss Plumpton plans to abandon you?'

Mary gave a hollow laugh. 'She never liked me—I am altogether too opinionated for her. She has made it clear that I must leave at the end of the month.'

Mrs Gray wrote something on the paper in front of her. 'I see.' She raised her gaze to pin Mary directly. 'What has happened to your father?'

Mary opened her mouth, but the lie about him

being taken ill would not come out. She hesitated, then her shoulders drooped. 'He has been sent to gaol.'

The agency owner's expression remained shuttered. 'Is he, then, a hardened criminal?'

Mary leapt to her feet. 'He is not a criminal at all, and never was!' Mrs Gray studied her for a moment, then made another note on the page before her. 'Be seated, Miss Smith, and tell me the whole.'

Mary did so, stumbling a little over the part where Miss Plumpton had revealed the contents of the housekeeper's letter. Saying it all aloud made Papa's plight seem more real, somehow. 'And so,' she concluded, 'I must go to him and try to assist him, but I shall need to earn money to do so. I—I cannot afford the stage fare to Norfolk.' She lifted her chin. 'I need your help. I assure you I shall work hard at whatever position I get, so that I may see my papa again.'

'What are your talents, Miss Smith? Can you clean, or sew, or teach?'

'I—I do not have any particular talent.' Mary shook her head and suddenly the impossibility of it all washed over her. 'This is hopeless. I apologise for wasting your time.'

Why did I think I could just walk in here and come away with a position, when there are so many other talented people?

She stood, determined not to give way to emotion. 'I shall have to think of another plan.'

'Sit down, Miss Smith.'

Mary sat, barely realising that she, who normally reacted to authority with immediate resistance, had obeyed Mrs Gray's command instantly.

'You understand, I think, the challenge for me in placing someone with no talents, no experience and, I assume, no references.' Mary simply nodded, her throat having swollen with pain, making it impossible to speak.

'Someone,' Mrs Gray continued, 'who has been described as—' she consulted her notes '—opinionated.'

Mary closed her eyes briefly. *This is dreadful.*

'And there is another problem. You had planned, I think, to seek a position here in London, then use your wages to travel to Norfolk by stage?' On Mary's nod, she shook her head. 'Most servants get only two days off per month, and it would take some time to save enough to travel to Norfolk. You could not hope to be there before April or May, I think—too late to be of use to your father. Which part of Norfolk, by the way?'

Mary blinked at this sudden aside. 'Er...my father's vicarage is in Houghton St Giles—near Walsingham. It is north of Fakenham, apparently.'

Mrs Gray's eyes widened briefly. 'Oh, I know *exactly* where Walsingham is. I even know of the village of Houghton St Giles. I found it on a map just yesterday.' Her gaze dropped to her notes and she ran a pensive finger along her chin.

There was a silence. In the background, a delicate clock ticked, and ticked. Mary's attention was given fully over to the ticking of the clock and to Mrs Gray's inscrutable expression. She held her breath.

'Miss Smith.'

'Yes?' All of Mary's hopes rested on this woman and whatever she would say next.

'Are you a good scholar? Can you read? And write?'

'I—yes. I adore books and learning.'

'Hmm…' For the next while, Mrs Gray quizzed her on her knowledge of mathematics, of geography and geometry and astronomy. Of languages, and history, and improving texts. Mary answered the questions as best she could, now feeling on firmer ground. This was her world. The world of knowledge and ideas. The world of book-learning.

'Good.'

Good? Her heart pounding with sudden hope, Mary kept her eyes fixed on Mrs Gray.

'I have recently received a commission to hire temporary servants for a house party in Norfolk. The house is, I believe, less than three miles from the village you mentioned. The post is for more than two months—until Easter, in fact, which probably suits your needs.'

'In Norfolk?' Mary's eyes widened as she realised the possibilities. 'If my work was there then I could visit Papa on my days off!'

'Precisely. Sir Nicholas Denny and his family live in Stiffkey Hall, near your father's village, which is why my instincts are telling me to consider including you in the hirelings as a governess. I have learned to trust my instincts, Miss Smith, and on this occasion I may be prepared to take a chance with you.'

'Oh, thank you, Mrs Gray! Thank you!'

Mrs Gray held up an age-spotted hand. 'You will thank me best by working hard. I understand your need to see your father and to try to assist him, but I am placing my trust in you. Do not compromise the reputation of this agency by being too distracted from your work.' Her dark eyes pinned Mary's. 'I need you to make a contract with me—not a legal contract, as men might make, but a moral contract. A vow, if you will. Placing you with this family when I know little of you is a decided risk for me. That risk becomes more acceptable if I have your word that you will complete the full term of the Denny family's requirements, and that you will fulfil your duties with diligence and care.'

Six or seven weeks with the chance to assist

Papa? Any position would be worth it! With a beaming smile, she nodded. 'I do so vow.'

'They may not welcome a governess who is *opinionated*.'

Mary considered this. *She is right*.

'I can manage to be demure and dull for a few weeks, in order to assist my father.'

'Can you?' The keen look in Mrs Gray's dark brown eyes penetrated Mary's confidence.

Mary lifted her head. 'I have no other option. I must.' She squared her shoulders. 'I vow to do nothing to threaten your reputation, nor that of your agency. I shall endeavour to be the ideal governess—efficient, effective and invisible. And I shall stay the full time if I am needed. Please choose me to be governess for Sir Nicholas Denny.'

Chapter Four

'Sir? May I disturb you?'

Nicholas, who had been quite ready to say that he might not be disturbed, realised who was there and set down his book. 'Bramber! You are returned.' He stretched a hand out and his secretary shook it with a pleased smile. 'Now, have you successfully concluded the business in London?'

'I have.' Bramber beamed with pride. 'Housemaids, a governess, footmen, nursemaids—even an extra groom! All appointed and all arriving in the next two days. The governess, Miss Smith, travelled with me in your coach. I thought it kinder than to force her to take the stage.'

Something in Bramber's tone piqued Nicholas's interest. 'Indeed? Is she, then, an *elderly* lady? I would not wish for someone who cannot keep up with my sister's enterprising offspring.'

'Um…no. She is not at all elderly.' The tips of Bramber's ears had gone an interesting shade of pink. 'In fact, she is—she is a young lady.'

'Is she indeed?' murmured Nicholas, remembering their previous conversation.

I should like to see Bramber settled. Perhaps this governess might suit him.

'And she is genteel? Well-mannered?'

'I found no fault in her,' Bramber replied. 'She is—' He checked himself. 'She behaves as she ought.'

'I am happy to hear it. Oh, and Bramber,' he added casually, 'I shall need you to dine with us during the house parties. And the governess, too, as my sister's eldest two girls are beginning to be exposed to company.'

There! That will throw the two of them together.

'Me, sir? But—'

'But nothing! You are the son of a gentleman, with every right to sit at the table. Besides, I shall need the reassurance of having at least one person present whom I know to be sensible.' Curiosity got the better of him. 'Now, go you and wash the dust of the journey away, and inform the governess, Miss—?'

'Miss Smith.'

'Miss Smith, that I shall receive her.'

'Yes, sir.'

Ten minutes later, a firm tapping on the door informed him that the governess had received his message. 'Enter!'

At first glance, he noticed nothing out of the

ordinary. She was a young lady of average height, neatly dressed in a cambric travelling gown. Her hair was dark and her features regular and pleasing. She was neither tall nor short, fat nor thin, buxom nor waif-like. She was simply a woman. Closing the door, she walked purposefully towards him. She had a no-nonsense air that he supposed would be helpful in her profession, but he quite failed to see why she had caused Bramber to be so incoherent.

He rose. 'Good day, Miss Smith, and welcome to Stiffkey Hall. I am Sir Nicholas Denny.'

She shook his hand briefly. 'Thank you, and thank you for allowing me to travel from London in your coach. It was so much more comfortable than the stage would have been.'

Her eyes are very blue, he noted, his pulse unaccountably skipping a little as their gaze met. *She is actually fairly attractive.*

He made a dismissive gesture. 'Your gratitude is misplaced. That decision was Bramber's.' He nodded. 'My secretary is a sensible fellow.'

'Indeed. He has been most kind to me.' Her tone was entirely neutral. If Bramber's *tendre* was returned, Miss Smith gave no sign of it. Quite right, too. A respectable lady would not allow her emotions to be on display.

'He has doubtless already apprised you of your task between now and Easter. My sister, Mrs Fenhurst, and her children will arrive in two days. Until then, you may take your leisure and acquaint yourself with the house and the area.'

Something briefly flashed in her eyes. 'Thank you, sir. I shall.'

'Good.' He picked up his book. 'We dine at six. Jarvis will show you to the dining room.'

'Yes, sir.' She turned and silently exited the room.

Quite a beauty, he mused, *though—apart from that brief flash—sadly lacking in any liveliness.*

Returning to Virgil, he promptly forgot her.

So far, all is well.

Despite desperately wanting to visit Papa and have him released immediately, Mary knew that she had to proceed carefully. In the days following her visit to Mrs Gray's agency, she had met with unexpected kindness—not once, but twice.

Firstly Jane, one of the housemaids in Miss Plumpton's school, had helped her pack her belongings into her two trunks. Miss Plumpton herself—possibly suffering from twinges of conscience—avoided Mary entirely. Mary did not take part in any further lessons and took her meals in her chamber. She had written to her father's housekeeper to explain that she had secured a position in Sir Nicholas Denny's household and would attempt to visit Miss Lutton as soon as she possibly could.

The second act of kindness—as she had discussed with Sir Nicholas—was Mr Bramber's offer to take Mary up in his employer's travelling coach. Naturally, Mary had accepted the offer with alacrity, reflecting afterwards that it would be the first time she had spent time with any man alone, apart from Papa. As a young lady, she could not have done so before. As a governess, she could do so now.

Despite her misgivings, the journey had been entirely comfortable. Mr Bramber was a pleasant companion and Mary had eventually become quite at ease with him—too much at ease, indeed, for something of her normal vivacity had begun to emerge. Once she realised, she had of course crushed it. She could not allow any deviation from the role of demure governess. Too much was at stake.

She had, however, taken the opportunity during the journey to enquire about both the household and her charges. Sir Nicholas, she had been surprised to hear, was quite a young gentleman, not yet thirty. He was as yet unmarried, so the children she was to teach were not his, but his sister's.

Mr Bramber was reluctant to provide many details about the children, but described some of them as 'high-spirited'. A little daunted by this, Mary reminded herself that the same epithet had frequently been assigned to her. She hoped the Fenhurst children would turn out to be high-spirited in a *good* way.

The chamber Mary had been given was small, but comfortable. The bed seemed firm, there was a table and a cupboard, and the window looked out over the side of the house. All in all, the perfect room for a governess. The house was impressive— substantial and well cared for, it indicated that Sir Nicholas was a man of means. As she changed her dress for dinner, she finally allowed herself to reflect on the man himself.

He was handsome, she allowed, with a square jaw, tousled dark hair and warm brown eyes. He had towered over her when he had stood— impressive shoulders and thighs framing a lean torso, yet her keen eye had noted that he had had a copy of Virgil's *Georgics* at his elbow.

He is no beef-witted Adonis, then.

Their brief meeting had left its mark on her and she was unclear why. Perhaps it was simply that he was her employer and therefore in a position of power over her. She squirmed inwardly at the notion. This was the moment when her fiery notions of freedom met the reality of society as it was.

Even Mrs Gray probably began as an employee, she reminded herself. One had to either inherit money, or earn it. And then a woman must somehow keep it from her menfolk. Mary's salary as a governess was paltry, but with Papa in prison, it was all hers.

Her thoughts returned, as they did constantly, to her father. How was he doing? Was he being badly treated? Was he ill, or in despair? She had made it to Norfolk—a challenge that had seemed impossible when she had first read Miss Lutton's letter. Her next action must be to visit the housekeeper. Thankfully, she would have time tomorrow to do so.

She lifted her chin with determination. *Papa, I am coming for you!*

Just three places had been set for dinner—a sight which made Mary briefly hesitate in the doorway of the dining room. Having hurried downstairs from her second-floor chamber on hearing the dinner gong, Mary had been directed to the correct room by Jarvis, the elderly butler. She thanked him, then hurried inside.

Sir Nicholas and Mr Bramber were just taking their seats and they greeted her easily, Sir Nicholas indicating that the place to his left would be hers. Mr Bramber, opposite, was to his right and he gave her a reassuring smile as the footmen began to serve the food. And what food! Having grown up in various vicarages before living in Miss Plumpton's Academy, Mary had always had enough to eat, but never had she tasted such a range of fine foods. Pies, soups and meats were flanked by side dishes such as omelette, cauliflower and olives. Conscious of not wishing to seem unpolished, Mary accepted a little of everything, enjoying tastes and textures she had never before experienced.

New experiences are always an opportunity to stimulate the mind, she told herself, enjoying the challenge of trying to guess what the grey material was before tasting it, or what the meat was in the delicious pie. Pigeon, she guessed.

Careful not to over-indulge—for her palate was unused to such rich food—she also took the opportunity to study her companions. The men chatted easily together, revealing a familiarity that had much amity in it. Bramber was a little stiffer and more formal than he had been, and respectful towards his employer. Mary had the impression that they did not normally dine together.

She played her part in the conversation when asked, but, unusually for her, tonight she was content to simply observe and listen. This was partly due to her determination to be uncontroversial, but she also recognised a nervousness that kept her tongue silent.

Is it because they are men and I am a woman?

The notion displeased her and she frowned at her plate.

'The blancmange is not to your liking?' Sir Nicholas was all polite concern.

He is too perceptive.

'Oh!' She could not possibly reveal the direction of her thoughts. 'I am admiring the detail on it. The mould must be intricate, indeed, to produce such a perfect shape.' In fact, the blancmange was, rather morbidly, in the shape of a canopic jar, such as the ancient Egyptians had used to store the viscera of their mummified aristocrats.

He gave a wry smile, replying, 'I had not given it much thought. Such domestic details sadly pass me by.'

Domestic details! Without intending to, she had given him the belief she was a domestic creature, inspired by moulds, rather than by the Egyptians. Well, at least it fit with the impression she had wanted to create.

I must remain colourless, hold no opinions on matters of note.

By this time, the conversation had moved on, with Sir Nicholas now quizzing his secretary on how challenging it had been to persuade nearly a dozen London servants to take employment in an obscure country house in the wilds of Norfolk.

Mr Bramber was quick to reassure his employer. 'It was not at all difficult, sir, for according to Mrs Gray, who owns the register office, there are more servants at present than there is work to offer them. Most were entirely grateful for the opportunity.'

Mary dropped her eyes to her blancmange again. This reminder had come at the perfect moment. Sir Nicholas's opinion of her was important, but only insomuch as it allowed her to have a post, with food and shelter, and the opportunity to try to help her father. The fact that he might imagine her to be as bird-witted as the typical young ladies in Miss Plumpton's Academy mattered not a jot. Indeed, her vow to Mrs Gray meant that bird-witted, in this instance, might be preferable to opinionated.

Do not forget, she told herself.

She was here to rescue Papa. Nothing must come in the way of that.

Sir Nicholas left the fields and took the back lane to Houghton village. It was one of his preferred routes for his morning ride, for it allowed him to return to Stiffkey Hall via the riverside fields. Enjoying pastoral views was one of his favourite indulgences. Even in winter, the green fields, babbling river and bare trees held beauty for him. Ahead, he noted a farm cart coming towards him and a person walking along the lane to the village. He slowed, hailing the farmer as he passed, then approached the lone walker from behind. It was a woman, and something about her no-nonsense gait struck a chord of memory.

It is the governess! he realised. He searched his memory for her name. *Something colourless. Smith.*

'Good day, Miss Smith.'

She jumped as if he had shot her. 'Oh! Sir Nicholas! I did not see you there. I did not expect—' Her blue eyes were wide, her expression shocked.

He chuckled. 'My apologies. I did not mean to startle you.'

Her eyes darted left, then right. 'Since I am new to Norfolk, I did not anticipate being hailed by name.'

Strangely, he had the immediate sense that she was not being fully open with him.

Why? What is she hiding?

He frowned.

'I enjoy walking,' she continued, her words a little hurried. 'Jarvis told me that this road leads to some fine villages and that Houghton St Giles is only a little more than two miles from the house. I thought it would make a good walk to go there and back.'

'Indeed,' he responded smoothly. 'You are almost arrived, for the first houses are just around the bend.' He tipped his hat. 'I shall wish you good day.'

'Good day, sir.'

Had he imagined she was relieved to see him go? He trotted on, pondering this. He was unused to such reactions. A genial, easy-tempered man, he was accustomed to cordial, gracious exchanges with those around him. Servants and other employees were generally entirely deferential—something he took for granted without ever having questioned it. It was simply what he was due as head of the Denny family.

Miss Smith's guardedness was unusual.

London people can be unfamiliar with our country ways, he reminded himself. Perhaps it was as uncomplicated as that.

He himself had lived in London as a young man, before his father's death. While enjoying all its delights—and many of its vices—for a few years, he had been content to retire to relative obscurity in Norfolk. Nowadays he travelled to the capital only when necessary and had come to think of it as a colder, harsher place than his beloved Norfolk. His life here was simple and uncomplicated. His servants did as they ought, Bramber looked after estate matters on his behalf, his family visited only occasionally and he had ample time for academic study.

Miss Smith might simply be a London girl, unused to rustic familiarity. He chuckled again at the memory of her deep blue eyes, wide with surprise at being addressed unexpectedly in a quiet country lane.

Her eyes, he reflected, were unusual and quite an attractive feature. Deep blue and framed by dark lashes, they lifted her face from ordinary to interesting and were the focus of her delicate beauty.

Overall, though, recalling the few conversations he had had with her, she had had no opinions to offer and was essentially forgettable. Quite what Bramber—a man whose taste and intelligence he admired—had seen in her, he was yet to discover. She must show herself to be worthy of Bramber, he decided. His secretary should not throw himself away on a tedious girl—even if she did have fine eyes.

Matchmaking was not a habit of his and he knew himself to be too indolent to do much to promote the match. He rarely put himself out for others. However, he was quite prepared to prevent the marriage if needed. As the fourth son of a distant relative from Sussex, Bramber had little in the way of fortune. He had, however, the benefit of a good education and he worked diligently in Nicholas's interests. In other circumstances, they might have been friends.

As it was, that was impossible. Nicholas had been raised with a strong sense of his own worth and, as head of the leading family in the district, he certainly could not encourage over-familiarity with servants—even those from well-bred backgrounds, like Bramber. Oh, he could be kind of course—there was no cost to it—but there was no one here who could match his status and therefore he was divided from those around him.

It meant that, apart from soirées such as the ones he would host during his sister's visit, he spent much of his time in solitude. Any friendships he had made at school and university were now distant memories. He shrugged. While occasionally he bemoaned the lack of company, he enjoyed life in his family home, with his books and his comforts.

His thoughts returned to Miss Smith. Bramber deserved a good woman, but Nicholas suspected that Miss Smith might well turn out to be unsuitable. She was neat, ladylike and pretty, but she had a flaw that Nicholas found fatal.

Quite simply, he found her dull.

Chapter Five

Mary exhaled in relief, watching Sir Nicholas's black horse disappear around the bend.

What if he had seen me entering the vicarage?

As far as they all knew, she had no connections in Norfolk—never mind a man taken up for treason! Her employment might be short-lived, indeed, should the truth be discovered. She had even suggested using a false name for her employment, but Mrs Gray would have none of it. 'What you do on your days off is none of my business,' she had said firmly, 'but I shall not knowingly lie to Sir Nicholas Denny.'

Knowing that Papa had been in residence in the Houghton St Giles vicarage for only a short time before his arrest, Mary was relying on his name and background not being widely known. Besides, Smith was a common enough name. There was no reason to connect the vicar now being held in

Walsingham gaol with a new governess lately arrived from London.

The vicarage, a pretty house with mullioned windows and a low roof, was in the grounds of St Giles's Church. Mary knocked at the front door, glancing furtively around as she waited for a response. Thankfully, no one was about and, a moment later, her father's housekeeper opened the door. As soon as she had made herself known, Miss Lutton, with an exclamation, ushered her inside.

'Oh, my dear Miss Smith, I am so relieved you are arrived!' She led Mary into a pleasant parlour. Winter sunshine arrowed its way through the window, pointing at the desk in the corner. With a pang, Mary recognised some of Papa's books piled there. After an initial exchange, consisting mostly of Miss Lutton expressing how shocked she had been at Mr Smith's arrest, she disappeared to make tea, leaving Mary alone in the parlour.

Unable to resist, Mary walked to the desk. There was Papa's much-loved copy of Dean Swift's sermon *On Doing Good*, along with his classical texts—many in the original Greek or Latin. Searching through them, Mary found what she had been looking for: Virgil's *Georgics*. Until she had seen Sir Nicholas's copy, the only version she had ever seen or touched had belonged to Papa.

'Oh, Papa,' she murmured, tears stinging her eyes. 'What will become of you? And what am I to do to rescue you?'

She had, she realised, been so focused on reaching Norfolk, and seeing Miss Lutton, that she had been unable to think beyond this moment. Yet now, in the vicarage, and having met Miss Lutton, she felt dejected and forlorn, unable to see how two women—and lowly women at that—could possibly put things right.

'Here you are, Miss Smith.' Miss Lutton was back, her tray laden with tea, cakes and even an orange. She was an attractive middle-aged woman, with twinkling blue eyes and a warm smile. 'I shall serve you, and then we shall think what must be done.'

An hour later, Mary left the house, no more confident, but at least a little better informed. Miss Lutton herself had opened the door to the officers, who had spent only a short time in the parlour before taking the vicar away. 'They took away a folder of papers that your father was protesting about, saying they were not his and he had not ordered them, but the Runners would not listen.' Miss Lutton shook her head sadly. 'Anyone can see that your papa is no villain, no traitor. As kindly a gentleman as I ever met!' she declared, with a decided tear in her eye.

'But why did they come here in the first place? And how did they know there would be papers here?'

Miss Lutton simply shrugged, having no answer to these or other questions.

Hearing that Miss Smith had only one more day of freedom until her charges arrived, the housekeeper gave detailed directions to Walsingham and urged Mary to try to visit her papa in the gaol on the morrow. 'You will need to be off bright and early, mind. They do not always allow visitors into the Bridewell, or you may have to await their pleasure.'

Mary promised to do her best and left the vicarage with more determination than confidence. As she trudged along the lanes back towards Stiffkey Hall, her mind was beset with worry. Papa languished in gaol, accused of treason, and she—a powerless maid employed as a governess—was expected to save him. It was impossible! It could not be done.

Yet, as she marched towards her current abode, with the weak warmth of a winter sun on her face, she could not help but feel a small sliver of hope. She was here in Norfolk, after all, and tomorrow she would see him. She must be resolute, and believe that good would somehow prevail.

Stiffkey Hall was located in the parish of Little Snoring, adjacent to Great Snoring, Houghton St

Giles and the Barshams. Walsingham itself was only a matter of two miles away—an easy walk for a country-bred girl like Mary. Yesterday, she had turned west at the edge of Great Snoring, taking the Barsham road to Papa's parish. Today, she continued straight on, towards the village where Papa was now incarcerated.

The road was narrow and in poor condition at times, the mud made worse by last night's rain. The way was flanked by unruly hedgerows where, Mary reminded herself, birds would soon begin to nest.

There is always hope of another spring.

In the darkest of winters, the world continued to turn and new life to emerge. It was almost miraculous that she was in Norfolk at all. Somehow, she would find a way to help her father. She *must*.

Her absence this morning might well be remarked upon, particularly as she had been gone from the house for so long yesterday. She had made a point of expressing a love of brisk walking during dinner last night. Sir Nicholas and Mr Bramber had listened with polite disinterest.

Oh, dear! she had thought. *I must appear quite eccentric!*

Still, it did not matter what opinion Sir Nicholas or anyone else held. Her quest was more important. With Sir Nicholas's sister due to arrive before nightfall, Mary might have little time after today with which to pursue Papa's comfort and safety.

Eventually, Walsingham came into view. It was a pretty village, with neat, half-timbered buildings, an old abbey and some interesting shops. At any other time, Mary might have enjoyed exploring its architecture and history. Today, however, she was in no mood to play the visitor, instead making directly for the gaol—Walsingham Bridewell.

The building looked relatively new, which was something of a relief. As a vicar's daughter, she had on occasion assisted him in his pastoral duties to care for the poor, the old, the hungry and the prisoners, and some of the older prisons had filled her with horror. This one was of brick, surrounded by high cobblestone walls.

Papa is in there!

Mary's stomach turned just looking at it. Gathering her courage, she walked around it until she found the way in.

'Good day, sir,' she offered, with a confidence she did not feel.

The guard behind the large wooden desk looked up. He was large and sullen, and unhealthy-looking.

'I am here to visit the prisoners.' Mary indicated the basket on her arm. Many was the time she had performed this same ritual, in many gaols. Just never before for Papa.

'And you are?'

'My name is Miss Stanton,' she lied, giving Mama's maiden name. Hopefully he would instantly forget it. 'I am working at Stiffkey Hall and have walked here in order to give succour to the unfortunate prisoners.'

'Unfortunate?' The man raised an eyebrow. 'They are here because of their own misdeeds and as such are to be punished.'

'Of course! And yet, the Bridewell is known as a house of correction, is it not? The Bible tells us to *aid* the sick, the hungry and the prisoner.'

She quoted Matthew's gospel at him, causing his eyes to narrow in suspicion. 'Are you a Dissenter?'

She laughed. 'Not at all! Merely doing good works as I was raised to do.'

Grumbling, he lurched to his feet. 'I shall have to search your basket.'

'Of course!' She held it out, remaining motionless as he rummaged through the napkin containing various ends of food she had purloined from the scraps at the breakfast table. He ignored the New Testament at the bottom of the basket.

Taking a piece of precious meat for himself, then stuffing a large piece of cheese into his pocket, the guard returned the basket to her. 'We have but four prisoners at present, all waiting for the next Quarter-Day sessions.'

'What will become of them?'

He shrugged. 'Sir Harold Gurney will decide their fate just before Easter.'

She nodded briskly. 'Are there any that might seek to do me harm?' Papa had never allowed her to visit violent prisoners.

He shook his head, absently scratching his groin. 'Nah. A poacher, a pair of burglars and a traitor.'

She feigned concern. 'A traitor, really? Is he or she a desperate character, then? Must I be on my guard?'

He laughed. 'The traitor is the easiest of all of them. Until the Bow Street Runners caught him, he was a vicar, no less!'

'A vicar? Truly?'

He nodded vigorously, seemingly pleased by her incredulity. 'So I was informed. Assisting enemies of the Crown at the very least. Treason at worst.'

She shook her head sadly. 'What a world we live in, that a man of the cloth should stoop so low.'

'You are right there.' He reached behind for a bunch of keys hanging on a nail. 'Follow me.'

He took her through two locked doors, securing each behind them as they passed through. Finally, they reached the cell corridor. Identical iron doors marched off at regular intervals to their right. Mary, scanning quickly, counted eight cells.

'This one is the Dark Cell, where I put them

if they misbehave.' He pointed to the first door. 'Our current bunch of ne'er-do-wells are in these four.' He indicated the cells furthest from the way out. 'I've put the traitor at the end and placed the poacher between the burglars.'

'Very well. I shall begin here.' She pointed to the nearest cell.

Wordlessly, the guard unlocked the door. 'Good day,' she announced cheerily. 'I am Miss Stanton, come to visit you today.'

The prisoner, a thin man of indeterminate years, eyed her sourly. 'What's in the basket?'

'Some food,' she replied, 'and a Bible that I may read to you some passages to ease your spirit.'

'I'll take the food,' he muttered, 'but you may keep your Bible reading.'

She nodded and passed him a share of the food. He grabbed it eagerly, stuffing it into his mouth as though he were afraid she would change her mind and take it back. 'Any more?'

'I'm afraid not. I shall try to return another day, though.'

She stepped back to the corridor and the guard locked the door. The ritual was repeated twice more, save that the third prisoner, who told her that he was the son of the man in the first cell, asked her to read something from the Bible for him. She did so, choosing passages that she hoped offered him some ease.

She spoke loudly, hoping that Papa might hear and recognise her voice. She needed him to be cautious when he first saw her, so that he would not reveal her true identity. If the guard realised she was the traitor's daughter, he might not allow her to see Papa at all.

Finally, it was time. The guard turned the key and opened the door to Papa's cell.

Pale winter light from the small window provided some illumination, yet at first Mary thought the cell was empty. The other prisoners, on hearing the key in the lock, had jumped up and were standing in the centre of the room when the guard opened the door. Papa had not.

Her eyes eventually picked him out, lying on the straw-strewn wooden platform that served as a bed. Apart from the foul bucket in the corner and the long iron chains fixing Papa to the wall, the cell was empty. The walls were pale, plastered brick and the floor littered with dirty straw.

As the door opened, Papa stirred, turning his head to face her. She knew him, of course, though shock rippled through her on seeing the change in him. His beard was long and unkempt, his cheekbones hollowed with hunger and the expression in his gaze one of utter hopelessness.

'Mary? Is that you, child?' He looked dazed, his speech slurred and unclear.

'My name is Miss Stanton,' she replied briskly, aware that her hands were gripping the basket so tightly that the knuckles were showing white. The guard remained behind her, listening to every word. 'I have come to visit all of the prisoners in this hopeless place.'

Papa raised himself up to a half-upright position, then swung his legs to the floor. When he looked at her again, his expression was guarded. 'I see. "Rejoicing in hope; patient in tribulation",' he quoted slowly.

'The letter to the Romans,' she responded. 'I am told you are a clergyman.'

'I was, at least. I do not know any more who or what I am.'

He is so thin!

She could see his breastbone and the top of his ribs, where the grubby shirt gave way to the wrinkled paleness of his neck and chest. 'I have brought some food.' She offered him some bread and their fingers touched briefly as he took it.

Papa!

With some effort, she managed to conceal the anguish piercing through her. 'I have also brought a Bible, in case you might welcome my reading it to you.'

'Thank you, child. I should welcome it. I never

thought to hear again—' He broke off, then continued in a different tone. 'I was used to being the one visiting those in prison. These tribulations have been sent to me for a reason. Perhaps I was too arrogant, too sure of my place. The Widow's Mite is worth more than the rich man's beneficence.'

She could not argue, though it pained her to see him so broken, in spirit as in body. So she did the only thing she could; she read to him—carefully selected passages she had prepared to offer hope, and comfort.

The guard had now been yawning in the corridor for quite ten minutes, so Mary was unsurprised when he called a halt to her visit. 'Enough!'

'Will you—can you return?' Papa's eyes were a mix of concern, fear and desperate hope.

'I shall try my best. What is your name?'

'Mr Smith.'

She gripped his hand briefly, eyes meeting eyes. 'I am working locally as a governess and I do not know when I shall have a day off. But I promise to try.'

He nodded, his throat working with emotion. Turning, she stepped outside the cell, wincing as she heard the clang of it closing behind her.

By the time they had returned to the guardroom she had her emotions under some control. It would, however, be reasonable for a gently-bred young lady to feel compassion for the prisoners and so she dared voice some of it to the guard. 'It always upsets me,' she offered, 'no matter how many prisoners I visit. Today, the young burglar and the old clergyman have been particularly affecting.'

He eyed her with incomprehension. 'Quite so, miss.'

'Since they will be here without even the benefit of a hearing for the next two months, I shall endeavour to visit as much as I may—which might not,' she acknowledged, 'be very often.' She handed him a precious coin. 'Thank you for allowing me to spend time with these unfortunate prisoners.'

With a wide, gap-toothed smile, the guard concealed the coin somewhere about his person. 'You will be most welcome, Miss. My name is Gedge, by the way.'

'Thank you, Mr Gedge. You have been most accommodating and so I shall inform the magistrate if I ever should meet him.'

With this final act, she hefted her basket and left the gaol.

Chapter Six

'A governess? But I already have a governess!'

There was a brief silence. Sir Nicholas had just introduced Mary to his sister, who had responded with something like shock. Mary, expecting a polite exchange, was entirely bewildered. She stood immobile by the salon fireplace, transfixed by the exchange between brother and sister.

Sir Nicholas seemed unperturbed. 'And a most estimable creature she is! Miss Cushion has been a great support to you, I know.'

Mrs Fenhurst's face was flushed with anger. 'Her name is *Cushing*, not Cushion! And she is going to be extremely displeased when she hears that you have appointed a second governess. As am I! You had no right to do it, Nicky. No right at all!'

'I meant only to assist you, my dear Susan,' he responded smoothly. 'Since you were determined to bring all your delightful offspring with you—'

'You make it sound as though I had a hundred children!'

'It does sometimes seem like it,' he murmured, then, in a louder tone, added, 'Besides, I shall need you to act as hostess and I cannot have you too distracted.'

This seemed to appease his sister momentarily. 'Oh, so you mean to entertain? Well...' she preened a little '...I dare say you shall need me in that case. I have developed quite the reputation for entertaining at home, you know. Although obviously my house is nothing like as extravagant as Stiffkey Hall. I assume soirées? Musicales? Perhaps some dancing? It would be good for Amabel and Beatrice to try their steps here before I take them to London after Easter. I mean to launch Amabel this year, you know.'

Sir Nicholas was listening with all the appearance of interest. 'Fascinating!'

Mary could not help but be a little diverted. Despite the fact that her very future—and her ability to assist Papa—depended upon Sir Nicholas securing Mrs Fenhurst's approval, it was clear that Sir Nicholas seemed confident he could manage his sister. The notion intrigued her.

'So it is all agreed then? Capital!' He rubbed his hands together, and turned to Mary. 'Miss Smith,' he said sternly. 'I must ask you to follow Mrs Fenhurst's directions to the letter. You have been employed as a governess, but if Miss Cushion—'

'Cushing!'

'If Miss *Cushing* can spare you, then I expect you to assist my sister in organising and hosting the various parties and entertainments.'

'Of course, sir.' Mary turned to Mrs Fenhurst. 'I shall be happy to assist in whatever way I can.'

'Hmmm. I suppose I shall find ways to make use of you,' Mrs Fenhurst replied flatly. Sir Nicholas closed his eyes briefly.

'Ah!' Mrs Fenhurst smiled. The dining room door had opened to admit an elderly lady accompanying two girls. 'Girls, come and make your curtsies to your uncle Nicky! Thank you, Cushing.'

Mary eyed them with interest. Both were dark-haired and dark-eyed, like their mother and their uncle. The older, a tall girl of about sixteen, was wearing an entirely unsuitable gown in a strange shade of puce, over-trimmed with heavy Spanish lace. 'Good evening, Uncle.' She fluttered her eyelashes at him and gave a false-looking smile. 'I am delighted to see you again.'

Sir Nicholas did not, it seemed, share the delight. Raising a quizzing-glass, he addressed his sister. 'What is that get-up the girl is wearing, Susan? She cannot go out in society looking like a matron, when she is only sixteen.'

'I shall be seventeen next month. And this

colour is all the crack!' the young lady declared defiantly.

'Amabel! Do not use such coarse language! I have told you a hundred times!' Mrs Fenhurst uttered the reproach in a mechanical way. 'And, Nicky, what would you know of female fashions? Although—' she cast a dubious eye on her daughter's gown. 'Is that your aunt's old dress that you were reworking? I am not sure it is entirely suitable.'

Miss Cushing, a thin, elderly lady in a dark grey gown, was wringing her hands in distress. 'Oh, Mrs Fenhurst, I do apologise. She did insist on wearing it, even though I was not sure it was an appropriate gown. I knew we should not have brought it!' She lifted a lace handkerchief and dabbed the corner of her eye.

'Oh, fie, Cushing, it is delightful! Why, I spent hours adding the lace—and I copied it from something I saw in *La Belle Assemblée*, so of course it is right!' Amabel, Mary noted, looked a little uncertain, despite the defiance in her tone. Meanwhile the younger girl—Mary had forgotten her name—was watching the exchange with all the appearance of terror.

Sir Nicholas snorted. 'Just because you saw it on a fashion plate does not mean it is suitable for a girl your age. Why, people will think your mother cannot afford to clothe you in printed muslins and colours suitable for a girl making her come-out! You would not want that, now would you, Amabel?'

His niece, much struck, uttered a surprised, 'No! Of course not!'

He nodded. 'Tonight, we have no visitors, so you may wear it with impunity. But you will need to be more appropriately clothed if I am to allow you to appear at the entertainments that I am planning.'

'Yes, Uncle,' Amabel replied demurely, her eyes lighting up. She thought for a moment. 'Mama, I shall need new dresses!'

Mrs Fenhurst's expression turned a little sly. 'Well, I do not know how I am to afford to buy them for you.' She shrugged her shoulders. 'I thought we were coming to Norfolk for a quiet sojourn. I had no idea there would be so much entertaining. Besides, I cannot be taking you to dressmakers and the like, as I shall be quite exhausted from acting as hostess for my brother.' She sighed. 'But then, I am happy to sacrifice myself, for I understand the importance of family.'

Sir Nicholas, listening to this exchange with a cynical expression, nodded. 'Very well, Susan. I shall pay for a couple of dresses for the girls— and for yourself, of course. I would not like it to be believed that I failed to understand the importance of family.'

Mrs Fenhurst was all delighted surprise. 'Why,

Nicky, how generous of you! Girls, do thank your uncle!'

They did so, Amabel with clear glee and her sister with some awkwardness.

She has not yet found her voice.

Recalling herself at fifteen, Mary understood a little of what the younger girl might be feeling. Thankfully, Mary had had Papa to believe in her and help her believe that she herself was capable and strong.

No. She must not think of Papa. She must remain strong while in company.

'—is Miss Smith.' With a start, Mary realised that Sir Nicholas was introducing her to his nieces and their governess. She curtsied, murmuring appropriate delight at making their acquaintance.

He continued, giving Mary their names. She noted that the younger girl was called Beatrice and that, this time, Sir Nicholas pronounced Miss Cushing's name correctly. Had he said 'Cushion' earlier just to vex his sister?

She eyed Sir Nicholas with a hint of interest, wondering for the first time what sort of man he was. A handsome face, strong frame and air of assurance had been her first impression. His choice of reading material had impressed her. Now, in the exchanges with his sister, he had revealed something more of himself. He was clever, clearly and seemed rather intolerant of stupidity and vulgarity—without being openly disdainful.

Mary sighed inwardly. She recognised the intolerance in Sir Nicholas because it was something she had long battled with in herself. Papa had instilled in her the importance of kindness, but she had felt unexpected sympathy with Sir Nicholas just now.

'Miss Smith will assist your mama—and you, Miss Cushing—in whatever way you need her,' Sir Nicholas continued smoothly. The word 'governess' was not uttered. 'I understand entirely that I am burdening you, Sister, with all of the responsibilities of acting as hostess. Miss Smith, you must ease those burdens.'

'I shall endeavour to do so, sir.' Mary's tone was even, but inside she was beginning to feel flutters of nervousness at the task before her.

Did he sense it? He gave her a level gaze, then nodded. 'I have every faith in you.'

Her throat tightened. This unexpected kindness threatened to sunder her fragile control. Thankfully, the salon door opened again, this time to admit Bramber. In the ensuing flurry of greetings, Mary regained her equanimity.

Soon afterwards the gong sounded for dinner, and they all walked through to the dining room. Sir Nicholas, naturally, led the way, his sister by his side. Her daughters followed, with Miss Cushing in train. That left Mary and Bramber to take up the rear.

'I trust you have had a good day, Miss Smith?' he enquired. 'I understand you went walking again.'

He is simply being polite, she told herself uneasily.

'I did,' she confirmed. 'This time I went as far as Walsingham.' She was determined to keep to the truth as much as possible. Thankfully, he did not ask what she did there, instead asking only for her opinion of the local landscape. She praised it, which seemed to please him.

They took their seats. Sir Nicholas was directly to Mary's right, with his sister opposite at the foot of the table. Amabel and Bramber, with Miss Cushing, were on one side, while Mary had Beatrice to her left, which pleased her. She was determined to do her best for Mrs Gray, who had given her this opportunity. That meant taking her duties as governess seriously.

Already she had taken the opportunity to visit Papa—something she could not have done without this position. Now she must work to be the best governess and companion that she could.

Dinner was served and Mrs Fenhurst struck up a conversation with Bramber and Miss Cushing, who were on her left-hand side. That left Sir Nicholas conversing with his older niece, while Mary took the opportunity to gently engage with Beatrice. They exchanged simple details about themselves—the Fenhursts lived in Cambridgeshire and often visited their uncle Nicholas at this time of year. The younger children did not normally come, too, usually only accompanying their mama when the whole family made a shorter visit each autumn. Mary explained that she had been in school in London until recently and that this was her first position.

'So I am a little anxious,' she confessed. 'I do hope you can help me understand what is required of me.'

Beatrice looked a little surprised. 'Me? Oh, but I do not know anything about—about *anything*!' she declared.

'Oh, but you do!' Mary countered. 'You know about your family, and I dare say you know something about Stiffkey Hall. I declare I get lost every time I come downstairs.'

This earned a shy smile. 'Well, I have been coming here since I was but a baby, so naturally it seems easy to me. Although,' she confessed, 'this is my first time not sleeping in the nursery. Amabel and I are sharing a bedroom on the second floor and it seems very grand!'

'I, too, am on the second floor.' Mary smiled. 'Tell me, will Miss Cushing continue your lessons while you are here?'

Beatrice sighed. 'Yes.' Seeing Mary's sympathetic gaze, she continued, 'Oh, please do not think I have been disrespectful to Miss Cushing. It is just—' She bit her lip.

'Yes? Do you dislike book-learning?' Most of the young ladies in Miss Plumpton's Academy had disliked book-learning.

'Oh, no—quite the contrary! But Miss Cushing does not seem able to help me with my Greek and Latin any more. And…but she is all that is estimable, of course.'

'Of course!' Mary agreed, but inside, a shard of hope appeared. Might Miss Beatrice be a promising student? 'I myself have studied Greek and Latin texts to quite a high level. Perhaps we could read something together?'

'Truly?' Beatrice's eyes were shining. 'I should like that very much,' she added, in laborious Latin.

'Well done!' Mary applauded her, adding a further couple of sentences in Latin. Beatrice understood them, responded appropriately and laughed at her own success.

At just that moment, Mrs Fenhurst turned to look at her daughter. 'Beatrice!' she adjured. 'Please maintain some decorum at the dinner table!' Her glare encompassed both Beatrice and Mary, who shifted uncomfortably. Propriety, manners and decorum were important, she knew, but she herself had often been chastised by Miss Plumpton for becoming too animated.

'I am sorry, Mama.' Beatrice, cowed, stared at her plate and would talk no more.

Mary set down her fork and reached for her wine glass. Her hand had tightened into a claw, so tightly she had been gripping the fork.

Poor Beatrice reminds me of myself at the Academy—except I had more spirit!

Amabel was now conversing with Bramber, leaving Sir Nicholas free, so it was unsurprising when he addressed Mary.

'Miss Smith,' he said, his voice low enough that only the two of them could hear, 'I could not help but notice how you brought Miss Beatrice out of her usual quiet timidity. Why, for a moment there she looked quite animated. I had not known that she was even capable of smiling!'

Was he displeased? He did not look it, so, bravely, she informed him about Miss Beatrice's love of Greek and Latin.

'Capital!' he declared. 'But—forgive me—how were you able to discover this scholarliness? I declare the girl barely looks me in the eye without quaking!'

Mary took another sip of wine, sending him a sideways glance that had a hint of archness in it. 'Are you roasting me, sir, or do you genuinely not know why she seems uncomfortable?'

'Enlighten me.' His expression was hooded.

'Well, you are—' She thought for a moment.

'You are quite an *imposing* person. Particularly to a girl of tender years.'

'Imposing?' His brow was furrowed. 'In what way?'

'Well, you are physically very—er—large, your voice is often quite loud and you are master of this house.'

He looked at her blankly. 'Are you accusing me simply of being a *man*, Miss Smith? For as far as I can discern, each of your complaints relates simply to the fact that I am male.'

She frowned. 'Not exactly.' Glancing across the table, inspiration came to her. 'Mr Bramber is also a man, yet he is different. He is less...' Her voice tailed away as she struggled to express herself without causing offence. *Arrogant* was the word on the tip of her tongue—but she must not say it. 'Less intimidating.'

For a moment she thought she had gone too far. Then, to her relief, he laughed. 'I never knew myself to be intimidating before. So that is why Miss Beatrice cannot speak to me without trembling?'

'I believe so, yes.'

'Yet you are not intimidated.' He spoke softly and something about his tone sent an unexpected shiver through her. It was unlike anything she had ever felt before.

Ignoring it, she twinkled at him. 'I believe I am made of sterner stuff, sir. We all of us are different.' She swept a hand around the table. 'You are different to Mr Bramber. Beatrice is different to Amabel.'

He was eyeing her closely. 'And you, Miss Smith, are clearly different to—to my assumptions.' He gave a wry smile. 'I believe I begin to understand why Bramber's ears were pink.'

'Bramber's ears?' Had she heard him correctly? 'What have Mr Bramber's ears to do with anything?'

He waved this away. 'What I should like to know, Miss Smith, is how you plan to usurp Miss Cushion in order to teach my niece advanced Latin?' He grinned.

'Cushing!' she retorted without thinking, then clapped a hand over her mouth.

His grin widened in surprised appreciation. 'Cushing,' he echoed. 'Now, do not deny it!' he chided. 'I can read this in you, I believe.'

She gave a rueful smile. 'I shall contrive it somehow.'

'Somehow, I do not doubt it, Miss Smith.' He raised his glass. 'This has been a most enlightening conversation!'

Belatedly, Mary realised that Mrs Fenhurst was staring at them. Something about her narrow-eyed gaze made Mary feel rather uncomfortable. Deciding she had had quite enough wine, she pushed her glass away and applied herself to her dinner.

Chapter Seven

Three days, three nights. Such a short time she had been here. Yet already, Stiffkey Hall was beginning to feel familiar, safe, homelike. As Mary entered her bedroom, she felt a wave of gratitude wash over her. At least she was in Norfolk. She had food, a place to live, the chance to see and possibly assist Papa, and now, a sense of purpose about her position here.

Miss Beatrice and she had continued their conversation in the salon, after the ladies had withdrawn from the dining room, and Mary had promised to find a way to assist the girl with her studies. Beatrice was naturally anxious about what her mama might say and whether Miss Cushing would like it, so Mary had promised to think about how best to approach the situation.

As she climbed into her comfortable bed, Mary's thoughts turned again to her papa and she finally allowed herself to feel the distress she had been denying ever since she had returned to the house after visiting him earlier. To see him had been terrible and wonderful at once.

It is February now, she reminded herself.

Somehow, she had to ensure that Papa remained alive and sound of mind until his appearance before the magistrate in April.

Right now, that seemed unlikely. Papa's frailty, dazed expression and dishevelled appearance had shaken her to the core. She cried a little, curled up on her side in the bed, then, with her usual sense of practicality, decided she would simply divert all of her concern into planning how best to help him.

As sleepiness overcame her, her rational mind began sending confused, half-awake thoughts featuring stern magistrates speaking Latin, Miss Cushing dabbing her eyes with a black handkerchief and Sir Nicholas telling her she was not to be intimidated. Holding to this last thought, she allowed herself to drift into sleep.

'What the deuce is this infernal racket?' Sir Nicholas's voice boomed through the house, causing Mary to suddenly stop on her way down the stairs for breakfast. Looking over the banister, she saw him emerge from his library, standing in the hallway with legs apart and a frown marring his handsome features. Mary's heart skipped a beat on seeing him. He was, she had already decided, the sort of person who was impossible to ignore.

It was not simply that he was physically imposing. He was *altogether* imposing. When he walked into the room the attention shifted. It was nothing to do with his status or his title, Mary had reasoned. It was to do with him. Had he been a blacksmith or a farmer, a duke or a bishop, it would have made no difference. He just had an indefinable presence that Mary had never encountered before.

Just now, his gaze was fixed unerringly on someone or something near the front door. Mary craned round to see. There, looking decidedly chagrined, were two young boys—one a little taller than the other. They were dressed in identical nankeens, with grey waistcoats and shirts already grubby at the collar. More Fenhurst children, then.

As Mary watched, the two London nursemaids appeared below in a flutter of aprons and apologies. The younger children had been quietly eating breakfast in the kitchen not more than a moment ago, they explained. Somehow, it seemed, the boys had slipped their leashes and come to the hallway to wreak some sort of havoc.

'If you are not capable of fulfilling your duties, then you should not be here!' bit out Sir Nicholas.

A cold shiver went down Mary's spine. She could only imagine how the nursemaids must be feeling.

And they might not even care about staying here!

She, who truly needed to be here, must be careful not to vex Sir Nicholas. The problem was that no one had told her exactly what her duties were.

Sir Nicholas glared at the nursemaids for another long moment, then turned his attention back to the two boys. 'Who broke the vase?'

Oh, dear! Is that what happened?

Quietly, Mary descended two more stairs and craned over the banister again. Sure enough, the black-and-white-tiled floor was strewn with china shards. There was a brief pause, then the taller boy squared his shoulders and spoke up.

'It was my fault, sir. I was chasing my brother and I should not have done it.'

The younger boy looked up at his uncle, a clear appeal in his expression. 'It was me what done it, though.'

Faced with two such remorseful faces, Sir Nicholas stood still for a moment. Mary was most interested to see what he would do.

'Very well,' he said gruffly. 'You have admitted your wrongdoing. Now, apologise and fetch a brush to sweep it up. Do not allow the servants to do it, mind!'

The boys made their apologies, faithfully

promised to brush away every shard, then the taller one added hopefully, 'Must we have lessons while we are here, Uncle?'

Sir Nicholas, it seemed, was well aware of the danger of undermining his sister. 'You must do as your mother wishes,' he pronounced, turning on his heel and seeking the sanctuary of his library.

Well! Mary released a breath before continuing down the sweeping staircase. She herself had no uncles or aunts, or nieces and nephews. There was only herself and Papa. To suddenly find herself in the company of a brother and sister, and the sister's numerous children, was both interesting and challenging at once.

I believe I am envious!

The Fenhurst boys were clearly in awe of their large, loud uncle, yet there was also some bond between them that had been clear to Mary. Despite his frustration, Sir Nicholas had handled the boys fairly well in the end. He had struck exactly the right note with them and had gone up in Mary's estimation. Quietly, she continued down the stairs towards the breakfast room, mulling it over in her mind.

Breakfast was an informal affair. When Mary entered the breakfast room, only Beatrice and Amabel were present. Helpfully, this gave her the chance to engage both of them in light conversation. Beatrice in particular seemed to have taken to her and smiled shyly as they chatted about their plans for the day.

I do like Beatrice!

A little later Sir Nicholas arrived, and Beatrice immediately and predictably went silent.

Sir Nicholas gave no sign of his earlier frustration with the boys and, indeed, seemed rather affable as he helped himself to tea, beef, eggs and bread. He talked of the weather and asked the girls what their plans were for the day.

Amabel answered for both of them. 'We are to spend some time at our lessons, then Mama has promised to look over some fashion plates with me.'

'Ah yes, the new dresses. They must be suitable, mind!'

'Of course. I was thinking pale pink silk for my evening gown—perhaps with roses and lace?'

Sir Nicholas had clearly already lost interest in discussions about gowns. 'As long as you do not overdo the trimmings,' he said dismissively, then turned to Beatrice. 'What of you, Beatrice? Do you also enjoy fashion?'

'Oh, no! That is to say, of course I—but I do not—' Beatrice lost herself in half-sentences and confusion.

'She would rather *read*,' said Amabel scathingly. Beatrice gave her a cross look.

'Well, I declare I am happy to hear it!' Sir Nicholas drained his tea and stood up. 'Miss Smith, I suggest you discover what Miss Beatrice would like to read. Feel free to borrow whatever books you need from my library.'

Mary, having caught only the briefest of glimpses of Sir Nicholas's well-stocked shelves during their first introduction, was thrilled at the thought. 'I shall indeed. Thank you!' His eyes met hers briefly, and she was surprised to feel a frisson of—*something* between them, like the shock one sometimes felt when brushing one's hair. This though, was entirely pleasurable—and altogether confusing. Strangely, she felt heat suffuse her face.

Why am I blushing?

Thankfully, Sir Nicholas had already turned to depart, meeting his sister in the doorway.

'Morning, Nicky! Are you done already? I have just been checking on the younger ones. They are eating in the kitchen and their nursemaids have everything well in hand.'

Sir Nicholas did not mention the broken vase. 'I am glad to hear it,' he replied drily. 'I shall be in the library if you need me.'

Mary was both glad and sorry to see him leave. Of all the people in Stiffkey Hall, he was the one that she felt most kinship with—apart from Beatrice. Their shared appreciation of books and scholarly pursuits was an obvious connection. Yet there was more to it. There was something indefinably personal about it.

Yes, there was something much too intense about her affinity to him and it made her decidedly nervous. She had never had much to do with men and had certainly never met anyone like Sir Nicholas before.

Perhaps that is precisely why I am drawn to him.

Her mind had not encountered his like before and it wished to study this new type of creature. Yet this did not explain why Mary felt such a strong physical response to him. Twice now she had experienced strange sensations when near him. It was unprecedented, confusing and unwelcome, so Mary did what any sensible person would do: she put it out of her mind.

'Miss Smith, come and meet my other children.' Mrs Fenhurst's tone was sharp, her posture unbending.

Have I displeased her?

Thinking back, Mary realised Mrs Fenhurst had not addressed her directly in the breakfast room. They were now in the Yellow Parlour, where Mrs Fenhurst had asked Mary to attend her after breakfast. Mary walked forward to where Mrs Fenhurst was seated near the parlour fireplace. Opposite, stiffly seated on a long straw-coloured satin sofa, were Amabel and Beatrice, alongside Miss Cushing and a younger girl.

'This is Miss Caroline, who is twelve years old since Yuletide.'

Mary greeted the girl, who eyed her calmly. 'Are you a governess?' she asked bluntly. Beside her, Miss Cushing showed definite signs of agitation, clutching her skirt and frowning.

'I can be, if needed,' Mary replied evenly. 'I am here to assist Mrs Fenhurst and Miss Cushing, as are these nursemaids.' She indicated the two nursemaids, who were clearly rather distracted by their charges. The boys were currently attempting to fence each other with invisible swords at the other side of the room. The nursemaids, conscious of the delicate furniture and ornaments in the parlour, were trying to prevent harm coming to anything.

Lord, the boys are full of vivacity!

Mrs Fenhurst pointed to the taller one. 'Master David is almost ten, while my baby, Master Edmond, is seven.'

'Seven and a half!' Master Edmond broke off from his swordplay to make the point with some indignation.

'That half is very important,' Mary agreed solemnly. 'I am happy to meet you both.'

The boys gave her the briefest of bows, then returned to their swordplay.

Mrs Fenhurst was not done. 'I have discussed matters with Miss Cushing and I have made a decision. Miss Smith, you will assist me with invitations and planning for the parties. You will also assist Cushing by taking responsibility for the boys' lessons.'

Mary's heart sank. She had hoped to be allowed to concentrate on Beatrice. While she had no difficulty with assisting Mrs Fenhurst in preparing for the entertainments, she suspected that she was being given responsibility for the boys simply because no one else was able to manage them.

What am I to do with them?

'I wish to make it clear that Cushing retains my full support, that she remains the governess for all my children and that your involvement is limited to our visit here in Norfolk. Is that understood?'

'Of course.' Mary had no desire to usurp poor Miss Cushing. Her aim was to do her best here in order to assist Papa. Nothing more, nothing less.

'You may begin the boys' lessons today—under Cushing's guidance, naturally.'

'Indeed.' Mary gave Miss Cushing what she hoped was a reassuring smile. 'Perhaps you could give me some information about the boys' proficiency in reading, writing and arithmetic.'

'Well, if you are going to be tedious, you may do it over there,' declared Mrs Fenhurst, waving towards a side table with two straight chairs beside it, by one of the long windows. Obediently, Mary and Miss Cushing moved to that part of the room.

Half an hour later, Mary was not reassured. The boys were, it seemed, reasonably proficient in reading and writing, but resisted number-work with passion, determination and some artful distraction. Miss Cushing was at her wits' end and quite lacking in suggestions as to how Mary could achieve success where she had failed.

'I have made it plain to Mrs Fenhurst, but she is unconcerned, repeating only that it will come to them eventually and that she herself detested all things mathematical!' Miss Cushing was wringing her hands at this point. 'I do worry that my dear Mr and Mrs Fenhurst will replace me with a tutor for the boys—indeed, it would be surprising if they did not do so. And then what shall I do?'

Mary touched the older woman's hand. 'I have no doubt they will treat you with kindness and provide a pension for you.' A thought struck her. 'Does Mr Fenhurst hope to join his family in the coming weeks?'

'Oh, no! For he says this is an opportunity for

some tranquillity—that is to say, his time is taken up with matters of business.'

'I understand completely.' They both looked to the bottom of the room, where Master David and Master Edmond were currently disagreeing hotly about some matter. The nursemaids seemed unable to manage them and the disagreement soon escalated to fisticuffs.

'Cushing! Miss Smith! Do something!' Mrs Fenhurst, clearly exasperated, instructed them from her throne near the fireplace.

Jumping up, Mary and the elderly governess approached the boys. Mary held back a little, wishing to observe how Miss Cushing would manage the situation. Since this seemed to be an ineffectual attempt at a lecture about good behaviour, Mary's heart once again sank. The boys barely heard the elderly lady, so intent were they in exchanging blows, while the nursemaids tried to stay their hands.

'Enough!' Remembering how well they had responded to Sir Nicholas's discipline earlier, Mary spoke loudly and forcefully. She stepped between them, taking a blow to her arm that was meant to land on Master David's chest. 'Who started this?'

As a way of disrupting the fight, it was immediately effective. Both brothers abandoned the bout in order to justify their angry actions. Mary spent quite five minutes listening to their reasoning, questioning them and checking the veracity of both accounts. By the end, the anger had subsided, as both looked to her for judgement.

'David,' she said, 'you should not have insulted your brother. Your words were designed to wound him and that is wrong.'

She turned to the younger boy. 'Edmond, instead of raising your fist, you should have challenged the falsity of his words.' She eyed both of them. 'Now, you are brothers. You will soon be gentlemen. You must each apologise for your part in this and shake hands.'

Grumbling, they did so. Mary turned to one of the nursemaids. 'Might I suggest that you take Edmond to change his shirt, for he has lost a button?'

'Yes, miss,' said the nursemaid, a respectful look in her eye. She found the missing button on the floor and led a protesting Edmond out of the room.

'Master David, come and sit with your mother and sisters,' added Miss Cushing. 'And I do not wish to see you playing at sword fighting in the parlour ever again!'

The boys needed to be separated for a while, thought Mary, relieved that her intervention had had the desired effect. Now, all she needed to do was teach them arithmetic!

'And then, according to the nursemaid, the two boys shook hands, placid as you like.' Bramber smiled. 'I am glad that Miss Smith is turning out to be good at managing children.'

Nicholas snorted. 'Well, she could hardly be worse than my sister and her elderly governess! It is not for me to interfere in how Susan handles her children, but it is of interest to me when they destroy the peace of everyone in this house.' He eyed Bramber closely. 'Miss Smith…is she…do you…?'

Damnation! How should I ask this?

'Are you asking if I have a *tendre* for her?' Despite flushing a little at the intimate turn of the conversation, Bramber shook his head decidedly. 'No, not at all. She is all that is admirable, but I must confess that—that another lady has been in my thoughts.' His ears were as bright as Nicholas had ever seen them.

'Another lady?' Relief warred with curiosity. Ignoring the former, Nicholas indulged the latter, asking bluntly, 'Who?'

'I am not going to tell you. With respect, sir.' Bramber lifted his chin.

'Fair enough. I have no right to pry.'

'In fact,' Bramber continued, 'I did wonder, while I was travelling home from London, if perhaps you…but no.' He clamped his mouth shut.

'If perhaps I what?'

If I know already which lady has taken your fancy?

Nicholas frowned in puzzlement. 'I have not

the faintest idea what you are referring to. Really, Bramber, you should learn to speak more plainly.'

'I shall give the matter my urgent attention,' offered Bramber wryly. 'Anyway, I need you to sign these papers for me. They relate to the new barn you are building in the West Farm.'

'A new barn? Why am I building a new barn?' Nicholas grinned, accepting the change of topic. 'Do not answer that. I shall sign them.'

Half an hour later, Bramber was gone and Nicholas was alone again. He picked up his book, but paused for a few moments, imagining the scene that had played out in the Yellow Parlour. Miss Smith had spirit, it seemed. Beauty, intelligence and spirit. Perhaps she was not so dull, after all.

Chapter Eight

Once again, Mary found herself seated between Sir Nicholas and Beatrice at dinner. Once again, she was conscious of that thrill of strange awareness in his presence.

I did not imagine it, then.

As she ate and conversed, and behaved—she hoped—in a natural way, she was curiously alert to his movements, his words, his nearness to her. Perhaps it was something to do with the wine, for she was unused to taking much alcohol. She tried another sip. It was truly delicious!

Sir Nicholas does have a formidable physical presence.

His height, the breadth of his shoulders and the banked strength in his frame was all strangely interesting to her. She found herself watching his hands while he cut his food—long fingers managing the utensils with practised ease. *Stop!* she told herself. How mortifying if he should see her watching him.

'Has my sister decided yet what she will re-quire of you, Miss Smith?' he asked politely.

'Yes. As well as assisting her to plan the par-ties, she wishes me to centre my attention on Master David and Master Edmond.' Strangely, the wine seemed to have created bubbles of mirth inside her chest.

How delightful!

Thankfully, her outward demeanour remained sensible.

'I wondered if she might,' he murmured. 'I have no doubt you are equal to the task.'

'Then you are more confident than I,' Mary re-torted frankly, 'for I do not have the faintest idea how I might manage them!'

He laughed at this. 'Your honesty does you credit, Miss Smith. It is refreshing to hear some-thing more real than bland platitudes.'

'I am sadly lacking in platitudes,' she replied forlornly. 'A deficiency which has frequently led to trouble for me.'

I should not be speaking to him with such open-ness.

Yet, somehow, she could not stop herself.

He grinned. 'I myself admire plain speaking, Miss Smith—except when speaking plainly might distress another.'

She tilted her head to one side, remember-ing Miss Plumpton's inconsistent approach to this very matter. 'That is true. I have frequently heard people defend inexcusable rudeness on the grounds of "honesty" or "plain speaking".' The footman refilled her wine glass and Mary thanked him absently.

'Precisely. Rudeness and downright vulgarity are not to be encouraged. Yet we agree, I think, that false solicitude is equally abhorrent.'

'Indeed. Honesty is a virtue, as we know, and yet *blunt* honesty is not always the best response in terms of morality.' She frowned, remembering that she had been less than honest with him and with the guard in the gaol.

I must, she reminded herself. *Papa's survival takes precedence.*

Yet her discomfort was acute.

'What are you thinking now?' he asked, clearly attempting to read the expressions on her face.

She looked at him blankly. 'I…' She paused. *Say nothing!*

'I do apologise, Miss Smith. You are entitled to the privacy of your thoughts.' His words were calmly uttered, yet somehow he had withdrawn from her. Gone was the open, teasing expression of a moment before, replaced by a cold, closed expression on his face. The affinity they had been sharing was lost, leaving a sick, empty feeling in Mary's stomach. They ate in silence after that, until the conversations turned and they each spoke to the Fenhurst sisters on the other side.

Morning brought Mary back to the Yellow Parlour, where the Fenhursts and Miss Cushing were gathered, along with the two harassed-looking nursemaids.

'Time for schooling,' announced Mrs Fenhurst. This brought exasperated sighs from the boys. 'Now, boys,' said their mama in a wheedling tone, 'you know you must continue with your lessons. Your papa expects it.'

Master David eyed Mary with suspicion. 'Will you force us to learn arithmetic?'

Mary shrugged. 'If Miss Cushing wishes it. But I believe that it is better if children enjoy their lessons.'

'Hurrah!' declared Master Edmond. 'That means no arithmetic!'

'Ah, but you are jumping to conclusions!' Mary kept her tone light.

The boy frowned. 'But I did not jump at all. I just stood here.'

Mary smiled. 'It is a way of saying that you came up with the wrong answer because you immediately assumed you knew exactly what I meant to say.'

'You said *enjoy* lessons. I heard you!'

'I did.'

David decided to join in the conversation. 'One cannot *enjoy* arithmetic—why, the very idea is nonsensical!' His tone was scathing. 'Therefore enjoying lessons means no arithmetic. Edmond is correct!'

'I like that you are using logic to explain your thinking, Master David.' She leaned closer. 'That is clever.'

He snorted. 'No, that is common sense!'

'But common sense may sometimes be wrong.' She thought for a moment, wondering if her unusual idea might work. 'Very well. I shall do this differently.' She looked him in the eye. 'Master David Fenhurst,' she declared, 'I hereby challenge you to an arithmetic quest!'

His eyes lit up, then he looked dubious. 'Is this a trick?'

'No, for I am happy to tell you openly that there will be arithmetic involved.'

'What would I have to do?' His tone was dripping with suspicion, but he was nevertheless intrigued. Mary was sure of it.

'I shall challenge you to complete three tasks. They all involve being outside in the gardens. At the end of each task, I shall ask about your enjoyment and we shall talk together about arithmetic. Do you accept the challenge?'

'Can I play, too?' Edmond, clearly liking the

sound of Mary's proposal, elbowed his way back into the conversation.

Miss Caroline, Mary noted, was listening intently. 'If Miss Cushing permits, all three of you may take part.'

Miss Caroline sniffed. 'It all sounds rather childish!' she declared, with all the defiant gravitas of a twelve-year-old. Yet, Mary noticed, the girl's eyes gleamed with curiosity.

'Caroline, you should stay here this morning,' said her mother, patting the seat beside her. 'I know Cushing is keen to work with you on your knowledge of the globe. This is the perfect opportunity, with Miss Smith diverting the boys.'

Miss Caroline, whose shoulders had slumped a little at the mention of Cushing's globe, shook her head. 'Actually, Mama, I think I should help Miss Smith with the boys.' Leaning confidentially in towards her mother, she added, 'For she will have no idea of the mischief they can get up to!'

Thankfully, the day was dry, clear and sunny, if cold. The frigid February wind whipped around them, tousling the boys' hair and flattening Mary's muslin gown against her. Miss Caroline, who had donned her cloak and bonnet with alacrity, now looked as though she regretted the impulse to take part. They all looked at Mary expectantly.

What on earth am I doing?

Still, it was worth attempting.

'I have created a series of challenges for you—three for you, Master David, and three for you, Master Edmond. The first is easy and, if you are successful, you will be deemed a Page. The second is more difficult, and will earn you the right to become a Squire. Only a true Knight will pass the third.'

The boys' eyes shone with excitement. 'I should love to be a knight,' declared Edmond, unsheathing his imaginary sword. 'I shall kill all the dragons!'

'No, for I shall kill the biggest, most fearsome ones!' argued his brother.

Intervening before Edmond could utter a frustrated retort, Mary adopted a confidential air. 'David, your first quest is near the kitchen door. Edmond, you must go to the Rose Garden. Wait!' for they had almost run straight off. 'You do not yet know what to look for.'

They paused, eyeing her eagerly. 'Here is a slate for each of you. Use it carefully.' She handed it to them with great solemnity and they took this most prosaic of items with much ceremony. 'I have hidden a note for each of you on parchment. You must find the note, read it and find the answer to my question. You may need to use the slate for the arithmetic part. Then you must run back here as soon as you have the answer. Do you understand?'

'Yes!'

'I shall complete my quest, fair lady!' David gave Mary a courtly bow, and she responded with a curtsy.

'Caroline, you may accompany Master Edmond—but do not help him with the answer. He must figure it out by himself. Now, when I drop my handkerchief, you may begin. Are you ready? Then—go!'

They ran at full pace, Caroline struggling to keep up with Edmond as they disappeared towards the Rose Garden. *Good!* Mary had discovered that the boys had had very few opportunities to run and play outside since their arrival.

Mary had asked for Mrs Fenhurst's permission to take her lesson outside, before suggesting it to the boys earlier. 'Highly irregular!' their mama had declared. 'But after this morning's fisticuffs, I declare I want them nowhere near me!'

Mary clapped her gloved hands together and paced up and down to avoid becoming cold. Despite the bright winter sunshine, the air was frigid and the morning frost had only just melted away. At this moment, she regretted donning only a spencer over her muslin gown. She thought wistfully of her cloak, currently in her bedchamber, and bit her lip.

Hopefully the boys would stay centred on their quests. She had deliberately sent them in different directions in order to prevent them distracting one another. She also knew that creating an air of contest between them would likely help.

A fleeting movement at one of the windows caught her eye. She glanced up—to see Sir Nicholas himself standing there. He was looking in her direction, so she raised a hand in acknowledgement. He returned the gesture, sending a warm feeling through her, then stepped away from the window.

What on earth ails me?

Sir Nicholas returned to his desk, despite wishing nothing more than to remain at the casement, gazing at the shapely figure of Miss Smith. Quite how he had failed to notice on first meeting her how perfectly proportioned she was now puzzled him enormously.

Modern ladies' fashions were for thin, fine, muslin dresses. They were surely an inconvenience to ladies for being so light, particularly in cold weather. At this moment, however, Sir Nicholas was immensely grateful to whoever had decreed it. Each time the wind blew, Miss Smith's dress pressed firmly to her figure, outlining clearly the shape of her divine form. Sir Nicholas had enjoyed both the front and rear views, as Miss

Smith, clearly attempting to keep warm, paced up and down. On this sunny winter's day, Miss Smith's long, shapely legs had also been clearly outlined. He groaned, closing his eyes briefly.

As a warm-blooded male, Nicholas had had his share of *affaires*, but he had not expected to find himself so interested in a governess! And it was not just her shapely figure that preoccupied him. Her face, too, he found fascinating. Her eyes— by far her best feature—danced with intelligence, a quality he had always admired. He liked her straightforward, no-nonsense way of speaking, too. He regretted being so cold to her at dinner. She made him laugh and made him think. He was glad Bramber had brought her.

He must, however, be careful. She was governess to his sister's children, nothing more. He should not be indulging his own foolishness. She was naturally, entirely unsuitable as a potential wife for someone like him. A gently-bred, likely impoverished female like Miss Smith would end up marrying someone like Bramber. Some younger son with a profession or a trade. A gentleman and a gentleman's daughter, it was true, yet both were limited by their financial status. Such were the ways of society.

And, he reminded himself, it was none of his concern whom she married. When he himself wed, it would be to some well-bred, wealthy maiden who had never needed to work to earn her keep. His position as master of Stiffkey Hall demanded it. He was in no hurry to marry, but would eventually find a suitable wife to carry on the Denny name and lineage.

In truth, she was little more than a servant and therefore entirely beneath him. Yes, despite this inconvenient fixation, he must think of Miss Smith only as a governess.

With determination, he forced himself to consider the challenge she had been set—that of somehow managing two lively boys. He had seen David and Edmond run off in different directions—Miss Caroline accompanying the youngest—and wondered what game the governess was playing with them. Whatever it was, the boys seemed to be finding it diverting.

Resisting the temptation to call for his boots and cloak, he picked up his book.

An hour later, having returned inside, Mary pronounced herself pleased with her first attempt at being a governess. The tasks she had set the boys contained only fairly simple addition and subtraction riddles and they had completed them easily. The fact they had done so without complaint was significant, she felt. Tomorrow's quests—involving both addition and multiplication—were more challenging, but they allowed her to see at what level the boys' learning was.

She herself knew that the greatest joy she had had in learning came from lessons which challenged her mind—but not too much. If the concepts were beyond her, she quickly became discouraged. She also knew that praise was a more powerful force than criticism and had already used this to full effect. Both boys had been delighted with their 'lesson', declaring that Miss Smith was a great gig and top-of-the-trees, even if she was a governess.

She had allowed them some time to play together once they had completed their tasks and all three children had run and whooped and shrieked delightedly for a good twenty minutes, before being called inside by their nursemaids for nuncheon, which they would take in the kitchens. Mary had asked them to come to the small parlour afterwards to continue their lessons and they had undertaken to do so with only a token protest.

She herself went to nuncheon upstairs with a feeling more of relief than satisfaction and, upon Mrs Fenhurst's questioning her, was able to say cautiously that she had made a beginning.

'I still say,' declared Miss Cushing with a sniff, 'that the children should not be outside in winter. What if they should catch a chill?' She eyed Mary with clear rancour.

Oh, dear! Miss Cushing, already feeling threatened by Mary's very presence, was now indicating her displeasure at Mary's first attempt at working with the children. Before Mary could formulate a response that couched what she really thought in more temperate language, she received assistance from an unexpected source.

'Oh, fie, Cushing! They are not made of glass, you know.' Mrs Fenhurst brushed a speck from her skirt. 'We had peace this morning for the first time and I was thankful for it!'

'The entire household is grateful.' Sir Nicholas, who had just entered, grinned at his sister. 'I cannot count the times the boys have caused havoc in this house—and they have been here less than two days.'

Mrs Fenhurst bristled a little. 'My boys are simply spirited. You are intolerant, Brother, and unused to children.'

Sir Nicholas nodded. 'It is true I am unused to children. I should say, however, that I am particularly unused to the mayhem that surrounds your children.'

She spread her hands wide. 'There is nothing my darling boys can do that would earn my displeasure.'

His eyes gleamed. 'Indeed? So when you despair at their behaviour and call on their nursemaids to remove them, that is not, then, displeasure?'

His sister's eyes narrowed, as she felt the hit. 'You are their uncle. You should welcome them here.'

He conceded this, but added, 'I shall welcome them more when they have learned how to behave like sensible creatures. The boys are in danger of being completely out of control at times. Surely you must see it?'

'I do not and *shall* not see any such thing! The boys are naturally a little boisterous, that is all. I declare they quite tire me out!'

Mary fixed her eyes on Sir Nicholas.

Oh, Lord, he is angry now.

'If they tire you out,' he declared, his eyes narrowed, 'I wonder that you have brought them here at all!'

Mrs Fenhurst stiffened. 'You must understand, Brother, that I would miss them terribly if I had come without them. Especially for so long a visit.'

'Quite.'

The air between them was charged with acrimony. Bramber had explained that both Sir Nicholas and his sister were motivated by a strong sense of pride in their family name, which was why this tradition of a prolonged visit was strictly observed, even if not always enjoyed.

Say something helpful!

Mary cleared her throat. 'Miss Caroline and the boys enjoyed some time to play after the lesson.'

'Well, I still cannot see how it was a lesson at all!' Miss Cushing looked decidedly cross. 'I do hope you intend to do some proper work with the boys!'

Oh, Lord! The tension in the air had not evaporated. Rather, it had moved to surround her.

'I shall be working with them after nuncheon, in the small parlour,' Mary responded, in a colourless tone.

'I am happy to hear it!' declared Miss Cushing. 'In fact, I shall observe your lesson, Miss Smith. After all, I must ensure that you are a capable teacher! And I remain, as my dear Mrs Fenhurst has confirmed, their true governess!'

'Of course,' Mary responded, hiding her hands under the table, since they had just bunched into fists.

I must mask my anger.

She could not pretend to welcome Miss Cushing's intended scrutiny, so merely added, 'I do hope you will be satisfied.'

'What were you doing with the boys outside earlier?' asked Sir Nicholas politely.

Mary explained, describing the tasks she had set and the arithmetic required for the boys to solve their riddles. Mrs Fenhurst, clearly indifferent to the discussion, applied herself to her ham and herring.

'But that is astounding!' Sir Nicholas declared,

causing Mary to glow with unanticipated pleasure. 'I wish my tutors had taken such an approach when I was a lad.'

Mary dimpled at him. 'I do not doubt, sir, that
you yourself could have been a handful at times.'

He understands why I did it! Why this gave her
such happiness was unclear, but it did.

He let out a bark of laughter. 'You have me
there, I'll admit!'

Miss Cushing, looking from one to the other
with alarm, was moved to say, 'But, sir! True
teaching must involve the discipline of the classroom!'

'Of course, of course,' he replied, seemingly
belatedly realising his error. 'But to have such a
game now and again cannot be harmful, surely?'

'As long as it is only an occasional lapse,' the
older woman conceded, 'but I myself shall continue to teach indoors, in a *sensible* way.' She
glared at Mary. 'These outlandish notions will
never take root, mark my words!'

Nicholas chuckled to himself as he walked to
the library. Miss Smith had, once again, enter-
tained him with her quick wit. He had been genuinely intrigued by her approach to teaching and
would have loved to see it underway, but resisted
the temptation.

She had also impressed him with her insight.

Of course it should be clear to anyone with discernment that he had been a strong-willed boy, but then he found himself sadly lacking in companions with the least amount of discernment. Until now, he had been entirely reliant on Bramber for wit, humour and intelligent conversation. Now, it seemed, he had Miss Smith, too.

The thought sent a confusing wave of warmth through him—warmth which instantly became desire, as he recalled again the tempting outline of her form, seen from the library window. Miss Smith was becoming all too distracting, and he was not sure he liked it.

Chapter Nine

Having survived Miss Cushing's critical scrutiny during her afternoon lessons with David and Edmond, Mary left the small parlour with a definite sense of relief. There was an hour yet until dinner and she wished nothing more than some solitude in her chamber. It was not to be, for a housemaid intercepted her to say that Mrs Fenhurst wished to see her in the Yellow Parlour, as soon as she had finished with the children.

Biting back a sigh, Mary thanked the maid and made her way to the Yellow Parlour.

'Ah, Miss Smith! Take a seat. How did the boys go on this afternoon?'

Mary gave a brief summary, omitting to mention the constant criticisms and interruption from Miss Cushing as she had tried to work with David and Edmond on their reading and penmanship. 'I believe,' she concluded, 'that they were better able to attend to the lesson simply because they had had the opportunity to play outside this morning.'

'Hmmm.' Mrs Fenhurst was clearly unconvinced. 'I would adjure you to take heed of Cushing. She has a lifetime of experience in dealing with children.'

'Yes, Mrs Fenhurst.' Not for anything would she mention the fact that Miss Cushing seemed entirely inept in managing David and Edmond. Particularly since Mrs Fenhurst seemed similarly incapable.

'Ring the bell for the housekeeper, please.'

Mary did so and only a few moments later they were joined by Mrs Kett, a plump, smiling woman who had already made efforts to make sure Mary had felt welcome in the house.

Mrs Fenhurst spoke to the housekeeper with great condescension. 'I wish to begin planning the various entertainments that my brother expects, Mrs Kett. I shall begin quietly, with a soirée musicale, then some card parties, perhaps some dancing evenings, and then we shall build towards a Grand Ball at Easter. If the weather improves towards spring, we can organise some al fresco gatherings for the daytime. Naturally, once Lent begins we must behave with appropriate restraint.'

'I am glad to hear it, ma'am,' offered Mrs Kett, 'for as a God-fearing woman I do not hold with celebrating too much during Lent.'

Mrs Fenhurst went on to detail the first few events, before asking Mrs Kett to send a house-maid to fetch Bramber. Mary made lists of all that was to be done—invitations, dates, musicians—while Mrs Kett noted the food preferences that Mrs Fenhurst outlined. Mary found the whole pro-cess most interesting.

When Bramber arrived, he and Mrs Fen-hurst made a list of people to be invited to the first event—a soirée, to be held in a fortnight. It seemed Sir Nicholas had already specified cer-tain of his friends who were to be invited. Mrs Fenhurst and Bramber then agreed on a few ad-ditional local families. The event was to include a dinner for selected guests, so Mrs Fenhurst asked Bramber to calculate the numbers of males and fe-males. Having done so, the number leaned slightly towards ladies.

'Hmmm…we need a few more unaccompa-nied males, then, as I do not wish to reduce the numbers,' declared Mrs Fenhurst. 'Is Mr Easton still in residence in the Great Snoring vicarage?'

'He is,' replied Bramber neutrally. Mary's ears pricked up at his tone. Bramber sounded decid-edly unenthusiastic at the prospect of including Mr Easton.

'Oh, I know my brother finds him tiresome,' added Mrs Fenhurst, with a dismissive wave of her hand, 'but we need some men to balance up all the ladies. Are any of the other local vicars suitable for company?'

'Indeed,' replied Bramber. 'Mr Fuller in Walsingham is a good sort. Actually,' he added, rubbing his chin thoughtfully, 'there is also a new man in Houghton St Giles. Sir Nicholas has met him on a couple of occasions and seems to like him.'

It took all of Mary's presence of mind not to gasp out loud. He was speaking of her papa—word had not then spread about his arrest. She said a silent prayer of thanks for Miss Lutton's discretion.

'Perfect!' declared Mrs Fenhurst. 'It is settled, then. You shall invite them all and we shall enjoy a veritable feast of vicars!'

A few moments later, as she finally climbed the stairs to her chamber to dress for dinner, Mary's mind was filled with one thought. Why it seemed so significant, she was unsure. But it made her heart sing with unnamed hope.

Sir Nicholas liked Papa.

Tonight, the seating arrangements at dinner had been altered. Mary's and Amabel's places were reversed, meaning that Mary was now seated between Sir Nicholas and Mr Bramber, while the Fenhurst sisters were side by side between their uncle and their mother. Beatrice, Mary noted, was next to Sir Nicholas.

While sorry to miss out on the opportunity to continue strengthening her own burgeoning connection with young Miss Beatrice, Mary was content to have been placed beside Mr Bramber. He was easy, uncomplicated company, conversing with affability on a range of topics while never straying into controversy.

How I wish sometimes that I could be so insipid! Mary thought, before chastising herself for being judgemental.

Mr Bramber was kind, gentle and moderate in all his opinions. Never would he dare to take arithmetic lessons outside, she was sure. No, nor call his employer intimidating!

Even if it were true.

She stole a glance at Sir Nicholas. He was looking at Bramber and seemed to be in a sombre mood tonight. Mary wondered what ailed him. Of course, it was none of her concern, but she could not help but wonder whom he confided his worries in. No one, she suspected. Although he was generally congenial, she sensed that none of the people around him, including his sister, were capable to engaging with him on an equal level. The thought made her sad.

She herself felt similarly alone. Since Papa's arrest, Mary had missed his wise counsel. It was frustrating not to even be able to write to him. For a moment, a vision of his cold hard cell came to her. She gripped her spoon hard and tried to regain control. Glancing around to check that no one had noticed her lapse, she was discomfited to find Sir Nicholas eyeing her, concern furrowing his brow. For an instant, she allowed the power of his brown eyes to penetrate her soul, before remembering where she was and how she must behave. Pasting a bright smile on her face, she asked if he had gone riding again today.

'It is my habit to ride every morning,' he replied, but his expression remained serious, thoughtful.

'I have never learned to ride a horse, though I have often wondered what it would be like. I am sure I should be frightened to be so far from the ground.'

'Miss Smith,' he declared, giving her a wicked look, 'I cannot imagine you being frightened of anything, or anyone.'

'Oh, but I am! Many things frighten me.'

'Things, not people?'

She considered this. She was currently frightened for Papa, for her own future…yet she could not recall being frightened of a *person*. Miss Plumpton had angered her, Mrs Gray had made her nervous, but only because she was so admirable. Sir Nicholas himself—no, he did not frighten her, exactly. It was not fear that caused her stomach to melt and her insides to clench in his presence. It was—something else.

Sir Nicholas was still watching her intently. Her heart was now pounding so loudly, she was sure it could be heard all around the room. Ignoring his question entirely, she attempted to distract him. 'Do you always follow the same route, or do you vary it?'

He hesitated, still looking at her, then almost visibly shook himself out of his inner thoughts. 'I generally go by Houghton St Giles, then back home along the river.'

Papa's parish! She had wanted to divert him from noticing her worries about Papa, but she had ended up asking exactly the wrong question. Thinking quickly, she took their discourse in a new direction. 'I always find I sharpen my ability to read or study after a brisk walk. I believe exercising the body can be good for the mind.'

'And for the spirit,' he agreed. 'Our local countryside has a most soothing effect on my temper.'

She grinned. 'Then you will own, I am certain, that it would be good for the boys to exercise outdoors each day.'

He leaned forwards, a ghost of a smile finally breaking his melancholy. 'You shall not trap me into stepping into that battlefield. I can deal with anything except the tears of a certain elderly governess!'

'Why, I am sure I do not understand you!' Her eyes danced with mischief.

'I am very sure that you do,' he retorted, throwing himself into the debate.

'And so,' she said deliberately, 'you ask *me* to step into duels that you would not consider for yourself.'

He grinned and she felt a thrill of happiness at having successfully diverted him. 'I do, and have, and I confess I am enjoying observing how the combat progresses! Sometimes one of you has the upper hand, sometimes the other. It is not clear yet who will be the victor, but if I were prone to gambling...'

'Yes?' She could not resist baiting him. 'If you were to bet, on whom would you place your coin?'

Oh, how exhilarating it is to be in his company!

He laughed, then replied with mock sternness, 'Gambling, Miss Smith? I would say that you would do well to remember that you, I understand, are the daughter of a vicar!'

'Who told you that?' she asked sharply, all humour leaving her.

'The register office, in their letter of recommendation.' He was frowning again. 'At the time, I thought it reassuring. Now...' His voice tailed away. 'You are something of an enigma, Miss Smith.'

Aware that she had erred, Mary decided to be

daring. To show weakness now could only harm her need for secrecy. 'An enigma…hmmm…' She tilted her head to one side. 'In a good sense, or a poor one?' she asked pertly, half-aware that she was hoping for some warmth from him.

'I hope, good.' He gave her *that* look again and this time she felt it in every inch of her body, right down to her toes.

'—of people who continue to rudely converse when I have already turned the table!' Mary became aware that Mrs Fenhurst was glaring at her and Sir Nicholas from the foot of the table and that everyone else was watching them. *Lord!*

With no acknowledgement of his sister's rebuke, Sir Nicholas merely turned to his left, throwing a genial question to Beatrice. Thankfully, Mr Bramber engaged Mary in conversation immediately afterwards and Mrs Fenhurst, thankfully, took her cross gaze away from her brother and Mary.

Oh, dear! There are hazards and entanglements in every direction, and I am not sure I am navigating them with any degree of success.

Nicholas absent-mindedly thanked his valet. The man departed, leaving Nicholas alone in his chamber. Nicholas extinguished all but one of the candles, then took his half-glass of brandy to the armchair by the fire. As he gazed into the orange glow, his thoughts drifted to Miss Smith. *Again.* He had noted the interesting intelligence that she had never ridden a horse before and, in fact, was nervous about the thought of doing so. He grinned. He should quite like to see the assured Miss Smith show nervousness.

His thoughts drifted to another fascinating glimpse into her mind. Did something trouble her? Earlier he had seen a shadow cross her face when she believed herself to be unobserved. Surprisingly, he had been in that moment quite overtaken with an urge to comfort her, to ease whatever it was that vexed her.

It was most unlike him to care much about other people. Apart from the occasional trouble of dealing with his sister Susan and her irksome brood, he was generally surrounded by straight-faced servants who, naturally, needed nothing from him. Finding himself concerned with another's unhappiness was a new experience for him. He wriggled uncomfortably, then finished his brandy in a single draught. Time for sleep.

Chapter Ten

Mary descended the servants' staircase to the lower floor, seeking Mrs Kett, the housekeeper. Following last night's near catastrophe at the dinner table, when she had been altogether too indiscreet in her conversation with Sir Nicholas, Mary was determined to do better from now on. The difficulty was, she acknowledged as she moved along the dimly lit passageway, when she was in Sir Nicholas's company she forgot things.

She forgot to be dull and discreet. Forgot that she was here under—well, not false colours, but with a lack of openness about her need to be in Norfolk. Forgot that the single most important matter she must manage while in Norfolk was to support her papa and hope for his release. Guilt flooded her as she realised that thoughts of Sir Nicholas quite drove her concerns for Papa from her mind at times.

Most worryingly, she frequently forgot that

Sir Nicholas was not some new friend, but her employer.

He already seems like a friend, was the answering thought, along with the fluttering in her stomach that she had come to associate with Sir Nicholas. It happened each time she thought of him and reached a crescendo in his company.

Not a friend like Papa. No, what she felt for Sir Nicholas was the most intense response she had ever experienced to another person. He fascinated her. She had now concluded that he was certainly the most handsome man she had ever beheld—even while dimly remembering that, on first meeting him, her impression had been of a handsome man, but nothing unusual. Each evening at dinner, when she sat near him, she revelled in the rumble of his voice, the dexterity of his hands, the impressive proportions of his frame.

These notions were most unlike her. Like most scholars, she had been raised to believe that the *mind* was to be celebrated, rather than the body. The body had its importance of course, along with the heart, but Mary's mind was the muscle that her papa had nurtured. Mary had grown up with a fixation on strengthening her intellect, celebrating thoughts and insights, while ignoring the needs of her physical self. Why, she and Papa had frequently forgotten to eat, ignoring hunger and thirst while engaged in some scholarly pursuit or debate.

Until recently, Mary herself had had no interest in the usual preoccupations of young ladies—how to dress their hair, what gown to wear, or how to avoid freckles. Papa, realising it, had sent her to Miss Plumpton's Academy in an attempt to right this imbalance. That had been failing spectacularly, right up until the moment Mary had escaped from there.

Yet here she was, fussing over her appearance for the first time in her life. Normally she dressed to please herself, and for comfort as much as fashion. In the past few days, however, she had begun to notice herself being a little more careful when choosing her clothing or dressing her hair. She had felt for the first time a feeling of satisfaction when she looked in the mirror and saw that her printed muslin was pretty, or that her blue silk evening gown matched the colour of her eyes.

This was not the only change. Since arriving in Stiffkey Hall, and for the first time in her adult life, Mary was continually aware of a man. Sir Nicholas's nearness had a potent effect on her body. The most wonderful sensations pursued her when he looked at her and when she thought of him. It was all most peculiar.

Straightening her shoulders and marshalling her wayward thoughts, Mary knocked on the door of the housekeeper's room. On hearing the command to enter, she stepped inside. The chamber was plain yet cosy, with a small fireplace, a metal bed in the corner and a table with two chairs. Mrs Kett was poised in the act of writing, her quill hovering over a long sheet of paper. On seeing Mary, she smiled and set her pen down.

'Why, Miss Smith, how nice of you to call! How may I assist you?'

Mary responded with a reference to Mrs Fenhurst's plans and they contentedly discussed the upcoming events together, finding agreement on all the important matters. Mrs Kett was, Mary realised, a sensible woman and her comment yesterday about Lent had given Mary an idea.

'There is one other matter I wished to discuss with you.'

'Yes?' Mrs Kett's kind face was beaming at her.

Oh, how wonderful it is to meet warm-hearted people!

'I walked as far as Walsingham the other day and I saw that there is a gaol there.'

'The Bridewell, yes. It is quite new, you know. They built it only ten or so years ago.'

'So that is why it is not as dingy as other gaols!' Responding to Mrs Kett's questioning look, she explained, 'I have made it my business to seek out the poor, the destitute and the needy wherever I have lived and I do what I may to aid them.' This was completely true.

Mrs Kett patted Mary's hand. 'Ah, I knew you for a God-fearing girl, the minute I met you!'

'My father is—was—a vicar.'

Is he yet? Mary did not know. What was the status of a vicar in gaol? Had Miss Lutton made the Bishop aware of Papa's arrest?

The housekeeper was eyeing her with approval. 'So what do you mean to do during your stay here?'

'I would like to visit the prisoners—give them food, and blankets, if permitted, and read to them from the Bible. I called in when I was there and I was shocked by how little they had.'

'Food we can always give. And we do have a couple of spare blankets…how many would be needed?'

'There were but four prisoners on Thursday.'

Mrs Kett nodded. 'Leave it to me. Let me know when you will be free to visit them next and I shall prepare everything for you.'

'Thank you. Also—'

'Yes?'

'Are there any other needy people in the district that I might assist?' Mary could not escape the feeling that she should not only be assisting Papa. Anyone might aid a loved one. There was no particular goodness in it.

'Mrs Skipper in the Home Farm has a sick child this week. I was going to bring her some beets and carrots, and perhaps a wheel of cheese, but I have not yet had the opportunity.'

'If I find myself with a free hour, I shall bring them for you.'

'You are a good girl,' said Mrs Kett. 'I am glad you came.'

I am not as good as you believe me to be, thought Mary.

The way she was deceiving everyone sent a shudder of discomfort through her. Yet she could not risk sharing the truth with anyone. Papa was depending on her.

'Miss Smith!' Sir Nicholas's voice sent a delicious shiver through her. They were filling their plates at what Mrs Fenhurst called a 'potluck' nuncheon. All the food was laid out on the sideboards and, instead of being served while seated, they were all helping themselves in a most informal way.

The others were already seated, leaving Mary, who had waited until last, and Sir Nicholas, who had just arrived, to select their food at the side of the room.

'Sir Nicholas?' she replied, looking up at him.

'I have done something that I hope will meet your approval.' His tone was low and she matched it, unsure what was coming next.

'Indeed?' She raised an eyebrow. 'My approval is not easily won, I shall have you know.'

'Now I am quaking in my boots!' His eyes were smiling, and she noted with great interest how it added to his charm. 'I have persuaded Miss Beatrice to join me for some Greek and Latin reading in my library.' He speared some beef with a serving fork, transferring it to his plate. 'Your jaw has loosened, Miss Smith—not a particularly attractive look.'

She snapped her mouth shut. 'How on earth did you manage it? Why, the girl seems terrified of you!'

'My powers of persuasion are equal to it!' He grinned. 'Very well—I said that you would also be there and that allowed her to agree.'

Mary frowned. 'Me? But what of your sister and Miss—' She glanced around, then added, in a near-whisper, 'Miss Cushing?'

He leaned down to whisper into her ear. 'Leave the Cushion to me!' His warm breath tickled her ear, sending frantic pleasure tingling though her body.

Doing her best to ignore it, she concentrated on his words. 'You have set yourself a severe challenge, for Miss Cushing is well on the way to detesting me.'

'Precisely!' he retorted, taking a step away and turning his attention to the ham.

'Oh, Sir Nicholas!' Mary called to him silkily. 'There is a thing you may be interested to know.'

'Yes?'

'I am not a woman who cares overmuch about how attractive she looks!' With this final, jesting barb, she walked to the table.

Chapter Eleven

Sir Nicholas wasted no time. Barely had the party all taken their seats than he addressed his sister. 'Susan, my dear, I am impressed to discover that one of your offspring is something of a scholar.'

'You are referring to my dear David, I collect,' Mrs Fenhurst responded, munching on a side dish of leeks. 'He is prodigiously clever—so much so that he frequently outruns dear Miss Cushing. Is it not so, my dear?'

Miss Cushing hesitated. To agree would perhaps lower the assembled group's notions of her abilities, yet to disagree with her adored employer was impossible. Recognising the governess's dilemma, Mary could not help but glance towards Sir Nicholas, wondering if he, too, was enjoying the moment. At precisely the same instant, his gaze had sought her out and they shared a glance that was brimful of humour.

Miss Cushing mumbled something non-committal and Mrs Fenhurst continued. 'I dare say he gets it from his papa, for as you will remember, Nicky, I was never bookish!'

'I do remember,' he murmured. 'But it was not David I was referring to. It was Beatrice.'

'Beatrice? *Beatrice?*' Mrs Fenhurst paused, her fork halfway to her mouth. 'Beatrice is clever?'

'I believe so.' Sir Nicholas continued to enjoy his repast. Beatrice herself had stopped eating, her face as red as a tomato.

'But, what use is it to have a *girl* who is clever? For she will never need to work, or speak in Parliament, or deal with matters of business!'

Quite before she knew what she was doing, Mary found herself responding. 'Oh, but it is wonderful for a female to be clever! We are denounced as the weaker sex, yet many women are scholars and study the sciences, and literature. Some have even written entire books! I believe it to be a myth when people say that women's brains are less capable than men's.'

There was a stunned silence. Belatedly, Mary realised that, in the present company, she might as well have tied her garter in public. Mrs Fenhurst looked horrified, Miss Cushing delightedly shocked. Amabel and Beatrice were gaping at her for her audacity and Sir Nicholas—nervously, she glanced towards him.

Sir Nicholas's expression was one of unholy glee.

'Well!' declared Mrs Fenhurst. 'You state your opinions with some force for so young a person, Miss Smith! Must I remind you that you are an *employee* here—a governess, in fact!'

Miss Cushing gave a small cough.

'I mean to say, of course, that you are not *my* governess,' Mrs Fenhurst continued hurriedly. 'And I am very glad of it! Thankfully, Miss Cushing has altogether more sensible notions of the female sex.'

'It is immaterial, Sister, whether you believe women should or should not write books, or use what intelligence they have in public life.' Sir Nicholas leaned back in his chair, the picture of studied indifference. 'The fact is that I am glad to have discovered it to be the case and I am going to allow Miss Beatrice to have access to my library.'

Mrs Fenhurst's eyes narrowed, and her expression took on a slightly calculating look. 'Well, since this is the first time you have shown any interest in your nieces and nephews—'

'That is not true!'

'*Any* interest at all,' she continued, 'I shall permit it. Who would have thought that it would be my quiet Beatrice who would finally be noticed by her uncle?'

Beatrice herself, while still looking deeply uncomfortable at unexpectedly being at the centre of the conversation, managed to mumble a few words of thanks.

Mrs Fenhurst herself clearly had bigger fish to fry. 'Do not forget, Brother, that you also promised we should all have new dresses.'

'I have not forgotten, I assure you,' he returned smoothly.

Mrs Fenhurst gave a satisfied nod. 'I am glad to hear it. We shall travel in the coach tomorrow to Norwich and visit the modiste there.' She sniffed. 'She is not what I am used to, but we shall have to make do.'

'I have every confidence that you will manage very well,' he replied drily. 'Spending money on dresses, if I remember correctly, is one of your particular talents, my dear.'

Next morning, Mrs Fenhurst, her two older daughters, and their governess all departed for Norwich in Sir Nicholas's largest carriage. Mary watched them go with a definite sense of relief. They had left a full two hours later than planned, after a great deal of fussing over cloaks and boots and reticules, and they would not return until after nightfall.

'Miss Smith!' It was Sir Nicholas, striding down the hallway as though he were Zeus himself. 'Have they finally gone?'

'They have.' Not wishing to say anything indiscreet, she closed her mouth firmly, making him grin.

'Come with me.' He would say no more, despite her questions, simply marching off towards the kitchens. She, bewildered yet strangely invigorated, accompanied him, almost skipping to keep up. Servants dived to the left and right as he strode through their domain. Mary greeted most of them by name, shrugging at the parlourmaid's raised eyebrows to indicate that she had no idea why the master was taking her through the servants' corridors.

'Mrs Kett!' he bellowed and the housekeeper appeared at the doorway of her room.

'Ah, there you are!' She seemed unperturbed. 'Come inside, Miss Smith.'

Mary did so and was astonished when Mrs Kett began unbuttoning her sleeves. Mary caught sight of Sir Nicholas's gleeful grin as he closed the door to the housekeeper's room, leaving the women alone.

What on earth is happening?

'I have the riding habit all ready for you, my dear. It was Miss Susan's when she was young and slim, and should fit you perfectly.'

'Riding habit? But—' Mary was all confusion.

'Turn around.' Automatically, Mary did so, and allowed Mrs Kett to help her out of her day dress and into a beautiful blue velvet habit. It was plainer than current fashions demanded, but it had clearly been made by a master of their craft.

'This shade of blue is a perfect match for your eyes, my dear.' Mrs Kett frowned. 'It is a little tight about the bust… I shall leave the upper buttons undone and you should manage.'

Mary glanced down. There, as if on a platter, were her breasts, only half-covered by the blue velvet fabric. The top two buttons were undone and the third was under considerable strain.

Mary clapped a hand to her chest, the vicar's daughter in her horrified by the amount of exposure. 'I need a fichu or something. A piece of lace…'

'Nonsense!' retorted Mrs Kett briskly. 'Why, you will see much worse at a ball! Now make haste, for Sir Nicholas awaits.'

'Awaits where?' Mary's mind was struggling to keep pace.

'In the stable yard, of course!' Mrs Kett smiled warmly. 'You would do well to hurry, for it is quite a kindness for him to take you riding.'

'Riding? *Me?* But I do not ride!'

'Which is precisely why he instructed the stableboys to saddle the quietest mare in the stable for you. Now, go, girl, quickly!'

Mrs Kett's tone brooked no opposition. Mary fled, holding her longish skirts off the ground as she walked. The fabric was heavy—much heavier than the sheer muslin she was accustomed to— and it swished against her with sensuous grace.

One of the stableboys met her at the kitchen door and offered her a selection of boots from which to try. Finding a pair that fit, she allowed one of the maids to help her don them, then she was ready.

Sir Nicholas was waiting just outside the door, and he seemed to catch his breath when he saw her. His eyes swept over her from head to toe and, while his gaze did not particularly linger on her bosom, she felt a tingle go through her as if he had touched her.

'My dear Miss Smith!' He bowed, taking her hand.

'I—' Her voice croaked and she cleared her throat. 'I told you I am frightened of riding.'

'You should understand,' he said confidentially, tucking her left hand into the crook of his arm, 'that I took your statement as something of a challenge.' He smiled down at her. 'To ride is such a wonderful part of my life that it seemed entirely unfitting that you should be deprived of it.'

She was barely listening. 'Lord, why must you be so *tall*?' she declared crossly, spreading her right hand over her cleavage, for of course, as they walked along together, he was almost *forced* to look directly down the front of her dress.

He threw his head back and laughed. 'Your dress is perfect, Miss Smith, but as a man, I would of course say so. Now, tell me honestly, should I lend you my handkerchief to protect your modesty?'

'I should appreciate that, sir.'

He took a spotless white kerchief from his pocket and watched carefully as she tucked it into the bodice of her shocking habit. Once she was satisfied he sighed dramatically, as if mourning the loss of her bosom, then offered her his arm again.

They walked on towards the stables, where a groom was holding the reins of two horses—Sir Nicholas's black stallion and a pretty bay mare.

'Oh, she's beautiful!' Mary could not help exclaiming. 'But—do you really think it is safe for me to sit on her back?'

'Nellie is her name,' said Sir Nicholas indulgently, 'and, yes, she is perfectly safe for you. Now, allow me to help you up.'

This was accomplished with a great deal of nerves on Mary's part and calm instructions on his. Mary hooked her knee across the side saddle and fitted her foot into the strap. Inwardly, she was storing up the memories of every touch between them. Her hand on his shoulder. His steadying hand on her waist, just for a moment. The scent of him, so close by. It was enough to distract her from the fact that she was, for the first time in her life, sitting on a horse. It was only when the groom offered her the reins that she felt a moment's panic. 'Must I?'

'Yes, you must,' insisted Sir Nicholas. 'Now, I shall hold her by the bridle, and we shall walk around the yard.' He clicked his tongue and the horse began a slow walk. Once they had gone around the yard a few times, he stood back, instructing Mary on her use of the reins, how to command the horse to walk and to stop.

'There! You are a natural!' he declared and Mary's heart swelled with pride. 'Now for the real adventure!'

His groom gave him a leg-up and he sat astride his magnificent horse. Now they were almost at eye level again and Mary could not help but give him a sunny smile. He grinned in return and together they rode slowly out of the stable yard and away from the house.

For a good half-hour they slowly rode through the gardens, Mary becoming increasingly confident as he drilled her in stopping, starting and directing the mare to go left, or right. Throughout, he gave Mary warm praise and she basked in the glow of it.

Daringly, they ventured a little further, to the beginnings of the woods. Mary's heart was pounding with excitement and a sense of wonder. Was it because she was riding a horse for the first time, or was it because of the warm looks he was giving her? She could not be sure.

The pale sunlight filtered through the trees, giving everything a verdant glow. The mare picked her way carefully through the undergrowth and Mary shifted her position slightly on the side saddle. The gap between the trees was narrower here and so Sir Nicholas fell in behind her. A little way ahead, she could see a clearing and she turned her horse in that direction.

Then it happened. Something rustled in the undergrowth, spooking the little mare, and she took off at a very fast trot, with Mary bouncing all over the place and desperately trying to keep her seat. A low tree branch loomed in front of her and she ducked to avoid it, pulling on the reins and squeezing the mare's side in a frantic attempt to get her to slow down. Terror threatened to overcome Mary. If she fell, the horse would likely drag her along, as her foot was firmly entangled with the stirrup. Grimly, she held on to the saddle, gripping it as best she could. The reins were now abandoned, as her priority was simply not to fall.

Then Sir Nicholas was there, reaching across to gasp the mare's bridle and stop her. The whole thing had taken only moments, but Mary's heart was pounding in fear and her body trembling from head to toe.

Bringing his horse close to hers, Sir Nicholas enveloped her in a tight one-armed hug. She, trembling, cowered against his hard chest and tried to slow her breathing. Never had she been so frightened.

He half-released her, keeping his hand on her elbow as if to steady her. 'All is well.' His brown eyes were pinning hers. 'You are safe and you managed to slow her down really well. Had it not been for the dense trees in this part of the woods, I'd have reached you sooner.'

She nodded mutely, unable in that moment to speak.

Abruptly, he reached out to stroke her face. His hand was warm, his touch gentle. 'You are safe,' he repeated.

Mary could only look at him. His touch, the fright she had just had, the nearness of him... never had she felt anything like it.

Subtly, the air between them changed. His unwavering gaze now became charged with desire— the same desire that Mary was also feeling.

Mary had not known until now that a woman could feel so alive, so on fire, simply because of how a man looked at her. Fire, flames, sparks...

He exhaled raggedly. 'Shall we go back?' His voice was husky. She knew—was absolutely *certain*—that he, like her, did not wish to go back at all.

She nodded and he reached for her hand. Taking it to his lips, he kissed it, then turned it over to kiss her palm. She gasped again, unable to help herself.

Taking a deep breath, he let go of her hand. After a moment's pause, he passed Mary her own reins, then clicked at his horse to walk on. The mare followed without Mary having to do anything and they accomplished the journey back in a thrilling shared silence.

In the yard he jumped down, relinquishing his stallion to the stableboy who had come running out, then held out his two arms to lift Mary down. She went to him gladly, thrilling in the sensation of both his hands on her waist.

'Thank you,' she said, a little breathlessly, once she felt the security of cobbles beneath her feet.

'I do hope that you have not been too frightened by Nellie's momentary panic?' His tone was normal, yet the air around them both tingled with awareness.

'No, not at all.' It was true. While it had been undoubtedly frightening, overall the experience had been enjoyable. 'It was worth it.'

'I am glad to hear it,' he replied seriously and again a shiver went through her. 'We shall do it again. Soon.' It sounded like a promise.

'And now I must begin today's lessons!' she offered, trying to bring back a sense of the commonplace again.

'Indeed.' He smiled wickedly. 'I wish you good luck!'

Chapter Twelve

Miss Cushing had, predictably, given Mary precise instructions about the lessons she was to lead with Caroline and the boys today, while the ladies were gone. Mary had no notion of obeying them.

Instead, she sent the children running and shrieking around the gardens with their slates, completing the various arithmetical challenges she had set, then asked the nursemaids to take them for a long walk in the woods after nuncheon. It gave her time to enjoy—and be mortified at—memories of her riding adventure with Sir Nicholas. She had known him such a short time, yet already he had become central to her thoughts. Thinking of Sir Nicholas left her entirely confused—desire, admiration, friendship and wariness all warring for superiority.

It would not do. He was her employer and she was here because of Papa's need of her, nothing more. Once she had changed out of the outrageous riding habit, she had carefully folded Sir Nicholas's handkerchief, intending to give it back as soon as she could. With determination, she vowed to put the entire episode behind her and focus entirely on being a good governess.

During the walk, the children were each to collect five objects of 'treasure' she had listed—including such items as an acorn, a willow twig and a pebble. A sweetmeat was to be awarded to anyone who brought back all of the items on their list.

She had already noticed that the younger three were all much kinder to each other—and more well-behaved generally—when they had had the chance to run, and explore, and simply be children. The nursemaids had also reported that bedtime was much easier on those days when the children were tired out by healthy activity. It seemed the riddle of the boys' reputation for challenging behaviour had been answered; they were simply normal children with a need for wildness and freedom to play.

Despite her initial tolerance for Mary's unusual approach, Mrs Fenhurst was becoming increasingly insistent on traditional lessons, egged on by the anxious Miss Cushing, who was clearly fearful of being outshone by her young rival. Mary, realising precisely how things stood, was determined to help the boys learn while playing, for as long as she could possibly manage it. Being a governess was turning out to be much more engaging than she had anticipated.

After her lessons were done, Mary realised with some surprise that there were still a couple of hours of daylight left. Taking the basket of provisions given to her by Mrs Kett, Mary set off for the Home Farm, where Mrs Skipper was glad to report some improvement in her little one's condition. Mary stayed a half-hour and drank a cup of tea, before setting off again—this time for the village and Papa's vicarage.

Miss Lutton was delighted to see her and had some helpful information. Yes, the Bishop had been informed of Papa's having been taken up by the officers. He had been, Miss Lutton understood, shocked by the arrest and was leaving the parish without a vicar for now, with the incumbents in the nearby parishes covering Houghton St Giles. He had indicated he would review the situation after Easter, when it would be known if Mary's papa would be released or convicted. Until then Miss Lutton was to maintain the empty vicarage in a tidy condition.

'Might he speak up on my papa's behalf?' A surge of hope ran through Mary. Surely, with a recommendation from a bishop, her papa would get a more receptive hearing.

Miss Lutton shook her head. 'I have been told

that he will not interfere. The possibility that Mr Smith will be charged with treason means it is too serious, apparently.' She bit her lip. 'My impression is that the primary consideration for the church is the need for discretion. I have been charged to say nothing more than that Mr Smith was called away urgently.'

'An accurate statement, in essence.'

'I believe—and I would not wish to speak ill of a man of God—but my impression is that the Bishop may be more concerned about the possible scandal than about your father himself.'

Mary sighed. 'Many will feel the same, I am sorry to say. Treason is no little charge. I still have no way of discovering why they have taken my papa, though. Was it simply the fact that some important papers were found in this house?'

Miss Lutton shrugged. 'If I am honest, I am not sure which papers were the treasonous ones. Your father has many, many books and papers and pamphlets—indeed, there are so many that dusting them is quite a chore—and he writes and receives dozens of letters, as you will know, miss.'

'But his interests are scholarly. He is a classicist and also enjoys sharing well-thought-through sermons. He has never engaged in anything seditious! What was in these so-called treasonous papers, do you know?'

The housekeeper shrugged. 'Something to do

with the War Office, the constables said. But I do not really understand these things.'

'The War Office? Yes, you had said so in your letter. But Papa has no interest in military matters. He barely mentions the Peninsular campaign, save to hope that too many men are not lost, or to comfort bereaved families.' She frowned. 'I simply do not understand it.'

Miss Lutton grimaced. 'And now he is lying in a gaol and all we can do is pray for him.'

Mary snorted. 'I do pray for him, but I intend to do much more than just pray!' She described her visit to Papa, and Miss Lutton—who had never been inside a prison in her life—was impressed enough to declare that she, too, would find the courage to visit him.

'I did not mention that I knew him,' Mary confessed, 'for fear they would not let me see him.'

'Well, I shall give my true name and discover what they will say to me.'

Mary thanked her, feeling relieved that Papa would see another kindly face in the coming days, 'For I do not know when I shall get the opportunity to visit him again myself. I had hoped to go today, but the ladies were late to leave and so there was not enough time.' Even if she had not gone riding in the woods, there still would not have been enough time.

Miss Lutton patted her hand. 'If your father

is truly innocent, then I cannot see how they can convict him.'

Mary wished she felt so certain about the outcome.

The excursion to Norwich was pronounced a success, with Mrs Fenhurst and Amabel both chattering excitedly about the dresses, bonnets, spencers and slippers they had commissioned. Mary descended to the hallway to greet them on their return and was happy to hear their tales. Beatrice confessed shyly to Mary that she, too, had become caught up in the excitement of trying things on and helping to choose fabrics, styles and trimmings. 'I do hope, Miss Smith, that you do not think me trivial or insipid for finding myself interested in such trifling matters.'

Mary, having recently discovered unexpected understandings within herself, could only say, 'Oh, no! Of course one can be scholarly and clever, and still enjoy pretty dresses.' As she said it, she was struck by how much she was changing by being here in Stiffkey Hall. Never would she have expected to see merit in any focus on a lady's appearance, beyond the requirements of practicality and basic propriety. Yet here she was, not only supporting Beatrice's youthful excitement, but genuinely understanding it. Her classmates in Miss Plumpton's Academy would be shocked if they knew.

In truth, Sir Nicholas was at the heart of her own transformation. It was, she knew, only a foolish thing and really she ought to be ashamed of herself for being so superficial, but she had come to enjoy the admiration in Sir Nicholas's expression when she descended for dinner some nights. She had taken to dressing with care and allowing one of the housemaids to cut and dress her hair. Last night at bedtime she had even tied her hair up in rags to ensure good curls, as her mama had used to do for her.

Thankfully, her wardrobe was nothing to be ashamed of; Papa had ensured she was able to hold her head high among the other young ladies in the Academy by sending her to a good dressmaker before she went away to school. Back then, it had been a frustrating waste of time away from her books. Now, she could only be grateful. Even her lack of a riding habit had turned out well, in an unexpected—yet delightful—way.

Tonight she was wearing an elegant evening gown of pale blue satin, trimmed along the front and the sleeves with white velvet, and worn with long white evening gloves. A matching white velvet bandeau was twined through her dark hair and she tweaked it slightly to ensure it was placed symmetrically. Had she imagined the particularly appreciative look in Sir Nicholas's eye when she had worn this dress last week at dinner?

'Vanity, vanity,' she murmured, checking her appearance in the cheval mirror. She could not find much to criticise, nor yet much to praise. She was reasonably attractive, she supposed, her dark curls and neat figure being nothing out of the ordinary. She had learned to discount compliments about her blue eyes, believing herself to be nothing out of the common way. Yet, tonight, she was forced to concede that perhaps there was something agreeable about their deep blue gaze. She shivered, remembering the look in his eyes earlier, then smiled mischievously at her reflection.

'I am becoming frivolous!' she declared. 'And conceited!' Yet nothing could quell the slight skip of her heart as she descended to the salon to await the call for dinner. This—sitting near him, conversing with him—was becoming the best part of her day.

It would pass, of course, this little *tendre*. She had read about it many times and understood that it was a common fancy, particularly among young ladies. It was an interesting experience, she told herself, and one which intrigued her on a purely rational level. How her body responded to his proximity. How her perception of him was changed by her own feelings. How her thoughts tended to dwell on him in quiet moments...

It is a useful amusement, she told herself, *nothing more.*

She must not add meaning where there was none. Perhaps the fact that this had happened now, when her heart was sick with worry for Papa, was no bad thing. She, like her father, had to survive these days and weeks until the day when Papa would protest his innocence before the magistrate. If her thoughts were to dwell endlessly on poor Papa, she could go quite mad. So she spent much of her days immersing herself in activity, that she might not have time to think about him, slumped eternally on that hard bed in a cold, cold cell.

Nights were more difficult. She was finding it increasingly difficult to sleep, and often woke early, nameless fears clutching at her heart. Now, a wave of terror washed through her briefly, and she shuddered, closing her eyes. Papa!

I can be strong, she told herself.

Opening her eyes, she gazed again at her reflection, this time seeing only resolute determination. She squared her shoulders and went downstairs.

Dinner had been put back because of the ladies' excursion, so when they met in the salon, awaiting the dinner gong, they all were able to exclaim how famished they were and how ready they were to enjoy their evening meal. Miss Cushing looked pale with tiredness and Mary felt a pang of compassion for her. She was quite elderly, Mary reminded herself, and the lack of confidence the governess displayed in her position was probably due, at least in part, to her advancing years and the worry that Mrs Fenhurst would one day no longer need her.

So it was with tolerance that Mary replied to Miss Cushing's sharp questions about the children's behaviour today. They had been, Mary assured her, well-behaved, and had worked hard at the tasks they had been set. Before she was forced to reveal the sylvan nature of the children's lessons, Mary attempted to divert Miss Cushing by asking if the carriage journey had not been too tiring for her.

'Oh, well, these old bones do not like to be jolted along,' Miss Cushing offered, before a look of alarm flashed briefly in her eyes, causing her to add, 'although of course I am fit to carry out my duties at my dear employer's side!'

'I can see that she values your wisdom and companionship,' Mary replied warmly.

Poor Miss Cushing!

An uncertain look flitted across the woman's face. 'Do you?'

Mary eyed her steadily. 'I do. Truly. I believe she relies on you.'

Miss Cushing's brow remained creased, but she nodded tightly.

'Miss Beatrice told me that the modiste was most helpful.'

'Indeed she was,' replied Miss Cushing, 'for she gave us tea and everything.'

'And so she should, for Mrs Fenhurst will likely spend a substantial sum!'

Of Sir Nicholas's money, she added silently.

It was none of her concern, naturally, but she could not help but reflect on the fact that Sir Nicholas seemed unaware of the privilege afforded to him by his riches. Honesty forced her to recognise that, until losing her place at Miss Plumpton's Academy, she, too, had taken her financial security for granted.

She frowned, as her infatuation had led her to start thinking of him as having all the virtues and none of the vices. Here, then, was a vice of sorts and an important signal that she had not fully lost her senses. Of course, it was not his fault that he was unaware of just how privileged he was. It was simply that, now she herself was living with insecurity for the first time, she noticed things she had never noticed before.

I do not think I will ever be able to go back to my old self.

The frown was still there as she took her place by his side at dinner. Naturally, he noted it immediately. 'Are you well, Miss Smith?' he asked, simultaneously thanking the footman who was serving him a large slice of pigeon pie.

Mary looked at the footman, then turned her gaze to Sir Nicholas.

Inwardly, her thoughts were flying furiously. *I have always taken servants for granted. We were not rich, but we always had a housemaid or a housekeeper. Why did I never think enough of what their lives must be like?*

Sir Nicholas was still waiting for her answer. Inwardly tutting at herself for allowing her emotions to display so openly, Mary immediately smoothed out her expression. 'I am quite well, thank you. And you, sir? Are you well?'

He ignored her question, instead sending her a cynical glance. 'I cannot force you to tell me what ails you, unfortunately.'

Now she was back on familiar territory. 'Unfortunately?' She sent him a wicked glance. 'Are my thoughts not my own?'

'That rather depends.'

'On what?'

'On whether it is I who have displeased you in some way. You were looking at me with an expression I can only describe as disdain!' His tone was jocular, but beneath it she sensed she had wounded him a little.

That will not do!

'Not at all,' she declared. 'I assure you, I hold you in—in high esteem!' She had been about to say 'the highest esteem', but that would have been far too gushing. And too revealing, particularly after this morning's incident while riding.

He looked at her for a long moment, then picked up his knife and fork again. 'I am relieved to hear it! Now tell me, will you be free to join me and Beatrice tomorrow in my library? I shall need your expertise, you know, as I have never before taught anyone. Tell me, what text should we offer her to begin with?'

'You forget, sir, that I myself am new to teaching.'

She bit her lip. *Should I have avoided reminding him of my inexperience?*

Thankfully, he brushed this off. 'Well, you clearly have a natural talent for it.' She managed a polite 'thank you', hoping that her inner glow at his words was not obvious. Companionably, they discussed a number of options before settling on Ovid's *Metamorphoses* as an interesting and easy reader. 'I have it in translation as well as in the original,' he added, 'so she can read both side by side to improve her Greek.'

'Perfect—that is how I improved my own learning of languages!'

Some extra sense caused Mary to glance down the table. Mrs Fenhurst was watching them.

*She does not approve of my conversations with
her brother. Why? Can Mrs Fenhurst sense my
interest in him?*

Suddenly unsure of herself, she fell silent and
was a little relieved when, a moment later, Sir
Nicholas turned his attention to Beatrice.

Chapter Thirteen

'Miss Smith! Come and sit by me!' Mrs Fenhurst's tone made it clear that this was an order, not a request. *Oh, dear.* Was she in trouble?

The ladies had withdrawn to the salon, leaving Sir Nicholas and Bramber to their port. They would come to join the ladies in a little while. Mrs Fenhurst made a show of directing Miss Cushing to sit with the girls on a sofa across the room. Clearly she wanted to speak to Mary herself and in private. Miss Cushing, naturally, displayed immediate signs of anxiety at being displaced from her employer's side and sent angry looks Mary's way from the other side of the salon.

Mrs Fenhurst sat silently for a time, seemingly engrossed in her sewing. Mary waited patiently, having no idea what was to come. Mrs Fenhurst then began to involve Mary in some empty conversation. Eventually, she gave a brief sidelong glance and sat up a little straighter.

Mary's awareness prickled into alertness. *Here it comes.*

'While we were in Norwich today...' Mrs Fenhurst began, with a casual air.

'Yes?'

This was a little confusing. *Is this to do with Papa?*

'Which, by the way, was a most successful trip—I have every hope that the modiste may create some creditable gowns for myself and my girls!' She nodded in a satisfied way. 'We shall return in a few days for another fitting, with the dresses being ready next week, in time for my first soirée.'

'That is reassuring.'

Mary's polite response masked her bewilderment. *I know all of this. Why should she repeat it?*

Mrs Fenhurst's next statement revealed her true purpose. 'While we were away, Miss Smith, what did you do?'

Mary froze for a moment.

I exchanged wanton looks with your brother and he hugged me and kissed my hand. I failed to provide formal lessons for the boys and Caroline. I visited my papa's housekeeper and talked of his imprisonment for treason.

'I—er—well, that is to say, I worked on some arithmetic with Caroline, Edmond and David. After that I visited the Home Farm—Mrs Kett gave me some provisions to pass on, as they have a sick baby.'

Mrs Fenhurst was listening with avid interest. 'What did you do after that?'

Mary took a breath.

Keep to the truth as much as you can.

'I walked to Houghton St Giles and called on the vicar's housekeeper.'

Mrs Fenhurst frowned. 'Yes, yes, all very laudable, no doubt. The sick and the poor and your Christian duty. But what did you do when you came back here, to Stiffkey Hall?'

Mary's brow knitted with confusion. 'I went to my chamber and read until I heard your carriage arriving. Then we all went upstairs to dress for dinner.'

'And that is everything? You did not read *with* anyone before going upstairs?'

Oh, Lord.

'No, ma'am.'

That is perfectly true, yet I am dishonest.

'Very well.' Mrs Fenhurst straightened, smoothing her skirt. 'I must be satisfied that you are spending your time in useful ways while you are in this household. I deplore idleness!'

'Of course.' Mary could not be sure, but she sensed that she had been in some danger just now. She could not afford to turn Mrs Fenhurst against her.

Sir Nicholas might well be her employer in name and he might enjoy dinner table conversations with her, but if Mrs Fenhurst wanted her gone, Mary could not imagine Sir Nicholas resisting his determined sister.

He is altogether too indolent to do so.

In truth, she could not imagine him suffering any personal discomfort in order to aid another. She frowned.

Am I judging him harshly? He would probably admit to his indolence.

In seeking to push against her attraction towards him, was she now leaning too far in the other direction and finding fault simply for the sake of it?

Remembering his kindness to her when her mare had bolted, Mary knew she was being unfair. Yet something within her persisted in seeking to criticise him. It would be a shield to counter these other, perilous feelings.

Still, when the gentlemen joined them, Mary deliberately focused her attention on Mr Bramber. Both Sir Nicholas and his sister felt dangerous to her just now. With both of them, she needed to be guarded—not just because of Papa, but because she was becoming much too drawn to Sir Nicholas and she wanted neither him nor Mrs Fenhurst to know it.

So she avoided his gaze, instead smiling politely at Mr Bramber and inviting him to sit by her. They passed a comfortable half-hour discussing matters of no moment, but his easy company was balm to Mary's troubled mind. Here was an uncomplicated conversation with someone who had no secrets, no hidden purpose and no desire to criticise her.

Gradually her shoulders dropped a little and after a while she was able to smile with natural enthusiasm. She did notice, as Mr Bramber was describing a conversation he had had with Miss Reeve outside church last Sunday, that his ears were a little pink. It made her recall Sir Nicholas's cryptic comment that night when the Fenhursts first arrived.

I have never noticed Mr Bramber's ears before! I wonder, is that their usual colour?

'—Do you think?'

She started, then flushed as she realised she had quite forgotten to listen to him.

How rude of me!

Impulsively, she laid a hand on his arm. 'Oh, Mr Bramber, I was momentarily wool-gathering. What was it you just said?'

The tips of his ears grew even pinker. 'Oh, I was simply prattling about unimportant matters. But tell me, what did you do with your free time today?'

Perhaps his ears grow pink when he is uncomfortable.

She withdrew her hand and, as she did so, something in Sir Nicholas's stillness across the room drew her eyes towards him. He was glaring at them, his face with an expression like thunder. To his left, his sister was talking, her eyes on her sewing.

Hopefully it is his sister who has angered him, not me or poor Mr Bramber!

Decidedly startled by Sir Nicholas's ferocious expression, Mary bit her lip and turned her attention back to her companion. 'I visited Mrs Skipper at the Home Farm,' she replied.

Mr Bramber beamed at her. 'Ah, you are a good person, Mary.'

She flushed, dropping her gaze. *If only you knew how I have been deceiving everyone.*

'Not in the least. The baby is much improved anyway—though Mrs Skipper was grateful for Mrs Kett's gifts of food.'

Bramber smiled at Mary. 'I am glad you have come here. I believe others are, too.'

Mary shook her head.

I am not so certain.

'I do not wish to be trouble to anyone.'

He leaned forwards, speaking confidentially. 'Trouble may be a good thing. Life in Stiffkey Hall has been too quiet for too long.'

'Bramber!' It was Mrs Fenhurst. 'We are to play a round of cards. Come and make up a four with Amabel and Nicky!'

'Very well, ma'am.' With a nod to Mary, he rose, helping Sir Nicholas set up the card table and draw the chairs around it. As they played, Mary moved to sit with Beatrice. Miss Cushing had already departed, probably relieved to be able to retire after such a long day.

'How do you, Beatrice?'

'I am sorely fatigued,' the girl replied frankly. 'Do you think I might go to bed?'

Mary glanced at the clock. 'Of course you may—and what is more, I shall retire, too.' She patted the girl's hand. 'You have had a long day.'

Beatrice yawned, bringing her hand up to cover her mouth. 'Indeed, it seems like forever since I rose this morning.' She gave Mary her familiar shy smile. 'My uncle told me at dinner that you and he are to help me with my Greek reading tomorrow.'

'If I have no other duties to attend to and Miss Cushing does not object,' Mary confirmed. Miss Cushing? It was Mrs Fenhurst herself who might object.

'But how can she object? You are saving her from having to do it.' Beatrice's guileless expression suddenly made Mary feel old.

You have no idea, child, of the currents that eddy and swirl beneath the still pool of this household.

Aloud she said only, 'I expect you are right.'

They stood and bade the card-players goodnight. Mary could not help but include Sir Nicholas in her general gaze. His expression was shuttered, his words no warmer than polite.

It is best that it is so, Mary told herself.

All else was foolishness.

Nicholas heard the click of the door closing behind them, the murmur of their voices in the hallway as they moved away. He still felt angry with Miss Smith and he was unclear why.

She was simply too…what? Too attractive? Certainly he benefitted from the pleasure of enjoying her pretty face and perfect form. This morning's episode while riding had been preoccupying him all day.

She seemed to be growing more beautiful by the day—though perhaps it was simply that he had been away from London too long. Yet, strangely, he had no desire to travel to the capital, even though it was full of brothels and willing courtesans. Somehow, a simple governess had caught his fancy.

Was she too fascinating? There was depth to her and character. She had what his grandmother would have called 'countenance'—a composed, self-assured disposition that was admirable in itself. And yet, there were moments, too, when he felt that her composure was but a mask and that hidden emotions and opinions agitated beneath her calm expression.

Tonight, he had definitely read disapproval in her arch look towards him, as they were taking their seats for dinner. She had denied it, of course, but he could not shake the impression that he had disappointed her in some way. Having racked his brains all evening, he was no closer to discovering what action or word of his had so displeased her. Could it have been the incident involving his handkerchief? She had undoubtedly been mortified and he would not have dreamed of taking advantage of the situation. She had seemed to welcome his spontaneous hug at the time. And she had trembled when he had kissed her hand. Had she been shivering still with fear, or was it something else?

She had given him back his handkerchief earlier, with a no-nonsense, 'Thank you'. It now rested in his pocket and he was conscious of the urge to make a treasure of it. It had, after all, adorned that bosom that so completely occupied his thoughts.

And then—then she had not as much as glanced his way when he and Bramber had joined the ladies, preferring instead to shower her attentions on Bramber.

Bramber! My secretary!

Nicholas was unused to being passed over in such a way. Somewhere he retained a dim memory of wondering if she would do for Bramber, but that was in the long distant past. Besides, Bramber had made it clear that another lady had taken his fancy.

Yet somehow, his logical brain had been suffocated by the swell of emotion he felt when he thought of Miss Smith.

She is my friend. I think.

Somehow they had already developed an amity which had helped alleviate the tedium of his sister's visit—and indeed, of the empty days preceding it. For the first time, he dared to question the choices he had made—his abhorrence of London, his decision to remain cooped up here, thinking only of scholarly pursuits. Miss Smith had reanimated something within him that he had not even noticed had died.

The friendship part is easy, he told himself, selecting and discarding cards with half a brain, *but I have never before been so drawn to an attractive woman in two ways at once.*

He paused to reflect on this. He had had easy friendships with women occasionally—his friends' sisters, usually, but it had only occurred with women he did not find particularly attractive. With Miss Smith, however, there was a heady mix of being drawn to her face and body, as well as to her mind and character. And yet, unaccountably, tonight she had seemed to favour his secretary. He glared at Bramber, who sat opposite him, paired with Miss Amabel.

'For goodness sake, Nicky, are you deliberately trying to lose us the trick?'

Surprised, he glanced down at his discard. 'Apologies, Sister, it is getting late and I confess I am becoming fatigued. I shall remain riveted to the cards for the rest of the game.'

She snorted. 'See that you do so. If I had known you would be so distracted, I should have partnered with Mr Bramber instead! Tonight, Bramber, you are by far Nicky's superior!'

'Why, thank you, ma'am.' Bramber grinned.

Nicholas's scowl deepened, as he was possessed by a sudden determination to win the game. Pushing thoughts of Miss Smith aside, he gave his full attention to the cards, mercilessly combining with his sister to thoroughly defeat Bramber and Amabel.

Bramber, who occasionally had been known to display a streak of rivalry during their card games, seemed tonight to be in a strange humour. The more ruthless Nicholas became, the more amused his secretary seemed to be. Nicholas could make no sense of it at all.

According to Jarvis, the elderly butler, the library at Stiffkey Hall had been the pride of three generations of Dennys. The walls had been shelved from floor to ceiling and there were in the room hundreds of books, pamphlets and scrolls. To Mary, it seemed like a treasure house. The Denny scholarly tradition had apparently been passed from father to son to grandson, and Sir Nicholas had talked to Mary of the vital importance of developing a well-informed mind. Like Papa, he seemed not to discriminate between males and females, although Mary was wary of assuming this.

Having been raised with a fine appreciation of knowledge and wisdom, Mary was now discovering within herself a genuine love of sharing learning with others. Miss Cushing was busy with the younger children this morning, so Mary, without informing either her or Mrs Fenhurst of her intentions, had simply repaired to the library with Miss Beatrice after breakfast.

Sir Nicholas was yet to join them, so they both enjoyed having a little time to explore the library's treasures. Like excited children they giggled and exclaimed their way around the room, marvelling at the sheer number of texts and discovering notable books everywhere they looked.

'Oh, my goodness, it is *The Divine Comedy*— and in the original Italian!' Mary breathed, stroking the book cover with reverence.

Beatrice's eyes grew round. 'I could never read a book in Italian.'

'Of course you can!' smiled Mary. 'It is simply a matter of practice. Ooh—look at this! *Much Ado About Nothing*—the one with your namesake in it. I must say I do prefer Mr Shakespeare's comedies over his tragedies!'

'I could not agree more.' It was Sir Nicholas, standing in the doorway. Mary's heart skipped, as it always did when she encountered him. 'The language in both the tragedies and the comedies is inspired, but at least at the end of one of the comedies there are characters yet living!' He stepped inside, closing the door behind him.

Mary laughed. 'Yes! And there is usually a love story, too, which always helps.'

His gaze steadied on her; his smile faded. 'I do not abhor a good love story.'

All at once Mary's mouth was dry. Beatrice, seemingly unaware of the sudden suspense in the air, skipped towards Sir Nicholas. 'Uncle Nicky, thank you so much for allowing me into your library! I cannot take in my good fortune!'

He smiled down indulgently at the girl, causing Mary's heart, already racing, to turn over with some unnamed emotion. 'Well, what are books for, if not to be read?'

'Indeed, and there are so many I wish to read!' Mary allowed her gaze to sweep around the shelves. 'I could spend a lifetime in this room,' she murmured.

Beatrice nodded. 'It would surely take a lifetime. What do you think, Uncle? May Miss Smith and I live here forever? I promise we should not be in the way!'

Mary watched him closely. It seemed as though his eyes widened briefly, before his customary neutral expression reasserted itself. He pretended to consider the matter, tilting his head on one side and rubbing his chin thoughtfully with one long finger. 'I suspect,' he said finally, 'that we three, if we lived together for always, would become the greatest scholars in Christendom!'

Beatrice clapped her hands at this and Mary was struck by how the girl's natural animation had revealed itself inside this world of books.

'Now, to work!' Sir Nicholas added, his tone denoting mock sternness. 'Miss Smith and I discussed your education last night, and we decided that you shall begin with Ovid.'

'*The Metamorphoses?* How exciting! I have read parts already—in English of course.' She sent Mary a dubious look. 'Some of it was very shocking!'

'Ah, well, they were like that, the ancients,' Sir Nicholas murmured, his voice sending a wicked shiver up Mary's spine. She could not help it; she caught his eye, then blushed at what she saw there. Heat. Desire. Passion.

She recognised it somewhere deep within her mammal body. How could she not, when she felt exactly the same? Really, Sir Nicholas was expanding her education in many unexpected ways.

They settled Beatrice down with side-by-side copies of *The Metamorphoses* in English and Greek, then picked up their own books to quietly read. Strangely, Mary could not sustain her attention on her own book. She, who normally craved moments like this—a good book, in a quiet place, and time to read.

Yet today she kept being distracted by the situation itself. By Sir Nicholas. Even by their shared responsibility for Beatrice. There was almost an air of family about it. She sighed. If only her papa could be here, safe and free. The scene would then be perfect.

Nicholas was conscious of the strangest feeling. Something about the conversation had profoundly unsettled him and he was unsure what it was. Amid the ticking of the library clock and the occasional rustle of a page being turned, he could feel his heart thrumming with emotion. Beatrice, at fifteen, was an engaging child and Mary, though not her mother, was being a better mother to her just now than Susan. He shook his head slightly.

Mary was a bare few years older than his niece. Why should he be thinking of her in such a way?

Instantly an image came to him, of Mary nursing a baby. Shockingly, the notion infused him with a sense of *rightness* he had never before felt.

Like a skittish horse, he shied away from the thought. *She is a good teacher and will some day make a good mother.*

No, he would not think of who the father of her child might be. It was none of his concern.

Chapter Fourteen

Mrs Fenhurst found them out, of course. While her outward complaint was about Beatrice being quite clever enough already, Mary knew that Mrs Fenhurst's disapproval also stemmed from her own involvement. It was Sir Nicholas's house and he had to be indulged, but she could not like it.

Days went by and Mrs Fenhurst grumbled, yet each morning, without fail, Sir Nicholas, Beatrice and Mary would gather in the library to read and learn together. Mary could sense a firm friendship building between uncle and niece and it warmed her heart to see it. He spoke of it one day, as they were leaving the library together and Beatrice hurried ahead.

'Thank you.' His voice was low and she turned to him in confusion.

'For what?'

'For helping me see the true Beatrice. The younger ones, too. It is only Amabel that I still feel I do not know—although perhaps it would always have been more difficult to be her friend, for she thinks only of fashion.'

Mary thought of Amabel—her brittleness, her fear of ridicule. 'Amabel needs you, too. Do not doubt it.'

He cast her a warm glance. 'If you say so, then I believe it. You have a sound head, Miss Smith.'

She flushed. His gaze added warmth to the words, reminding her of things unspoken. Her mortification about the riding habit incident had faded a little, but her desire for Sir Nicholas had not. There had been no opportunity for them to ride again—there was an unspoken understanding between Mary and Sir Nicholas that to do so under Mrs Fenhurst's eye would be madness. However, they had taken the opportunity to walk in the gardens occasionally, discussing anything and everything that occurred to them. By unspoken agreement, they tended to walk in the gardens behind the house, which were not overlooked by Mrs Fenhurst's chamber, or the Yellow Parlour, where she tended to sit in the afternoons.

These past two weeks, Mary knew, had served to strengthen a sense of companionship between them, as they shared their joint passion for scholarly pursuits and a simple enjoyment in each other's company. It gave her a delightful feeling of warmth to know that she had found a friend.

Helpfully, Mrs Fenhurst's attention was becoming increasingly engaged by the events she was planning, the first of which—a soirée musicale—was to take place tomorrow night. Mary had been busy assisting with the guest lists and planning with the housekeeper, cook and butler. She now felt she knew most of the staff reasonably well, particularly Seth and James, the shy footmen, Sally, the pert scullery maid, and Mrs Kett, the warm-hearted housekeeper.

Mrs Fenhurst, like her brother, seemed to make no effort to engage with servants as people. The Dennys had clearly been raised with a firm notion of their place in the world. However, Mrs Fenhurst did seem to genuinely find it helpful that Mary was helping with her planning.

'Miss Cushing is a dear,' she declared confidentially to Mary, after a successful review of the plans with the staff, 'but she has no head for organising!'

Mary was simply relieved that Mrs Fenhurst had admitted she found her useful. That night sleep came a little more easily, although she woke early, threads of a delicious dream just out of reach.

'Today is the day!' declared Beatrice, with an air of excitement. They had all three convened as usual in the library after breakfast and were reaching for their books and finding their places. 'The soirée musicale is tonight and I am to be included!'

'Is this, then, your first grown-up party, little one?' Sir Nicholas's tone was indulgent. It did Mary's heart good to see this softer side to him. Beatrice, too, was continuing to grow in confidence and Mary delighted in the bond forming between the girl and Sir Nicholas. She, too, was forging strong bonds with both of them—it felt now as though she and Sir Nicholas shared a sense of pride in their protegée, Beatrice.

'It is! Our new gowns are not yet ready—indeed, we are to return to Norwich next week for a final fitting—so I shall wear my green satin evening dress. And Amabel has fixed her gown so that it will be quite presentable.'

'I am delighted to hear it!' His tone was dry. 'Miss Smith, do you enjoy social events?'

Mary considered this. 'A few short weeks ago, I would have replied with an unhesitating "no". And yet, I do find myself looking forward to tonight. I am a fickle creature, I suppose.'

'Not at all! For a few weeks ago you had not yet sampled the delights of residing in Stiffkey Hall!' His eyes danced with humour.

'True! And all its fascinating residents!'

'The reclusive uncle…the shy maiden…' He indicated Beatrice, who joined in with glee.

'Miss Smith, you shall play the put-upon governess in this scene!'

'Oh, no!' Devilment glinted in Sir Nicholas's eye. 'That role has already been claimed by Miss Cushion!'

'Cushing!' Mary and Beatrice corrected him in unison and they all laughed aloud.

Mary was struck by how much in charity with them she felt. Despite everything—her desperate worries about Papa, the anxiety about being found out as the daughter of a man accused of treason—she was glad that fate had brought her here, to this house and these people.

That glow of rightness sustained her through afternoon lessons with two devil-may-care boys, under the watchful eye of Miss Cushing. It took her through Miss Cushing's lecture afterwards, highlighting all of the things she had failed to do correctly and should try to do better tomorrow.

It became a little rickety when Mrs Fenhurst snapped at her during afternoon tea, having discovered that no one had dyed her spare gloves purple, as she had apparently requested. Mary had no recollection of any such request and it was not anywhere on her list of tasks for the staff, but she knew better than to argue. Taking a breath and biting back the words she truly wanted to say, instead she simply apologised.

'Hrrmph! You must do better, Mary. How am I to rely on you when you forget the most important tasks?'

Mary diverted her a little by asking what dress Mrs Fenhurst planned to wear and persuading her that her white evening gloves would be just the thing. 'If you are planning to wear a purple gown, ma'am, with purple feathers and purple gloves, then who knows, the gloves may have made your ensemble too purple, in effect.'

'Too purple? Hmmm, perhaps.' She wagged a finger. 'But I have not forgotten that you failed to ensure it was done!'

Lord! She could dismiss me on a whim and there is nothing I could do about it.

Mary was unused to this lack of security, having always had a home with Papa to fall back on. Constantly biting back her words and hiding her spontaneous thoughts was proving to be more challenging than she had anticipated. Yet, giving in to an impulse to speak freely could lead to disaster.

Finally, it was time for their dinner guests to arrive. Mary's stomach fluttered as she descended the staircase and saw, for the first time, Sir Nicholas in full evening wear in the hallway below.

My, he is handsome!

He looked up at her, his gaze sweeping over

her elegant hairstyle, bare neck and silk gown in a pretty shade of primrose.

'You look delightful, Miss Smith!' he declared, taking her hand as she reached the second step from the bottom. He bent over her hand and she felt the warmth of his lips through her thin evening glove. Her heart was pounding and, as he straightened, she realised that his face was directly level with hers. Level and close, so close.

Her breath caught in her chest. In fact, she could not breathe. Time stood still as she gazed into his dark eyes, unable to speak.

He wants to kiss me!

To Mary's left, someone walked towards the front door, breaking the spell. She glanced across to see the footman open the door. The first of the guests had arrived. Sir Nicholas, his expression shuttered, bowed and turned away.

Mary took the final steps down into the hall, then made for the salon. It was Sir Nicholas's duty to welcome his guests, but his sister should stand with him as hostess. 'Ma'am, someone is arriving,' she reported.

Mrs Fenhurst rose, a vision in purple, her feather headdress nodding as she walked. 'Punctuality is a virtue, I suppose. Sit up straight, girls!' This was directed at Amabel and Beatrice, bookending Miss Cushing on their usual sofa. They both looked nervous, so Mary sent them a kind smile.

A moment later, the footman directed the first two guests into the salon and the soirée began. By the time the gong sounded for dinner, fourteen people were gathered in the salon. Mary tried to recall who they all were. As well as the family, herself, Miss Cushing and Mr Bramber, there were two married couples, a middle-aged gentleman called Sir Harold Gurney, and not one, but two vicars. Including Sir Nicholas and Mr Bramber, that meant there were seven men to match the seven women, five of whom resided currently in Stiffkey Hall, two of whom were governesses. Mrs Fenhurst had made it plain that Mary should not expect to be automatically included in all of the dinners and was there simply to make up the numbers.

'Fourteen is a goodish number for my first soirée,' she had declared, all self-satisfaction, 'particularly as it is Beatrice's first engagement. I shall place you, Mary, between the two vicars, for as a vicar's daughter yourself you were raised to not find sermons tedious.'

Mary had simply looked at her, unwilling to protest. There would be no point in doing so.

I am becoming altogether too compliant, she thought.

She must be careful not to let this temporary

need for discretion become a habit with her. Still, at least her earlier worries—that she would be unable to hold back from expressing unaccept-able opinions—had receded. Yes, on occasion, her true opinions had become known, but—so far, at least—they had not fatally damaged her position here.

And so she found herself seated between the two vicars—Mr Easton and Mr Fuller. The two clergymen could not have been more different. Mr Fuller was plump, smiling and congenial, while his colleague was lath-thin, unreadable and taci-turn.

Mary did her best to converse with both of them equally, but Mr Fuller's outgoing nature made her task much more straightforward. He was a widower, with three grown-up children and a brace of grandchildren. Once she had discov-ered this, Mary needed only to encourage him to describe the children's character and achieve-ments and he was content to do so. At length, and in quite some detail.

In marked contrast, Mr Easton revealed no par-ticular hobbies or interests and, once he discov-ered she was a governess, seemed to decide that she could have nothing to say that might be of interest to him. Mary resorted to making empty comments on the weather and the food. Even then, she was largely unsuccessful, for Easton seemed to eat without tasting and expressed no preference for any of Cook's lovingly prepared dishes. He was much younger than his colleague, but his world-weary expression and permanent frown suggested an older soul.

Her papa probably knew both of them. Strange to think that they would probably all have met together, before Papa's arrest. Did they know why Papa had disappeared? Miss Lutton had suggested the Bishop had covered up the entire story, so they might genuinely think Papa was away visiting someone. She imagined how she might discuss both men with Papa and the thought made her happy and sad at the same time. She and her father shared the same enjoyment of the ridiculous and Mary knew that, had Papa been here, he would have teased her about being trapped between two such dull men.

That is unkind of me, she thought.

Both gentlemen were perfectly cordial and Mr Fuller in particular was warm and engaging. Glancing up, she happened to catch Sir Nicholas's eye. There was a glint of humour there, which she found reassuring.

He knows!

Sir Nicholas was not Papa, but right now he was the next best thing.

She frowned. *No.* He was the *best* thing, in a different way entirely. Unwilling to examine the thought, instead she asked Mr Easton if he had spent much time in London. 'I have been at school there until recently,' she explained.

'I do visit the capital on occasion, but I was last there in the autumn, so hardly recent.'

'And do you enjoy the city?' she prompted politely.

'Not at all. It is full of vice and vulgarity. Why should riches rest with such unworthy people? And why should they consider themselves to be better than others?' He snorted. 'The *haut ton*, as they style themselves, are sinners and the worst of reprobates. The fact that they drive around in expensive carriages and wear expensive clothes matters little.' He took another draught of wine, then applied himself to his blancmange.

Well. Finally, Mr Easton had expressed an opinion and in no uncertain terms. Mary, however, was in no position to argue with him. Nor, frankly, did she wish to. She had already recognised that Easton was unimaginative and judgemental. Such persons were not persuadable. Reason meant nothing to someone whose opinion was already fixed. Indeed, any suggestion that the truth might be different to what they believed tended to lead them to vigorous stubbornness. So she pretended polite interest, sipped a little of her own wine, then returned to commenting on the dinner.

* * *

Thankfully, the ordeal finally ended and Mary escaped with the other ladies to the salon, leaving the gentlemen to shake off whatever remained of their sobriety with bottles of the finest port.

'Well, Beatrice? How did you enjoy your first grown-up dinner?'

'If I am honest, it was not nearly as exciting as I believed it would be,' the girl admitted. 'Sir Harold was rather formidable—although he did not mean to be, I am sure. He talked of his responsibilities as Justice of the Peace and I was glad to have Mr Bramber on my other side to reassure me with gentle conversation.'

There was a roaring in Mary's ears. Sir Harold Gurney, Justice of the Peace. The man who would pronounce judgement on her father. Of course he would be part of the family's set. In a small rural community, all of the gentry would know each other. She cursed herself for her stupidity. When Mrs Fenhurst had added Sir Harold to her guest list, Mary had thought the name familiar, but had assumed some of the family must have mentioned him. No. It had been the prison guard.

Her heart pounding, Mary tried to think of what to do. This was a heaven-sent opportunity, yet how should she use it? No one here knew about Papa and one could hardly mention a prisoner facing a possible charge of treason without exciting interest.

'Are you unwell, Miss Smith?' Beatrice had laid a hand on her arm and was looking vexed.

'Actually, Beatrice, I do feel a little warm.'

Beatrice beckoned a nearby housemaid, who had been serving ratafia and punch to the ladies. Even Miss Cushing had accepted a small glass. 'Please fetch some cold punch for Miss Smith.'

'Yes, miss.'

'I do not wish to make a fuss,' Mary protested weakly.

In truth her mind was awhirl. *Papa's judge is here!*

'Not at all,' murmured Beatrice as they moved to sit near the terrace doors, which had been opened to allow some cooling air into the room.

'How do you now, Miss Smith?' Beatrice was regarding her anxiously.

'Much better.' She attempted a smile. 'Thank you. I must say, I am grateful for your care and attention. It is a sign of the excellence of your character.'

'Rather, it is a sign of my regard for you, Miss Smith,' Beatrice replied quietly. 'Indeed, were it not for you and my uncle, this whole visit would have been something of an ordeal. Generally I prefer books to real people, but it is good to be reminded that real people have much to commend them!'

Mary smiled. 'I am also learning much about myself and about the world by being here in Stiffkey Hall. And you are one of my favourite people here.'

Beatrice glowed at the praise. 'I have sadly little in common with Mama or Amabel, so I always believed myself to be defective in some way.'

'I felt the same way at school. You are very wise, Beatrice, to understand this truth at such a young age. I do hope you understand that we are neither of us defective and that it is natural to be different. Besides…' she grinned '…we are both learning to enjoy fripperies and fashion and to be excited by social events, so perhaps we are not so different from other ladies after all!'

Just then, Beatrice's mama called her across to sit with her. Mary bade her go. 'I am still a little warm and so will follow you in a few minutes,' she promised.

In truth, she needed a moment's solitude. The shock of Sir Harold's identity had begun to dissipate, but Mary was no closer to knowing how to use the information to Papa's advantage.

Too late! The door was opened and the gentlemen were joining them. Her palms sticky with sudden anxiety, Mary moved to sit with the main party.

Chapter Fifteen

'Delighted to make your acquaintance, Miss Smith!' Sir Harold had reached the flushed, exuberant stage of boskiness—a state shared by many of the gentlemen who had been in a raucous mood as they joined the ladies after what must have been copious amounts of port. Only Mr Easton and Sir Nicholas maintained the appearance of sobriety—although Mary had noted that the dour vicar was swaying a little on his feet. She sighed inwardly. One got such little sense out of gentlemen at the best of times. Why did they compound it by imbibing so much alcohol?

'What a delightful dinner party!' Sir Harold added. He was clearly determined to be delighted about everyone and everything, so perhaps this might be a good moment to engage him in conversation about his prisoners.

She took a breath. 'Indeed, sir. Miss Beatrice tells me you are a Justice of the Peace.'

His chest swelled. 'I am indeed. All of the local miscreants and no-goods come before me eventually.'

This was hardly a promising beginning. 'I have been visiting the prisoners in the Walsingham Bridewell. It is, I think, quite a modern building?'

He nodded. 'Built after the model devised by John Howard himself.' He named the great prison reformer—the man who had insisted that single cells would cut down on prisoner sickness. Mary fervently hoped that Mr Howard was right and that Papa would be spared the curse of prison fever.

'I do believe that we must treat prisoners with kindness—particularly those who have not yet been convicted of any crime.'

He gave her a pitying smile. 'You ladies are far too soft-hearted! I am certain I have rarely seen an innocent man or woman in my court. No, it is my lot to judge and to punish them—or occasionally to send them on to London if needs be.'

Mary's heart sank. Sir Harold was clearly one of those who believed that innocence should be proven, rather than guilt.

How will Papa fare before such a man? She shuddered at the thought.

'But we should not speak of such tedious matters when we have wine and congenial company!' He grinned at her. 'Come now, Miss Smith, will you take some wine?'

Wine was the last thing she wished for right now, but she agreed in order to not argue with him. She sipped at it slowly, listening to his tales of hunting success, until Mrs Fenhurst rescued her by opening the pianoforte and calling on Amabel to play. By the time all the ladies had performed—including Mary herself, who had completed a creditable performance of a Haydn piece—Sir Harold had taken to the red-striped sofa in the corner, where he was snoring fitfully.

Her frustrated glance towards him was seen by Sir Nicholas, who approached her with a raised eyebrow and a crooked smile. 'You do not approve of Sir Harold?'

Mary felt herself flush. This was their first conversation since he had kissed her hand on the stairs earlier.

He is so handsome!

'It is not my place to approve or disapprove of any of your guests, sir.'

'Tosh! I know you too well now, Miss Smith. What has Sir Harold done to attract your disapprobation?'

Sir Harold is drunk and snoring in a corner while Beatrice is singing. And he is likely to deal harshly with poor Papa. She opened her mouth, then closed it again. *I cannot say that out loud.*

'Your niece is singing just now,' she offered carefully.

'She is.' He leaned closer and spoke quietly into her ear. 'I am determined to subdue the impact on my tortured senses.'

She sent him a cross look. 'Oh, stop! She is just a little anxious, that is all.'

'Anxious?' he said, his eyes full of amusement, then, seeing a disapproving glance from his sister, spoke a little more quietly. 'So she should be, with a singing voice like that!'

'I thought you liked Beatrice.'

He snorted. 'I am not so blinded by familial loyalty that I have lost my sense of hearing!'

She stifled a laugh. 'Do not be unkind, sir. How would you like to be asked to sing, in front of all of these people?'

'Unkind? I am merely speaking the truth. Why, Beatrice's tuneless keening has even sent poor Sir Harold into oblivion.'

Sir Harold. She frowned. 'I do not think it is right to fall asleep during a performance, no matter what you say.'

'You seemed to be engaging in some debate with him earlier.' He sent her a glance. 'What were you discussing?'

'The treatment of prisoners,' she replied shortly. She still felt cross with him.

'Ah! Let me guess. You hoped to find some softness in him and he disappointed you.'

'He assumes that everyone who comes before

him is a miscreant who must be punished!' She could feel her anger rise. 'Surely it is his responsibility to judge who may be innocent, as well as the guilty?'

Beatrice's song had come to an end, so they paused to applaud her efforts. One of the guests—a married lady—then took her seat at the pianoforte and began shuffling through the music sheets there. Mrs Fenhurst joined her to assist her in choosing her piece.

'Lord! When will this end?' Sir Nicholas murmured in Mary's ear.

Ignoring the delightful shivers going through her, which were confusingly mixed with increasing ire, she turned to look him full in the eye. 'You have no taste for music?'

'I enjoy it when there is a certain level of proficiency.'

She raised an ironic eyebrow. 'Are you yourself proficient with any instrument?'

I would wager he gave little time to music as a student. Lord, he could be so much more understanding!

'I am not. I lacked...' he gave a rueful smile 'application.'

'I knew it! That is just what I thought you would say.' Abruptly, frustration with Sir Harold and frustration with Sir Nicholas merged into one. Part of her knew that it was mostly Sir Harold she was cross with and that it was fuelled by concern for Papa, but she could not help herself.

'How so?' His brow creased.

'Well, you seem so…' Her voice tailed away.

'Pray, continue. I seem so—what?'

She could not hold the words back. 'You have everything you need. Wealth, a comfortable home, servants, a family who admire you. And yet I sense a—a lack in you.'

She bit her lip. *Stop talking!*

He was eyeing her keenly, eyebrow raised. 'You interest me greatly. What is this "lack" your wisdom has seen fit to identify?'

She flushed. 'I should not be speaking so frankly. It is a failing of mine. In truth, I have surprised myself by how long I have kept my tongue silent since I came here.'

He ignored this. 'I insist on hearing your opinion. It is a rare chance for me to understand how another might see me.'

She shook her head. 'I must not say any more.'

He was definitely frowning. 'It is too late for that now. I must insist as your employer that you continue.'

Oh, Lord! She straightened, eyeing him levelly. *I shall tell him.*

'Very well. You lack purpose, sir, and insight. I sense great power in you—the potential to be someone who can make his mark upon the world.

Yet here you stay, with your books and your comfort.' She shrugged. 'I know that you visit London occasionally, that you hunt with the rest in season, that you welcome your sister here each year at this time and her whole family in the autumn. But apart from that, I have not been able to discover that you actually *do* anything.'

'I do plenty, I shall have you know!' he retorted, clearly stung. 'You yourself understand the importance of the mind and of scholarly learning.'

'Of course, and that is why I can see you so clearly, I believe. As a scholar myself and the daughter of a scholar—' she faltered a little '—I enjoy studying and learning, and I understand its value. But I also understand that I have a responsibility to my fellow man.'

He grimaced. 'Oh, spare me from charitable benevolence. I am as much a philanthropist as any other gentleman. I pay a substantial amount every year to sustain the orphans and my housekeeper provides food and gifts for the local needy.'

'And that is exactly what a man might say who has no true idea of the suffering of others and his duty to help.' Her right hand was gripping and releasing a fold of her dress.

Like me before my change in circumstances, he barely notices the servants.

'There are many like you, sir. The difference is that I believe you do have a heart and so you have potential. That is why it is frustrating to be around you!'

He kept looking at her, his expression now half-hurt, half-angry. 'No one dares to speak to me as you have!'

'Ah, but you bade me do so, as your employee,' she returned. 'You cannot turn me off for it, as I was simply following your instructions!'

He gave a bark of laughter. 'And that is how you shall get away with it—for tonight, at least!' He shook his head slowly. 'Miss Smith, you are an unusual woman. You are sent into my life to try me, I think.'

'Not at all, sir,' she replied primly. 'I am simply a governess, that is all.'

He stilled, his gaze fixing hers. 'No. You are not.'

Not a governess? What does he mean?

'Uncle! Miss Smith!' It was Beatrice. 'I am so relieved that my turn is done. I have been dreading this musicale, for I have no talent, yet Mama insisted I must perform.'

By the time Mary had sympathised and reassured the girl, Miss Cushing had come to join them and all opportunity for further private speech with Sir Nicholas was lost. The party continued on, endlessly it seemed to Mary. As the men became louder and the ladies more bemused, Mary gradually sank into her own thoughts. Her preoccupation was not only on Papa's plight and her disappointing encounter with Sir Harold, but on her own conversation with Sir Nicholas. She had spoken freely when every instinct in her had been urging silence.

It was still too warm in the salon and no one was paying her any attention. Impulsively, she picked up her shawl and slipped out on to the terrace, closing the door gently behind her. Standing in silence in the blessed darkness, she took some cooling breaths and tried to steady her inner turmoil. Why did he fill her thoughts so completely?

Wrapping the shawl more tightly around herself, she gazed up at the countless stars as if she might find an answer there. Their silence, eternal and magnificent, reminded her of the small scale of her concerns in the greatness of the heavens. There was peace in the feeling. Gradually her breathing slowed, and her mind became calmer. She half-registered a brief increase in the light and noise emanating from the salon behind her, then all was dark and quiet again.

'They are beautiful, are they not?' Sir Nicholas's voice sounded softly to her right, but strangely, she was not in the least bit startled. It was as if she had known he must be here, simply because the stars were so perfect.

'They are wondrous,' she affirmed, keeping her

gaze aloft. With each passing moment it seemed that more and more heavenly lights appeared. Rationally she knew it was because her eyes were becoming accustomed to the near-darkness. But her rational mind had gone away, it seemed, for she felt overwhelmed by the magic and miracles of the universe.

She sensed him approach, felt him stop beside her. Her right arm tingled with awareness of his nearness. Time seemed to stand still as silence settled around them.

In all of time, there was only now. In all the world, there was only this place. He and she, side by side, gazing at the stars.

His arm moved a little, the back of his hand brushing hers. She responded and their fingers entwined. Mary was conscious only of him, her anchor to the universe. He and the stars and the night and the silence merged into a single, all-encompassing moment of perfect contentment.

'Mary,' he murmured and her heart sang at the sound of her name on his lips. She turned towards him and his eyes fixed on hers, his glittering with darkness and some unnamed emotion. A moment later his arms slid around her, and she lifted her face to receive his kiss.

When he had stepped on to the terrace, having noticed her quiet departure, Nicholas's pulse had skipped on seeing her there. Her face had been lifted up to the stars, their pale light giving her an unearthly quality that had momentarily stopped his heart.

Although she must have known someone was there, she had not turned her head. Quite without thinking about it, he had walked towards her and joined her in looking at the heavens.

Although he frequently stood on his own terrace in the darkness, something about her stillness had drawn him to her. As he allowed the beauty of the night sky to wash over him, he had been moved to seek the warmth of her hand. She had reciprocated, and the urge to kiss her had then been irresistible.

Lost in the moment, he gave himself over to the kiss. It began gently, almost awkwardly. After only moments, ardour took over and they embraced fervently. He lost himself in exploring her mouth, crushing her close to him as he realised that she was equalling and matching his passion. Vaguely, he was aware that his response to her was not just physical in nature—although his body was on fire with need of her. No, this was more. This was *her*.

Eventually, they paused, the sound of their ragged breathing amplified by the intense silence. He lifted a hand to touch her face, wishing there was light enough to read her expression.

Abruptly, she broke away from him, wordlessly dashing for the safety of the house, trailing her shawl behind her.

Finally. The guests were departed, the family gone to bed and the house was quiet. Sir Nicholas sat before the fire, swilling smuggled French brandy in a Bristol green glass, rolling its delicate stem in his long fingers. He had dismissed his valet, needing solitude before seeking his own bed. The valet had not demurred, knowing that his master frequently stayed up reading late into the night, even after a party.

All would appear normal on the surface—the jacket, waistcoat and cravat discarded, the comfortable armchair pulled close to the fireplace, the carafe of brandy on the side table. Yet tonight was different, for inwardly, Nicholas was in turmoil.

Miss Mary Smith was the cause. In truth, Miss Mary Smith was giving him discomfort in numerous ways. Her comments earlier tonight had been outrageous, of course. And completely unfounded.

She is a vicar's daughter, he reminded himself.

Such families were frequently prone to muddled notions of benevolent patronage. He knew himself to be a generous, if distant, benefactor. He was perfectly content to do good by proxy, and his conscience was clear. Of course it was. His housekeeper supported the tenants and villagers when needed indeed, he understood that Miss Smith herself was assisting Mrs Kett by visiting sick babies and such.

Did she not know who paid for the food she gave to these families? The more he thought about it, the more his indignation rose. Bramber, his loyal secretary, also ensured that regular donations were made on his behalf to the parish for the care of orphans and the destitute. What on earth did Miss Smith expect? That he spent all his time visiting orphanages and hospitals, when he had work to do?

Ridiculous.

And she, a scholar, should understand the importance of serious study. Had she not contributed to a piece he was writing on the *Georgics*, to be shared with other scholars of the great Roman poet? It required laborious analysis, systematic note-taking and cross-referencing with other analysis of Virgil's work. It was work. Important work.

In his head, he prepared a long speech, outlining in great detail every flaw in Miss Smith's assertions, yet all he could see in his mind's eye was her neutral expression—the one she adopted when she disapproved of someone or something. She would be unconvinced.

His attention shifted to their more recent encounter on the terrace. Now he was on firmer ground. Kissing women was a skill in which he had, he knew, some proficiency. Kissing Mary in particular had been an unexpected joy.

It had been an impulse of the moment, naturally, nothing more. He squirmed a little at the realisation that he really should not have been embracing a woman who was in his employ. He ought to have been more careful of her reputation. Why, anyone might have come out to the terrace and seen them!

She will be here only a short time, he reminded himself.

Strangely, the thought gave him no comfort.

He shifted in his seat as he relived their passionate embrace in his memory. He was unsure why it seemed so intense. Perhaps it was simply the setting—the cloak of darkness, the silver stars…perhaps the poets were right, after all.

Or perhaps it was because he had been kissing Mary, not any other woman.

Why did she run away?

He had stood there, momentarily bereft, his body calling for her and his mind full of a thousand questions.

Eventually, of course, he had come to his senses, reminding himself not to refine too much upon an insignificant encounter, then joining his friends and family in the salon. She had already retired, along with his nieces, and his sister had given him a narrow-cyed glare that she no doubt intended to be intimidating.

An insignificant encounter.

He would do well to keep his distance in future. Yet right now, hours after the kiss, the feeling that remained with him was one of having lost something precious.

Chapter Sixteen

'Papa!' Mary hugged her father close, uncaring of the noxious smells emanating from his person and their surroundings. He had now been in this filthy cell for nigh on two months and it showed. He grew thinner each time she saw him, his beard was now long and matted, and his grey hair unkempt. Yet his blue eyes blazed with emotion as he put her from him to gaze at her.

'Mary! It is a joy to behold you, Daughter.' His voice rasped with lack of use. Mary dried her tears with a handkerchief, then took both his hands.

For the first time, the prison guard had left them alone together. With Mary's permission, he had locked her inside Papa's cell, stating that he had tasks to complete and had not the time to stand around waiting for her. He had assured her that, in his opinion, this prisoner was harmless. Finally, her patience and diligence had been rewarded. After many constrained visits, the guard had finally had enough of the tedium of listening to Bible passages and had left them alone together.

'Oh, Papa! It is so unjust that you are here!'

He eyed her steadily. 'There is a meaning in it, I am sure. When I passed the initial stupor, I became overcome with anger, which stayed with me for many, many weeks. Thank the Lord I am now in a calmer state of mind. I know myself to be innocent, yet here I am in this cell. My soul is at peace and I am content now to wait and see what my fate will be.'

Mary frowned. 'I do not understand. Are you—are you in despair, Papa?'

Her heart sank. *How can I care for him if his spirit is broken?*

He shook his head. 'Truly, no. I am composed now. I am ready.'

'But you still have hope? You know that you have done nothing wrong, so you can be set free by the judge?'

'What the judge may or may not do is not in my hands. I shall, of course, speak the truth to him when my day in the Shirehall comes, but I am ready for all outcomes, my dear.'

She bit her lip, but did not argue. 'Tell me, what is the evidence against you?'

'If truth be told, I do not know for certain. I recall opening a package containing strange lists—numbers, places in Spain... I understand now that it represents something to do with the movement of our armies and ships against the French, but at the time I thought it a puzzle unworthy of deciphering. I set the papers aside and thought little about them.'

'But how did they come to be in your possession?'

'They appeared at a time when I was receiving numerous papers. I had not long settled into the new vicarage, as you know, and I had ordered pamphlets, sermons and periodicals from numerous sources. Various messengers had called on six or seven occasions in the preceding fortnight. There was no way to discover which messenger had brought that particular package, nor when it had arrived. Miss Lutton, my housekeeper, also visits me, but I have not yet had the opportunity for private speech with her.' He patted her hand. 'But tell me, Daughter, how did you come to be here? You mentioned working as a governess? Is that true?'

She beamed at him. 'It is. When I received Miss Lutton's letter I left Miss Plumpton's Academy—a great relief to her, I am sure—and sought work as a governess with an agency. I was honest with the agency owner—a most interesting woman, Papa. You would like her, I think. I was right to do so, for she had a vacant position here in Norfolk, just a few miles from here!'

He nodded. 'I begin to see meaning in many things, these days. Such a coincidence is telling, I think. So who are your employers? Do they treat you well?'

Strangely, she felt a slow flush build in her cheeks. 'My employer is Sir Nicholas Denny, of Stiffkey Hall.'

'I have met him.' He tilted his head to one side, considering. 'A gentleman of quality, I believe. And a good mind, to boot. When I called on him we had a most stimulating discussion about Virgil's *Georgics*.'

She smiled. 'He is still reading them—and in the original Greek.'

Papa was frowning. 'But I was given to understand that Sir Nicholas is a bachelor. Why, then, does he need a governess?'

She explained and went on to provide an entertaining account of Mrs Fenhurst, her children and the much-put-upon Miss Cushing.

He shook his head in wonderment. 'I always knew, my Mary, how discerning you are, with quickness of mind and goodness of heart. It does me good to hear you manage so well with all these people and in such challenging circumstances. I am proud of you, child.' He frowned. 'What does Sir Nicholas make of my situation?'

'I have not spoken of it with anyone here, save Miss Lutton. Apart from her, no one knows of my connection with you. Even the guard here believes me to be a Christian visitor, nothing more.' She grimaced. 'It does not sit well with me to deceive anyone, but this is not a usual situation.'

He spread his hands wide. 'There is something—I know I should not consider such worldly matters as reputation, yet I am small-minded enough to do so.' He swallowed. 'So I shall ask you—is my shame widely discussed?'

'Not at all! Indeed, my understanding is that only the Bishop himself is aware of what has happened and he has charged Miss Lutton to tell no one. She is discreet and so far not one person has spoken of it to me. The other local vicars are covering your parish for now and the Bishop is awaiting Sir Harold Gurney's decision at the Quarter-Day session.'

'I assume Sir Harold Gurney is the magistrate?' She nodded. 'So he is the man who holds my life in his hands. I know little of legal procedures, but I do believe that local Justices of the Peace cannot preside over serious crimes such as the ones I am accused of. I expect he will simply wash his hands of me and send me to London for trial.'

'I think so, too—unless he believes you to be innocent. But that means Newgate, and—oh, Papa, I do worry about what will happen to you!'

'Meanwhile my first concern has always been for you, child.' He gripped her hands tightly. 'You must petition the Bishop to provide an allowance for you, should the worst happen to me. Your dowry is safe, of course, and my investments in the funds, such as they are, but I—'

'Oh, no, Papa!' A tear rolled down her cheek. Distantly, she heard the sound of the outer door clanging. 'The guard is returning! Here, take these!' She thrust a package at him, wiping her tears away at the same time. 'It is your own Bible, along with writing materials, and the rest of the food. I shall try to visit again, very soon.'

Papa set the precious items down in the corner, behind where the door would open. They embraced briefly and, when the guard unlocked the cell door, they were standing a respectable distance apart, with Mary quoting part of the Twenty-Third Psalm from memory and in a pious tone. She wished the prisoner a polite farewell, hefted her now-empty basket, and left the cell without a backward glance.

'I have left him a Bible,' she informed the guard, once they had reached the guardroom. 'If it is not permitted, please return it to me.'

She could read in his expression the impulse to confiscate it, then the thought of the effort it would take to unlock and relock all the doors again. 'It is normally not permitted, but as he is a clergyman I shall allow it for him.'

'Thank you, Mr Gedge.'

She passed him a coin and he smiled briefly. 'When will you return?'

'I hope every Sunday from now on. I believe my employer will permit me to do so.' She bit her lip. 'Unfortunately, if I visit more regularly, I shall be unable to maintain my current—er—generosity. But I can bring food?'

He nodded. 'Very well. I am partial to a nice cheese or a fresh loaf.'

In perfect accord, they bid each other good day and Mary stepped outside. The skies were heavy with threatened rain and she drew her cloak tightly around her. As she trudged down the High Street towards the Fakenham road, despair threatened to overcome her. Why was Papa, an innocent man who had done no harm, incarcerated in gaol, and how on earth was she to help secure his release?

'Miss Smith!' It was Sir Nicholas, on horseback. He was smartly dressed in the palest breeches, gleaming Hoby boots and a superfine coat. He looked like a hero straight out of the ancient texts.

She halted, gaping at him. For a moment it felt as though she had been caught stealing, or disobeying her parents by being somewhere she ought not to be.

'Sir—Sir Nicholas!'

'Good day, Miss Smith. What do you here in Walsingham and at the Bridewell, no less?'

'The Bridewell?' *How stupid I sound.* 'Oh, I have been visiting.' She indicated her empty basket.

He shook his head slowly. 'More good works?' He sounded rather disapproving and she flushed, recalling her unnecessarily candid discussion of his character a few nights ago at the musicale.

'Yes,' she replied shortly, conscious now of an added wave of guilt that she was not being fully honest.

There was a tense silence. Mary knew not what to say. It seemed as though he did not, either. 'Well,' he said, tipping his hat, 'good day to you.'

She murmured a polite reply, her eyes never leaving him as he rode away. As she walked through the village and took the road towards home, her spirits were low. Visiting Papa had been wonderful, yet disheartening at the same time, and the encounter with a frosty Sir Nicholas had now completed her distress.

She saw him every day, of course—at meals and during their time reading with Beatrice. At times they assisted the girl with Greek translation, but often they all three simply sat together in companionable silence. There was, naturally, no opportunity for private speech.

Indeed, this was the first time that Mary had

been alone with Sir Nicholas since that kiss on the night of Mrs Fenhurst's musicale. The kiss that haunted her memory, interfered with her sleep, and confused her in every possible way. It felt as though there were two of her—the one who thought endlessly of Sir Nicholas and the one who worried about Papa, taught children and made polite, empty conversation.

Mrs Fenhurst had numerous guests for dinner almost every evening now and somehow Mary was never placed beside Sir Nicholas. There was to be a dancing evening on Friday and the ladies were due to return to Norwich tomorrow for another dress fitting.

Will he take the opportunity to speak with me tomorrow, while they are gone? Might there be another riding lesson, or a walk in the gardens?

She shook her head. Probably not. He had not sought her out for days.

How perplexing everything was! Her mind was already in turmoil over Papa, yet she also felt heartsore over this unexpected estrangement from Sir Nicholas. The comments she had made about him that evening had been ill-judged, she knew, and she deeply regretted them. Oh, not because they were particularly untrue. Because they were unkind.

Papa would have no reason to be proud of her if he knew what she had done. Indeed, Papa had cautioned her many times about stating her opinions in too blunt a manner.

This is not new.

On numerous occasions in her life, she had had cause to regret an intemperate response.

This, though, was worse than any she could remember, simply because it had, she believed, left a crack in her friendship with Sir Nicholas. He had not deserved her judgement of him. She recalled the injured look in his eye that night. Why, she was no better than Sir Harold! Yes, she must have hurt Sir Nicholas deeply, judging by his coolness towards her since that night. And she had no easy opportunity to make amends.

She trudged along the country lane, gripping her cloak tightly against a bitterly cold wind that had sprung up and was blowing in her face. Remembering her harshly spoken words was easier than allowing herself to recall the other memory from that evening—their kiss on the terrace. Immediately, the usual heat ran through her—yet still the cold wind bit at her nose and ears.

How foolish she had been, to risk her position by allowing him to kiss her. There were some gentlemen, she knew, who made a habit of seducing their employees, often turning them off when they got with child. Sir Nicholas was not such a man, she believed. He was truly a man of integrity.

So why had he kissed her that night? He must

have known, as much as she, how impossible it was. Had she made his acquaintance as a guest— perhaps as the dowried daughter of the new vicar, a gentleman by birth—then they might have been more equal in the eyes of society. Money and position, as well as birth, mattered. As it was, as a poor governess she had given up her status in society. She had no business to be kissing any gentleman, least of all her employer.

When he embraced her, had he still been irate about her assessment of him? Had the kiss, for him, been borne out of anger? She squirmed at the possibility. At the time, it had seemed pure, almost heavenly—although earthly, too, in terms of the animalistic passion that had flared between them and which had frightened her into running from him.

Now the rain began to fall, icy droplets that gathered and increased until she was leaning into a veritable downpour. The empty basket became a nuisance as she held on to her hood with one hand, the front of her cloak with the other.

Today's encounter had confirmed what she had suspected. Sir Nicholas had abandoned his former warmth towards her and he was now determined to treat her with a cold formality that should not have stung, but did. Hot tears mingled with freezing rain as she pressed on, feeling pity for herself and her situation.

I have lost a friend, she thought. *A friend that I had only just come to appreciate. I wish I had never kissed him, never spoken aloud my thoughts on his character.*

That night had changed everything.

Hearing the rumble of an approaching carriage, she stepped off the road and into the ditch to await its passing. The hedgerow behind her dripped cold down her back, while her left foot felt suddenly damp. She glanced down, then shuffled sideways to get out of the puddle. The carriage appeared around the corner, coming towards her, and she had only enough time to recognise it before it stopped, a little further along.

The door opened. 'Well, come on then, Miss Smith! Or do you intend to stand there all day in this infernal rain?'

She started forwards. 'Oh, Sir Nicholas! But I am going home, to Stiffkey Hall.'

'Yes, and I am here to fetch you,' he retorted brusquely.

John, the coachman, well-protected in oilskins and a broad-brimmed hat, had jumped down to lower the step. Mary thanked him gratefully as he handed her in to the rear-facing seat, her mind still disordered by the notion that Sir Nicholas had put out his carriage in the rain simply to bring home his governess. 'I—thank you, sir. But there was no need. I could have walked.'

The carriage set off again, the coachman carefully turning it at the nearby crossroads. Sir Nicholas did not respond until the carriage had departed back in the direction it had come. He then said simply, 'Well, of course you could. But you should not.'

Mary sat back and looked at him. He was staring out of the window, scowling. His frustration was palpable—indeed, he was showing all the signs of a man beset by foolishness on all sides. Yet he had just inconvenienced himself—and his coachman—for the sake of a woman who was, essentially, a servant.

'Thank you,' she said again, this time quietly.

He turned his head to look at her and his eyes softened. 'Think nothing of it. By the time I arrived home the rain had started. I could not leave you to get drenched when I could do something to rescue you. It is of no matter.'

She shook her head. 'On the contrary, it matters very much. You sacrificed your own comfort for another.'

The merest hint of colour rose along his cheekbone. 'Oh, I believe I am still the same indolent, selfish knave I have ever been.'

'Oh, no! You were never that!' Without thinking, she leaned forwards and grasped his hand. 'Indeed, I hold you in the highest esteem!' This time, she put no restraint on the warm words.

He looked down at her gloved hand on his, then shifted his gaze to her face. She froze, as his eyes locked with hers and time seemed to stand still.

Recalling herself to the moment, she withdrew her hand as if stung. Flushing, she looked out of the window, using all of her will to slow her breathing and maintain a neutral expression.

We almost kissed again.

The hunger in his eyes had called to her, and every moment of her upbringing as a lady and as the daughter of a respectable clergyman had been needed to prevent her from encouraging his embrace.

I could have done it! she thought fiercely. *If I had simply looked at him unwaveringly, or looked at his mouth, then...*

A sense of heady power rushed through her. She knew instinctively that, in that moment, he had needed only the smallest encouragement from her. Had she given it, they would even now be locked in an embrace as wonderful as the one they had shared on the terrace. Grimly, Mary bunched her hands into fists and pressed her knees together, determined to fight against the unwanted desire within her.

I must not!

The rattling carriage wheeled into the drive of Stiffkey Hall. Too late. Disappointment washed through her.

I should have kissed him.

Immediately, she chastised herself. Of course she should not have done so. As wonderful as the kiss would have been, she would have been flooded with regret and worry afterwards. It was better this way.

The coachman handed her down and Sir Nicholas jumped lightly down behind her. Neither of them noticed Mrs Fenhurst, who happened to be looking out of the window just then. Had they seen her, they might have been struck by her stiffened posture and icy expression.

'Thank you again,' Mary said as they entered the hallway. She undid her cloak, relieved to be shedding its sodden weight.

'Please stop thanking me,' he replied tersely. He bowed politely, then stomped off to allow one of the footmen to relieve him of his boots. Mary watched his retreating back, resisting the unaccountable urge to smile in a relieved way. Something had shifted. She was not sure exactly what. She just knew that, somehow, she had found again the connection to him.

Mrs Fenhurst had agreed that Mary could have this afternoon off, for the purpose of visiting the poor and the needy. This had partly been influenced, Mary knew, by Miss Cushing's anxieties, for the elderly governess did not like to see the growing bond between Mary and Beatrice, or the way in which the younger children sought her out to play with them. Mary suspected Mrs Fenhurst was also content to see Mary away from the family when she was not being personally useful to her.

Yet it was still a little surprising when, after dinner, Mrs Fenhurst decided to quiz Mary on her activities that afternoon. Such an interrogation had not happened since the day of the ladies' trip to Norwich.

'I visited the Bridewell in Walsingham,' Mary said carefully, in response to Mrs Fenhurst's sharp question. 'Mrs Kett provided food which I gave to the prisoners.'

'And where else did you go?'

Mary frowned. 'Nowhere.'

'I saw you arrive back here in my brother's carriage.'

Mary's brow cleared. 'Ah, yes. It was raining, so he took me up in his carriage for a short distance.'

'Hmmm.' Mrs Fenhurst was clearly unconvinced, yet seemed unsure as to what question she would ask next. Mary sat very still, inwardly praying that her hostess would focus neither on her brother's interactions with her, nor on the prisoners in the Bridewell. Luckily, Amabel chose that moment to distract her mama with talk of the dresses that were being made for them, their return trip to the modiste planned for tomorrow and the plans for the dancing. Mrs Fenhurst became caught up in this new topic and her attention to Mary was deflected for now.

Chapter Seventeen

⁂

The next morning, as the ladies were setting off, despite the rain, Mrs Fenhurst took Mary aside. Gripping Mary's arm tightly, she admonished her to remain with the children at all times while they were gone. 'Promise me that you will do so, for I have a terror of something ill befalling them!' she declared.

That is a lie. You wish to keep me from your brother.

Biting back her true thoughts, Mary promised dutifully, but could not resist a thankful sigh as the carriage finally departed. The house felt lighter without them—although Beatrice would be missed.

She turned in towards the hallway, when she was surprised by a dark voice above her. 'Miss Smith.' Sir Nicholas was becoming more handsome by the day. This morning, his hair was a little damp.

He must have had a bath.

The thought sent delicious shivers through her.

'Good morning, Sir Nicholas,' she replied primly, her eyes secretly devouring him as he descended the staircase.

Thank goodness he cannot see my thoughts!

'We missed you at breakfast.'

'I ate in my chamber,' he said shortly. 'Are we studying together as usual? I know Miss Beatrice has travelled with her sister and her mother—and of course, the indomitable Miss Cushion! That should not mean we forgo the pleasure of companionable study.' His tone was light, but the fact he had even asked pleased Mary immeasurably.

'I promised Mrs Fenhurst I would not let the children out of my sight,' she replied ruefully. 'I am even now on my way to fetch them.'

'My sister is remarkably enthusiastic about her children's education.' His tone was wry. 'What are your plans for them?'

'The weather is unfortunately too poor to spend much time outside this morning, although I shall watch for any break in the rain. I am planning to paint and sketch with them.'

'Yes, it is too wet for a riding lesson, too.' He paused. 'There will be a fire already lit in my library and the light is remarkably good in there. Please feel free to bring the children if you wish.'

Her heart skipping at the memory of the previous riding lesson and how he had looked at her that day, Mary took great care to speak in a colourless tone. 'You will not be disturbed by their presence? I assume you mean to read, as usual.'

'I do and, in answer to your question, I shall manfully tolerate any disturbance to my train of thought.' He sent her a meaningful glance that managed to combine humour and heat. A warm glow went through her as she reached the inescapable conclusion that he wished to spend time with her.

While he was getting to know and appreciate Beatrice, he was only distantly tolerant of the younger children and would not have normally sought their company.

It seems he has indeed forgiven me for my plain speaking.

The relief that flooded through her at the thought was much stronger than it ought to have been. Somehow, his good opinion of her had come to matter very, very much.

Half an hour later, an awed Caroline, Edmond and David sat at Sir Nicholas's large table, setting to with pencils and pastels. Mary had arranged a still life for them in the centre of the table—a bowl of apples, a milk jug and a crumpled cloth. Sir Nicholas took his usual seat by the fireplace and Mary sat with the children. She gave gentle encouragement and noticed Sir Nicholas lifting his head from his book each time she spoke.

After a time, as the children became more riveted on their art, they all lapsed into silence. The clock ticked, the fire crackled and the children's pencils scratched rhythmically on their sketchbooks.

All is well.

A sense of unexpected well-being settled over Mary. The children were happy. She was safe and warm. She would see Papa again on Sunday. Sir Nicholas was once more her friend.

She glanced at him, enjoying the sight of his intent expression as he focused on his book, his eyes downcast. His hair had dried and was long enough to curl a little over his collar. His pose was relaxed, long legs stretched out before him, hugged by tightly-fitting breeches.

He is so beautiful.

Just then, he looked up, making her flush. Wordlessly, he beckoned her to come and sit with him. Heart pounding, she rose from the table and moved towards him, conscious of his intent gaze.

Am I walking differently?

Something new and unexpected was happening in her body. There was something fluid and beguiling in her own movements, she realised, something that she was doing naturally, without conscious thought.

My goodness, this tendre *has opened my mind and body to so many new thoughts and experiences!*

Gratifyingly, the blaze of hunger in Sir Nicholas's eyes revealed that her unstudied impulse had kindled an answering response in him.

He rose, his eyes never leaving hers as he pulled the second armchair close to his own. He held out a hand to her and she took it briefly, allowing him to seat her close beside him. She murmured a word of thanks, glancing towards the children. They had not, it seemed, even noticed that she had left the table, so intent were they on their task.

'I have never seen the children so quiet,' he murmured in her ear. She knew well that he did not need to do so. It was simply a ruse to lean physically close to her. His breath was warm on her face, and his nearness was sending a thrill of delight through her body.

'Art usually has that effect,' she replied softly, turning her head to look at him. He had not retreated and their faces were agonisingly close.

They continued to converse about nothing, enjoying the tortuous agony of exquisite proximity. Their bodies spoke to each other—a language of leaning close, of looking into each other's eyes for much too long, of 'chance' touches. Arm against arm. His foot touching hers momentarily. His fingers 'accidentally' brushing her arm. Every part of Mary's body was alive and tingling, her mind and heart on fire with his nearness.

The magic could not last forever. Eventually, the spell was broken by little Edmond, who called on Miss Smith to view his drawing. She rose immediately and went to him, thereafter remaining with the children and admiring their work. Emboldened by this, they began making conversation with their large uncle, going as far as to shyly show him their work, which he admired with great enthusiasm.

When the clock chimed for nuncheon, Mary accompanied the children to the dining room, asking them to thank their uncle for allowing them into his library. He bade them enjoy their nuncheon, mentioned that he might join in their games one day, then added, 'Miss Smith, I have never known the children to be so well-behaved. What magic do you have in your person, that you can so bewitch people?'

Knowing he was not only referring to the children, her heart sang. *He thinks me bewitching!*

Aloud, she said only, 'They are good children, sir. I believe you have been misinformed.'

He smiled, tousled Edmond's hair and nodded. 'So it would seem. I must do better and avoid judging people on my first impressions of them.

I am learning that there is more to people than I sometimes realise.'

He watched her as she followed the children from the library. She felt the touch of his gaze on her back, enjoying the sensation.

It is a promise. We have agreed to kiss again, when we find the opportunity.

The notion sent her heart pounding.

After nuncheon the rain gave way to sullen cloud, so she was able to take the children outside. They rampaged through the woods, shrieking and playing, developing rosy cheeks and happy smiles. By the time they returned Sir Nicholas had gone—riding out as was his usual habit. He had not offered her another riding lesson.

Swallowing her disappointment, Mary hugged the memories of this morning's encounter close.

I shall see him again in less than an hour.

The knowledge sat warmly somewhere behind her breastbone, glowing like an ember.

She finished the afternoon with a more formal lesson in which the children, contented by their day of art and play, were remarkably focused. Indeed, she thought she had achieved more with them in that final hour than she had done in any of her previous schoolroom periods. She told them so and their little faces glowed with happiness at the praise. And when their mama and sisters returned, along with Miss Cushing, they were able to show their progress with arithmetic and geography, as well as their sketches. Mrs Fenhurst had to be impressed and said so. Miss Cushing, on the other hand, looked decidedly put out.

'And has Miss Smith been with you all day long?' Mrs Fenhurst asked, with an innocent air.

'Why, yes,' replied David. 'And she has not told us off even once!'

'We were good all day,' emphasised Edmond.

'I am glad to hear it, my darling,' said his mama, embracing him. 'Now, go you and find your nurses, for we ladies must dress for dinner.'

She watched them depart, then turned to Mary. 'David is advancing well with his arithmetic, is he not?'

'He is indeed,' Mary enthused. 'And what is more, he fears it less. Today he positively enjoyed his multiplications and divisions—something I would have thought would be nigh on impossible a month ago.'

They moved into the hallway. 'And Edmond's sketch showed real promise.' Mrs Fenhurst's voice thrummed with pride.

Mary smiled. 'Given he is only seven, his sketch was as good as the others, I think.'

Mrs Fenhurst patted her on the arm. 'Thank you, my dear.'

Well—this was progress indeed! While Mrs Fenhurst spent little time with the younger children and was entirely hopeless in managing the boys, it seemed she was susceptible to maternal pride.

Miss Cushing was regarding them both in dismay. 'I have always recognised Edmond's talent for art. Why, if it had not been for my tutelage, he would not have the skill he currently displays!'

Mrs Fenhurst, realising she had erred, made haste to reassure her governess. 'So true! And I am so glad you were with me today, to help me with parcels and reminding the girls how to go on!'

Miss Cushing looked a little mollified. 'Miss Amabel in particular is developing a propensity for pertness. And Beatrice needs to spend more time in the dressmaker's and less time in the library!' She glared at Mary. 'Why, if she is not careful, the girl will become a bluestocking and utterly unmarriageable.'

Mary's hackles rose. *And what of it? Can she not choose to be unwed? She has a good mind— why can she not use it?*

Summoning all her resolve, she bit her tongue. To her surprise Beatrice, who had been silent until now, spoke in her own defence.

'Can I not enjoy both? Pretty dresses are a pleasure to wear and reading a good book is a gratifying experience for my mind. Why, Miss Cushing, you yourself enjoy reading novels on occasion.'

Miss Cushing spluttered in outrage. 'Novels? I think not. Sermons, histories and improving texts, never novels!'

Beatrice and Amabel exchanged a dubious glance, while Mrs Fenhurst absent-mindedly remarked that she herself enjoyed a novel from time to time.

'Where is my brother?' she added unexpectedly.

'I know not,' Mary answered truthfully. 'I believe he went out riding earlier and I am unsure if he has returned.' They moved towards the staircase, Mary holding her breath in case Mrs Fenhurst should ask another question about Sir Nicholas. Thankfully, she seemed satisfied and they all separated on the upper floor to dress for dinner.

Chapter Eighteen

❦

The salon and the parlour next to it were separated by gilt-trimmed doors which could fold away and hide in the wall, but tonight they had been thrown open for the Stiffkey Hall dancing evening. It was to be a modest affair, with the Grand Ball now planned for Easter, and Mrs Fenhurst, Mary and the servants were all treating it as a chance to try things out, in preparation for the larger event to come.

Mary had been hard at work since before dawn, helping and supervising the servants as they worked together to ensure all was ready. Most of the furniture had been taken out to leave space for dancing and all of the sofas and chairs had been placed around the edges of the room. Additional candles had been purchased and the room blazed with warm light.

Mary gave a nod of satisfaction and moved back to the hallway. The first guests would begin to arrive shortly and Sir Nicholas and Mrs Fen-hurst would need to be ready to greet them.

She herself had completed her toilette more than an hour ago and was now almost accustomed to the rustle and swish of her evening gown—a white satin dream, worn with an overdress of dark blue gauze and trimmed with silver thread. One of the housemaids had dressed her hair, creating elegant side-curls and even threading a silver fillet through Mary's dark curls.

Beatrice is right, she reflected, catching sight of herself in a gilt-framed mirror. *There is something gratifying about wearing an elegant ballgown and feeling pretty.*

Sensing a movement on the staircase above, she glanced up. Just like on that recent morning, Sir Nicholas was descending and the sight of him left Mary rather breathless. He looked magnificent in his black evening coat, white shirt and evening breeches, his clothing plain and unadorned, save for a single diamond pin in his crisp cravat. His clothes clung to his form, accentuating the muscular thighs, lean torso and broad shoulders.

What a specimen!

Her objective eye could see the beauty of his figure—Michelangelo's *David* reproduced in living form. Her subjective body came alive at the sight of him—particularly as her gaze swept upwards to meet his. In his brown eyes she saw a heady mix of admiration and desire.

The promise was still there, thrumming between them. For days now they had looked at each other, guarding their desires from others when in company. So far, they had had no opportunity to be alone—and, if she were honest, Mary was as much glad of it as she was sorry. Although she wanted nothing more than to kiss him again, she was also aware of her own frailty when it came to Sir Nicholas. He was dangerous.

'Good evening!' He continued to descend until he had reached her. 'How beautiful you look!' Lifting her right hand, he pressed his lips to it. Even through her glove, the effect was potent. Mary's knees promptly turned to water.

'Thank you,' she said huskily, then cleared her throat. 'You look beautiful, too.' Hearing her unguarded words, she instantly brought a hand to her mouth. 'I should not have said that!' Mortification flooded her face and neck with heat.

He had thrown back his head and was laughing. 'Miss Smith, you are a treasure—and good for my soul, I think. Let us agree that we both look beautiful tonight. Now tell me, is everything in hand?'

This was safer ground. 'I believe so.' Conscious of the footman, James, standing to her right, eyes kept rigidly forward, she went on to give Sir Nicholas a summary of the preparations and his sister's plans, adding, 'Mrs Fenhurst means to include a waltz, which is very daring of her.'

'Do you disapprove?' He gazed at her intently.

'Not at all! I think it unexceptionable and I fail to understand why some in society think it so shocking.'

'Have you yourself learned the waltz and danced it?'

'I have learned it, certainly, but have never danced it at a ball.' She smiled. 'Admittedly, I have only waltzed with other young ladies and with the dancing master at my school, who must be seventy if he is a day!'

'I see. Well, if you both believe it to be unexceptional, I can have no objection.'

The housekeeper appeared then, seeking Mary's assistance, and she departed with a polite farewell to Sir Nicholas. By the time she had attended to Mrs Kett's queries about which serving plates to use for the main supper dishes and assisted Mr Bramber with the final list of guests, she heard the first carriage arrive, so hurried into the salon to ask the musicians to begin to play quietly.

An hour passed, then another. The evening was an undoubted success.

'An absolute crush!' Mrs Fenhurst called it, with an air of satisfaction. 'They all came—and why should they not? We are still the leading family in the district.'

Supper was served and was pronounced a delight. Slowly, Mary felt her nerves begin to slacken a little. This was the biggest and most elaborate event she had so far co-ordinated for Mrs Fenhurst. Afterwards, the dancing began anew and Mary was approached by Mr Bramber.

'Well, Miss Smith, are you content?'

She returned his smile. 'I believe I am. There is little now that can go wrong—and most of the guests have drunk so much that they would not even care if it did!' She grimaced. 'Oops! I mean no disrespect. I—'

'Think nothing of it. You have spoken only truth.' He hesitated. 'When I asked earlier, you would not dance for you said you had too much to worry about. Will you dance with me now?'

Mary glanced at the smiling couples on the dance floor. 'I should love to dance,' she replied frankly. 'Are you certain that it is permissible?'

He shrugged. 'Sir Nicholas has declared that he will not need my services any further tonight, and has bid me find enjoyment by dancing with all the pretty girls in the room.' He grinned. 'I am fortunate to have such a benign employer.'

She snorted. 'Perhaps he has only given you freedom because he has no need of you.' She still believed that Sir Nicholas did not think enough of his servants' needs and wishes—including Bramber's.

'And why should he not? He is our employer, after all, and entitled to do as he pleases.' He eyed her keenly. 'You are hard on him, Miss Smith. Why is that?'

Because he could be a better man, if he chose to be. It still bothered her.

'Because,' she said carefully, 'he could choose to do more for others than he currently tries.'

He laughed. 'But I have told you, he has bade me dance and make merry! I assure you, I am most grateful to him!'

She would argue the point no further. 'Yet you have not danced at all so far.'

Glancing across to where the young ladies had gathered, he opened his mouth to say something, then closed it again. After a moment, he said only, 'Perhaps, like you, I had too much to worry about earlier.'

'The footmen have been faultless,' she reassured him, 'the guests are content and Mrs Fenhurst is brimming with pride. I declare it is probably safe for you to dance now.' She smiled. 'And for me.'

'Very well.' He grinned and offered her his hand. 'Let us venture on to the dance floor together.'

Inwardly, Mary remained a little wary of earning Mrs Fenhurst's disapproval and was relieved to see only calm unconcern on that lady's face when she noticed Mary and Mr Bramber dancing together. Her worries eased, Mary gave herself over to the country dance, realising how much she enjoyed dancing and how agreeable it was to dance in a candlelit ballroom wearing an elegant gown and with a pleasant partner.

She whirled round, exchanging places with Beatrice who was dancing next to her, then returned to Mr Bramber. As she did so she noticed Sir Nicholas out of the corner of her eye. He was standing near the musicians—and something about his stance sent alarm through her. She stole a glance in his direction. He was looking at them and was positively glowering!

Oh, no! Should I not be dancing? Have I overstepped my place as a governess?

Mary bit her lip. She was used to socialising as a young lady, daughter of a respectable gentleman. Life as a governess had not yet sunk fully into her consciousness. Maybe he was cross with Beatrice? Or Mr Bramber, perhaps?

'Mr Bramber,' she ventured. 'Sir Nicholas looks displeased.'

He turned his head, frowning as he noticed his employer's thunderous expression. 'Naturally,' he declared, as the dance brought him back to Mary. 'He bade me dance with all the pretty ladies,

yet failed to mention that you were excluded!'
Amusement flickered across his face, followed
by a chuckle.

'What? I do not understand you.'

*At least, I pray I do not. I hope he is referring
to my role as governess. Otherwise—does everyone know of Sir Nicholas's partiality for me?*

'We spoke of inevitability before,' he replied,
shaking his head. 'A man may take some time to
understand that the Fates have spun him a different life.'

This, despite the reference to the ancient Greek
tales, was entirely too cryptic. 'You are making
no sense, Mr Bramber. Come, tell me what you
mean.'

He shrugged. 'Perhaps you should ask him
yourself.' The music stopped and he took her
hand, deliberately bending over to kiss it. Yet
the look in his eyes as he did so was mischie-
vous rather than lover-like. 'I wish you well, Miss
Smith.'

'You wish me well? That sounds like a farewell, yet neither of us is departing.' She laughed.
'I suspect, Mr Bramber, that you have also been
imbibing some of Sir Nicholas's fine wine.'

'Well, I have,' he admitted, 'but that is not it.
Ah, here he comes.'

'Who?'

'Very well, Bramber, that is quite enough for

now.' It was Sir Nicholas. 'Go and dance with Miss Reeve,' he continued, his tone somewhere between a growl and an order. Mr Bramber bowed and promised to obey with alacrity, his devilish smile causing the frown on Sir Nicholas's brow to deepen further.

Mary watched as Sir Nicholas's secretary approached the pretty, fair-haired Miss Reeve, who replied shyly and allowed Mr Bramber to lead her to the dancing floor. As the girl smiled up at him, Mary noticed the tips of Bramber's ears had developed an interesting rosy hue.

'Wait here!' Sir Nicholas declared curtly, before spinning on his heel and heading for the far side of the room.

Mary was completely bewildered. Now what? Had she erred in some way? Sir Nicholas seemed to be in a foul temper, yet he had been in high humour for most of the evening. Mr Bramber had seemed unconcerned though, which she found reassuring. Perhaps Sir Nicholas, like the others, had taken too much drink.

Confused, she saw him speak to the musicians, then thread his way through the crowd to return to her side. The musicians struck up for the next set and a ripple of excitement went around the room. 'Come, Miss Smith.' He held out an imperious hand. 'Dance the waltz with me.'

For a moment, she considered refusing him.

His high-handed manner, her bewilderment, Mr Bramber's amusement…there were undercurrents here that she could not grasp, but knew that she did not like. Contrariness rose up within her.

He noticed her hesitation, saw that she was not minded to obey him. A disconcerted expression flitted across his handsome features, which then resettled into an inscrutable mask. Her heart turned over as she sensed his brittleness. She could not rebuke or reject him here, now. Not in front of all his friends and neighbours.

Besides, she realised with surprising fierceness, she *wanted* to waltz with him. 'Very well,' she replied coolly, allowing him to lead her to the centre of the room. 'Though only because I wish to dance. Not because you have ordered me to.'

'I am pleased that you are dancing because of your own desire to do so.'

She remained cool with him. 'Yet you cannot know if I am only dancing with you because I must, or simply because I wish to dance the waltz.'

This was something of a test. Naturally, he realised it. The frown that crossed his face as the music began properly was worth all the indignation she had felt at his autocratic manner.

Sometimes I can read him as easily as if he were a children's book!

'So,' he growled, as they began moving together to the music, 'did you truly wish to dance with me, or not?'

His proximity was causing havoc with her ability to think in straight lines. So this was why the waltz was so much debated among the dowagers! His hand was entwined with hers, their bodies close together, and when he looked down at her, his gaze was of necessity angled directly towards her décolletage.

Thankfully, her dress was no more shocking than those of the other ladies— bosoms were on display in every part of the room. Daringly, tonight there was no need for a handkerchief! She had the presence of mind to be relieved that she was not waltzing with some of the less savoury gentlemen who were here tonight, before a rush of desire built within her.

She felt alive, womanly, powerful—as though the essence of Venus, the Roman goddess of love, was flowing through her.

Venus, or Jezebel?

The thought, born of years of Bible studies, was fleeting and discarded. This was entirely natural. This was how things ought to be between two people.

'Can you not answer me?'

Startled, she looked up at him. His face was almost as close as when they had kissed on the terrace. His hand gripped hers as he read the desire in her eyes. 'Mary!' he muttered and the sound of her name on his lips was almost her undoing. Mutely, she gazed at him, knowing he already had the answer to his question.

Vaguely, she was aware that they were in a crowded ballroom. In reality, there was only his handsome face and the heat from his body, and the places where their bodies were touching. The music was part of it, too, swirling around them with a heady vivacity that added to the air of dreamy unreality. They spun around the room in perfect harmony, moving as one, as though they had been dancing the waltz together since the beginning of time. There were no missteps, no faltering, no hesitation. It was as though they were one creature.

Eventually, the dream subsided and the music ended. Recovering herself, Mary made the required curtsy, murmured a word of thanks, then preceded him in walking from the dance floor.

An air of unreality surrounded her, as the magic of waltzing with Sir Nicholas permeated every part of her. Physical desire, the attuning of minds and…something more. Something wonderful.

Gradually she began to notice the everyday world. Miss Cushing, she noted, was seated beside her mistress and the two women were watching Mary intently. Abruptly, the dreamlike quality left her. She shivered, feeling a little like a mouse under the gaze of a pair of merciless hawks.

Sir Nicholas secured refreshment for her from a passing footman and they stood together at the side of the room. Their eyes met once, as they sipped their drinks, and Mary felt a sliver of magic spear through her.

It is still there!

Beatrice bounded up to them, curls bouncing. 'Oh, Uncle! They played the waltz! Can you believe it? I have never seen it danced before. Miss Smith, I was never so excited in my whole life!'

Mary smiled at her charge's enthusiasm, delighted to see such animation. 'In truth, Beatrice, I have just danced it in public for the first time myself.'

'I saw you. You dance so well together.' Beatrice beamed at them both. 'As did Mr Bramber and Miss Reeve. She was fortunate to have Mr Bramber as a partner, for I saw him steer her on two occasions when she almost went wrong.'

'I am glad to hear it,' murmured Sir Nicholas. 'He deserves it.'

Mary sent him an admonishing look and he acknowledged it, eyes dancing. Amabel joined them then and there was no further opportunity for private conversation. But as she moved mechanically through the rest of the evening, dancing, talking and watching others, Mary hugged the memory of the waltz close to her heart.

No matter what came next, what trials she would face in her life, she would always have this one perfect memory. That time she had waltzed with Sir Nicholas Denny.

Chapter Nineteen

Although it had been late in the night when the ball finally ended, Mary found herself awake at her usual time. It mattered not that she had had so little sleep, for she felt happy. She lay for a while in the near-darkness, savouring the memories from the night before.

The moment he had said she looked beautiful. The deliberate way he had ensured the musicians would play the waltz next. The waltz itself and the ever-increasing desire that had flared between them.

Oh, if only circumstances were different! She lost herself again in her favourite daydream—the one where Papa had not been arrested, where she had met Sir Nicholas through social connections, where she had danced with him not as his governess, his paid employee, but as the daughter of a respectable vicar. Simply a gentleman and a gentleman's daughter. How might that have made a difference?

When she had run in haste to Mrs Gray, seeking employment, she had not realised how thoroughly it would change her station in life. A governess remained a lady, yet was immediately also of the servant class. There were, she supposed, some gentlemen who would consider marrying a governess, but Mary suspected the proud head of the Denny family would never dream of it. Oh, if only there had been some other way to aid Papa!

And why was she even thinking of marriage? He had kissed her and danced with her. He desired her. That was all. Gentlemen, she knew, might have numerous flirts and *tendres*, none of which remotely influenced who they would eventually marry. No, such a dream was impossible. She must be content with what she had. So why did she feel so dashed *happy*?

Questions fluttered through her head like leaves in autumn, yet no answers came to her. Knowing the family planned to stay abed until noon, Mary tried to sleep again, but oblivion eluded her. Eventually, she admitted defeat and rose. Padding to the window, she drew back the heavy curtains and looked outside. The morning sun was shining, pale and weak, yet welcome. Spring was everywhere to be seen, with new buds on the trees, busy birds building nests and tiny snowdrops adding welcome colour next to the solid reassurance of the oak trees. Thankfully, the relentless rain of recent days had briefly ceased.

Country-bred, she opened the window to better enjoy the fresh air and spring sounds. As she did so, her eye caught a movement below.

It is him!

He was leading his horse to the mounting-block near the terrace below her and had automatically glanced upwards when he had heard her window slide open. Now he stood transfixed, as did she.

Somewhere inside, she knew she should step back, that she should not allow him to see her thus, with her hair tumbling in unruly curls about her half-bare shoulders and her body barely hidden by her thin white nightgown. Yet the same spirit of Venus that had gripped her last night now did so again. She thrilled in the knowledge that he desired her. Never had she felt so alive, so vital, so full.

His eyes devoured her, his gaze sweeping over her body, then focusing on her face. He half-lifted his left hand in a greeting and automatically she reciprocated. His horse, failing to understand the sudden delay, walked on and Sir Nicholas, as if recalling himself to his surroundings, allowed it. Mary, finally finding the ability to move, stepped backwards before sinking down on to the bed, her breathing ragged and her mind all disorder.

One thought came to her clearly; he was going riding and would return within the hour. The ladies were abed. Here was an opportunity.

A slow smile spread across her face as she rose again, this time with purpose.

* * *

Sir Nicholas's heart was thumping wildly. As he rode out along his usual route through the woods and towards the river, he reflected that he had never—no, not even in the throes of his awakenings to manhood—*never* been so taken with a woman. She enthralled him. Thoughts of her body dominated his mind when alone. Seeing her almost naked in the window frame just now was almost his undoing.

Yet, he acknowledged, his obsession was more than simple lust. Her beauty captivated him and her character fascinated him. Why was it that the opinion of a simple governess—and one whom he had initially thought to be unremarkable—should be so vital to him? Why should he be filled with jealousy when she had smiled at Bramber and allowed him to lead her to the dance floor? Irrational, for Bramber had told him that he preferred another lady.

More questions. Why should her criticism of him sting so deeply? And *why* had waltzing with her felt so wonderful?

He had no answers. Nothing but yet more uncertainties, each piling on top of the last until he had quite lost his ability to reason. Abandoning any attempt to find peace, he spurred his horse to a gallop, enjoying the feeling of wind on his face, weak sun on his back. Finally, he turned for home and entered the woods. He had yet no clarity about what was transpiring or what he should do about it. He continued, his horse picking its way through a dappled mosaic of shadow and sunlight—nature's very own stained glass.

As he reached the last section of the woods— the part that led directly to his gardens—his eye was drawn to a flash of colour on his right.

He caught his breath. Miss Smith, wearing a silk cloak in a dramatic shade of yellow-gold, standing still and calm in a delightful oak grove.

Now. Here. Alone. Unobserved.

He knew exactly why she was there. Knew why she had timed her walk to this moment. Knew why she had worn the gold evening domino rather than her usual black day cloak. Knew that their guards—most notably his sister and her elderly assistant—were likely still in their beds.

Now is the moment!

He turned the horse towards her, halting right beside her. Sliding off, he abandoned the horse and stepped towards his Mary.

An instant later, he swept her into his arms. No words were needed, for they had both hungered for this moment for far too long. Their language was that of tongues. Of lips against lips. Of hands seeking and touching and discovering what they might. He gloried in her—in her mouth and her hair, and her breasts and her derrière. He gloried in her soft skin, her ragged breath, her murmuring his name. 'Mary!' he muttered, as he had last night. 'Mary!'

'Nicky,' she groaned, pulling him even closer, as if she could by will alone merge them into one being.

In the end it was he who put a stop to it. Not because he wished to, but because he knew, even if she did not, what might happen in this place if they did not stop. Some vestige of gentlemanliness remained within him. He could not use his Mary so. Not without first placing his ring upon her finger.

Marriage? Really?

Had he lost his mind?

Perhaps I have, he acknowledged ruefully.

He must think about this. He must be sure that he was not driven to make a long-time decision based on a short-time fancy. So he held his tongue and said nothing of the tremendous thoughts that were whirling around inside his disordered mind, the tremendous feelings that had taken hold of his heart.

She was still there, real and lovely and breathing raggedly not a foot away from him.

What a fix! Her puzzled expression hinted of hurt. *She feels rejected.*

'Mary,' he said, trying to find the right words. 'You are a delight. But I am your employer and you are in my care, and this—' he gestured vaguely '—cannot be right.'

'What do you mean?' Her voice was husky. She looked at him in bewilderment.

Lord! She was only twenty, with no one to protect her. *I am a damn fool!*

He drew himself back, dropping his arms to his sides. 'We cannot and should not do this again.'

Leastways, not until I know what I am doing.

Tears sprang to her eyes, but she lifted her chin proudly. 'You are right. I have been foolish. Please promise me you will not speak of this to anyone.'

'Of course I shall not speak of it! What do you take me for?'

'At this moment,' she flashed back at him, sudden anger in her expression, 'I honestly do not know!'

She whirled around, all gold silk, fury and pride, and stomped off southwards, away from the house. Sir Nicholas watched her go, using every ounce of self-control to stop himself from running after her and proposing marriage. *Madness!*

He took a deep breath and scanned the area for his horse. There he was, contentedly munching sweet spring grass. Recapturing the stallion, Sir Nicholas mounted with the aid of a nearby rock and galloped the half-mile back to the stables. He had much to consider.

* * *

Mary heard him go, yet refused to turn her head to watch him. Her mind, heart and body were all in disorder and she knew she needed time to restore herself—away from the insanity that had overcome her. She wandered through the woods, choosing to focus on the beauties of nature that were all around her. It took some time, but eventually a sense of calmness returned. It could only be maintained, she knew, if she did not think of him, or of what had occurred between them. She could not allow herself to recall the glory of his hands on her, of their tongues dancing, of his strangled uttering of her name.

Stop! Once again, she chose to notice the yellow celandines beside the brook, the robin on the nearby tree limb, the crunch of bracken beneath her feet. Once again, her breathing steadied and her spirits regained their equilibrium.

Finally, knowing it must be almost noon, she went back to the house. Handing her cloak to the footman, she divested herself of her stout walking boots and donned her house slippers, before asking calmly where the family were at present.

The footman informed her that the ladies had recently come downstairs and were even now in the breakfast room. Realising she was hungry—for she had been too excited to eat earlier when she had dressed for him—she made her way to the breakfast room, where she filled a plate of eggs, rolls and ham.

The ladies were already aware that she had been out walking and Mrs Fenhurst commented disapprovingly on her windswept hair and pink cheeks. 'Really, Miss Smith, you ought to do better! I must say I have been extremely disappointed in you lately.'

Mary, flushing even more, promised to fix her hair just as soon as she could. Thankfully, Sir Nicholas did not join them and his sister reported that he was presently enclosed with his secretary. Mary's shoulders relaxed a little on hearing this. She had no desire to encounter Sir Nicholas any time soon.

Oh, how foolish she had been! Like a wanton, she would have done whatever he had wished earlier in the woods. Stupidly, she had wrapped herself in daydreams and it had almost undone her.

Remember, she told herself, *all of his flaws.*

Deliberately, she sat, chewing food that tasted like sawdust and thinking of all of the things he had ever done or said that were less than ideal. His insularity. His lack of awareness of the privileges given to him by his wealth and his birth. His lack of engagement with the wider world and everyone he could help if he chose to do so.

It helped, a little, for it quieted the hurt within her heart. Vaguely, she was aware that she was being unfair to him but, in this moment, being angry was better than being heartbroken.

Just then, the door opened, admitting Seth, the same footman who had been at the front door earlier. He looked decidedly uncomfortable.

'Ma'am, I apologise, but there is a person here.'

'Yes?' Mrs Fenhurst's brow was creased. The footman's choice of words indicated that the visitor was not of the gentry. 'You may direct this person to Mrs Kett, or Mr Bramber. Why are you informing me of it?'

'He says he is seeking Miss Smith.'

All eyes turned to Mary, who could say only, 'Me? But I know no one in the area!'

The footman coughed. 'I believe him to have travelled from London yesterday.'

Mary frowned in puzzlement. Could he be something to do with Mrs Plumpton? Or Mrs Gray, perhaps? What on earth could someone from London want with her?

Mrs Fenhurst was all vexation. 'Where have you put him?'

'In the small parlour.'

Mary rose. 'I shall go to him, although I cannot think who he might be.' Conscious of the interested gaze of the four ladies, she followed Seth to the parlour. Stepping inside, she closed the door behind her. The man who stood to greet her was of average height, with a weather-beaten face, a balding pate and a purple waistcoat. Mary had never seen him before in her life.

'Miss Mary Smith?'

'I do not believe I have made your acquaintance?'

He fished in his pocket for a card. 'The name is Potter. John Potter.' Mary looked at the card. John Potter, it read. Principal Officer.

'You are a Bow Street Runner?'

He bristled a little. 'That is not a title that we officers answer to. Ours is important work and we answer only to the title of Officer.'

Mary's senses were now fully alert.

Is this the man who arrested Papa?

She forced herself to smile. 'I apologise, Officer. Please be seated. Now, how can I assist you?'

He took out a notebook and set it down on the side table near his chair. 'Are you aware that a certain vicar, Reverend William Smith, was taken from the vicarage at Houghton St Giles to the Walsingham Bridewell, having been accused of a serious crime?'

Mary could only nod, distress at his words having momentarily closed her throat.

'A messenger, who is being watched as part of this investigation, was observed delivering a letter to this vicar some weeks ago. However I—we have not been able to establish the connection between this messenger and this traitorous vicar.'

He drew himself up, hooking his thumbs into the top of his breeches. 'This day, I have interviewed Miss Sarah Lutton at the same vicarage and she has informed me that you are the man's daughter.'

'I am.'

He picked up his book and made a note in it. 'She attests that the vicar in question was not known to be of a political persuasion, nor was he short of a shilling.'

'Er—that is correct. My father has never been active in politics and has an independent income. He is a clergyman through choice, not financial need. Why do you ask?'

He ignored her question, and made another note. 'I have been working on this case for a number of months and so far I have been unable to track how and why your father might have become part of a conspiracy against King and country.'

Mary could not help it. She snorted. 'Well, the solution to your conundrum is obvious. It is because he was not part of any such conspiracy!'

The man's eyes narrowed. 'Who were his acquaintances in London and how often did he visit there? I believe you yourself lived in the capital until very recently?'

'I was at school in London, yes. And my father never visited me there because he hated the place. Smoke and noise, and bad smells, he would say. He has, as far as I know, no acquaintances in London at all.'

'It is your duty to assist me with my questions, Miss Smith.'

'And it is your duty to find the true traitor, rather than hound a poor man who has done nothing wrong!'

Mr Potter stayed a full twenty minutes, asking Mary stupid, pointed questions that invited her to incriminate her own father. Why, even if he had been guilty, she would not have done so! Eventually, he rose to leave, clearly unsatisfied. He appeared convinced of Papa's guilt and seemed not to even consider other possibilities. No matter what Mary said, he stuck to his belief that her father was guilty.

Once the footman—his curiosity apparent—had shown the man out, Mary sank back down on to the satin-covered sofa. She had had only a few hours' sleep, had nearly been compromised by Sir Nicholas in the woods, had been rejected by him and had now endured a rigorous inquisition from a Bow Street Runner. She put a hand to her head. She could not even begin to think clearly.

Surely this day could not become any worse?

Chapter Twenty

Nicholas paced restlessly in his library, his thoughts interrupting each other like greedy gannets diving after elusive prey. Mary was wonderful. Mary was a governess in his employ. If he had not halted their amorous activities in the woods… If anyone had seen them! Was she distressed?

Lord, I should have behaved better!

Oh, but he wanted her, even now. His heart ached to think he had vexed her.

More confusing questions followed. Why on earth had he thought of marriage? He had no notion of becoming leg-shackled any time soon. Was the notion driven by simple lust?

He took a breath. Until he was calmer, he could not know if his desire to wed Mary was real or simply a figment of his heated passion. There was danger in acting on the impulse of the moment. All his life he had valued rationality, reason, temperance, moderation. Now…he barely recognised himself. Losing control with an innocent maid in the woods, almost blurting out a marriage proposal, even now having to restrain himself from seeking her out…

No. There was a better way. He must find himself again. His rationality. His true self, not this crazed madman.

'I must subdue this!' he declared aloud, glancing guiltily around as if he might be heard. With deliberation, he sat in his usual armchair and picked up his book. Normally, Mary and Beatrice would be with him at this time. But the ladies were not long awake and he did not know where Mary might be. He pictured her then, her eyes heavy with desire, and squirmed uncomfortably in his seat. He started reading the same passage again, as he had not taken it in before.

No. Exasperated with himself, he uttered an expletive. This time, his mind had wandered back to a concern for her present well-being. Had she returned safely to the house? Lord, why had he not thought to check with the servants? The library door opened, causing him to lift his head in anticipation.

It was his sister. Resisting the urge to take out his irritation and disappointment on her, he gave a bland greeting.

It was not well-received. Bristling with indignation, she sat opposite him, clearly ready to divulge some Gothic complaint.

'Please be seated, Sister,' he murmured, his tone dripping with sarcasm at her intrusion.

'Sister? *Sister*, is it? Is that what you have to say to me?'

He refused to rise to this provocation. 'Are you not my sister?'

'Indeed I am and as such I believe I have the right to censure you when deserved!'

Now she had his full attention. 'Censure me? For what reason?'

Lord, did someone see us in the woods?

She raised a sceptical eyebrow. 'Do not trifle with me, Nicky. I can give you five years, you know, and I was not born yesterday.'

'Indeed not. Why, you are now almost elderly, I would say.'

'Elderly?' Her chest heaved with outrage. '*Elderly?* How dare you?'

'Apologies. Not elderly, no. Perhaps, older?'

'My age has nothing to do with the case!'

'Why, then, did you bring it up?' He frowned. 'Really, Susan, if this is how you behave with Mr Fenhurst then I can understand why he sends you here for so long each spring.'

Two angry red spots had appeared on her cheeks. 'Mr Fenhurst does not *send* me here. I shall have you know that he is very fond of me and misses me when I am gone.'

'Would that I had such felicity,' he murmured.

'What do you mean by that?' Her tone was sharp. 'Never mind. I shall not allow you to divert me. I mean to speak of Miss Smith, the governess that you hired and whom I never asked for!'

'Miss Smith?' His heart sank. Hoping he was displaying something approaching genuine puzzlement, he asked, 'Why should you speak of her?'

'Because, Brother dear, you and she were seen at the dancing ogling each other and in full view of my impressionable daughters!'

Damnation.

'Ogling?' he said lazily. 'My dear, such an inelegant word. Vulgar, almost.'

'Then you do not deny it?'

He shrugged. 'Miss Smith is an attractive young woman, I will allow. Both Bramber and myself have noted it. We both danced with her last night. Really...' he laughed '...you cannot expect us to not notice an attractive young lady. Besides...' he leaned back in his chair '...what business it is of yours I do not know.'

'It is my business when you waltz with her before any other lady in the district—and she a governess! It is my business when she might influence my innocent daughters with wantonness!'

Thank goodness they had not been seen in the woods. What if he had not stopped? 'My dear sister,' he drawled, 'I believe you may trust me as a gentleman to behave with honour.'

Even as he said it, he was conscious of his own dissimulation.

I have no choice!

He had to protect Miss Smith's reputation by pretending no interest in her. At least Susan was only outraged by the waltz. At least she did not know the rest.

She leaned forwards. 'Ah, but therein lies the problem, Nicky. I know you well enough to see that you are besotted with the chit. I am sure that you will not throw yourself away on a governess, but I want your assurance that you will not do anything to demean the Denny name!'

He eyed her blankly. 'Besotted? No!' Even to himself, it sounded unconvincing.

She shook her head sadly. 'Tell me truly—if I were to say to you that I no longer need her to assist with the children, would you not fight to keep her here?'

Yes! With everything that is in me!

Aloud he replied, 'Of course not. She is a passing fancy, nothing more. I should forget her within a half-hour of her leaving.'

Her eyes narrowed. 'I do hope you are telling me the truth, Nicky.' He remained expressionless.

'Very well. But I beg you, pay her no more attention. It is being noticed— and that is not good for our family reputation.' She hesitated. 'And there is something else.'

Lord, what more?

'Yes?'

'A person called to see Miss Smith today who, according to the London footman, had all the appearance of a Bow Street Runner. Now, we have no way of knowing what he spoke to her about. Equally, we cannot be sure that she can be trusted. My children are my most prized possessions and if I cannot be safe leaving them with her, then…' Her voice tailed off.

Nicholas was frowning. 'Did Miss Smith say why the person had called?'

'She did not. Indeed, she went straight to her room after his departure, and no one has seen her since. She will have to come down for nuncheon shortly, though.'

'I see.' He did not see, not at all. Was Mary in some sort of difficulty? His heart turned over at the thought.

'I shall leave you to consider my words, Brother. I assure you, I did not speak them lightly.'

She departed in a rustle of self-righteousness, leaving him alone with thoughts even more disordered than before. He was angry with his sister and with himself. He should have behaved better. As a gentleman, and as head of the family, he ought to have been more responsible. Now a Bow Street Runner had entered the stage. Thinking back, there had been times when he had noticed a worried furrow on Mary's brow. Each time he had asked her what was vexing her, she had laughed it away, or made some excuse. Now, his instincts told him there might be more to it.

'You are a damned fool, Nicky!' he said aloud. If only he had not kissed her today, not put her away from him, he might have been able to call her here and ask her directly about whatever was troubling her. As it was, he had no doubt that her justifiable anger against him following their encounter in the woods would make that impossible. For now.

Somehow, he needed to make things right between them again. He needed to regain their fragile friendship and protect Mary from his sister's ire. Briefly, he put his head in his hands. This mess was entirely of his own making.

'Damnation!' He recalled his sister's words, her scathing tone. He must not let Mary be hurt by anyone.

A Bow Street Runner! No doubt his sister was just as curious as he about the man's reasons for speaking to Mary today. He glanced at the clock. Nearly time for their late nuncheon. Having intended to stay away, he abruptly changed his mind. Mary would need to be protected from his sister's barbs and pointed questions. Knowing that he himself was in a discomposed frame of mind, he yet understood that he needed to do everything in his power to protect Mary from an instant's distress. He rose, determination commanding the rabble of thoughts and emotions within.

Silence! he told them. *She needs me. All else must wait.*

The gong sounded for nuncheon. To Mary, it had a funereal tone. Not only might she be forced to face Sir Nicholas, but the ladies would no doubt question her on her visitor, and she had no idea what to say. Squaring her shoulders, she set off for the dining room.

Unusually, they were all there before her. As she entered, her gaze swept around them all, noting their various expressions: Mrs Fenhurst with a face like thunder, her daughters curious, Miss Cushing gleeful. No surprises there, then.

Sir Nicholas was seated in his usual chair, being served by a footman. He showed no emotion, displaying a bland affability that pierced Mary's heart. He did not as much as look in her direction.

Motherless herself since childhood, she had heard enough advice from well-meaning matrons to understand that men often became overcome by their body's needs and did not always have any attachment to the lady concerned. That was why, she understood, so many serving maids were sent away to the country to raise fatherless children. It had always seemed unfair to her.

But this is different! she told herself, as she slipped into an empty seat. *We have a meeting of minds, as well as bodies!*

Yet doubt remained. He had put her away from him so decidedly, so finally. 'I am your employer,' he had said. 'We cannot and should not do this again.'

Because, the undeniable conclusion presented itself, *he does not wish to get me with child.*

As a gentleman he was attempting to behave honourably by ending it. Discovering evidence of his sense of honour could not have come in a more distressing manner. He clearly had no thought of marriage—and why should he? Instead he sought only to save her from her own lustful folly.

She was still angry with him, but half-knew that her rage came from hurt. The Bow Street Runner had added to her distress and her mind, hampered by lack of sleep, seemed unable to handle the various conundrums before it.

Cutting a piece of fish on her plate in an attempt to disguise her distress, Mary carefully diverted her thoughts away from her troubles. It would not do to exhibit waterworks at the dining table. So she avoided looking at anyone, desperately trying to present an air of calm unconcern.

The others were chattering away about last night's party. Miss Amabel and Miss Beatrice were discussing with great animation who they had danced with and how many people had been there, and how wonderful it was to dance in real life and not just with each other.

Oh, I know, thought Mary sadly. She felt a hundred years older than them.

'I believe you had a caller earlier, Miss Smith.' It was Miss Cushing, the excited gleam in her eyes not matching her casual air. 'I did not know you had acquaintances in the district.'

Instantly the air in the room seemed to sharpen. To her right, Mary sensed Sir Nicholas stiffen slightly, while the girls glanced at each other and Mrs Fenhurst eyed Mary with a steady malevolence.

'Actually, I now have a number of acquaintances in the area,' replied Mary, with a calm she did not feel.

'Really?' Miss Cushing was now openly disdainful. 'Are they all as well-bred as the man who called this morning?'

Mary opened her mouth to answer, but nothing came out. The viciousness of Miss Cushing's barbed question had entirely pierced her already wounded heart.

'Enough!' Sir Nicholas threw down his cutlery and glared at Miss Cushing. The words seemed to erupt from him. 'I have endured for weeks now your jealousy, your crushing remarks, your attempts to undermine Miss Smith with my sister. It is plain as a pikestaff that she is a hundred times the better governess, but you refuse to be grateful for her efforts, or her assistance. Because of your own fears, you hurt others. If you wish to remain welcome in this house, you will treat Miss Smith with respect!'

There was a stunned silence, as the shock of Sir Nicholas's intervention sank in. Mrs Fenhurst gasped, as did her daughters. Miss Cushing herself, realising the enormity of his rebuke, looked at him, slack-jawed and pale for a moment. Then her face crumpled and the tears began to flow.

'Oh, spare me the Cheltenham tragedy,' Sir Nicholas retorted, pushing back his seat and standing. 'I shall be in my library.' He threw his napkin on to his chair. 'Feel free to keep her to yourselves until she is ready to behave in a more rational manner!'

He stalked out, leaving the door open. Both footmen in the room stared steadily ahead, as if nothing out of the ordinary was occurring.

As soon as he had gone all of the ladies, including Mary, jumped up and went to Miss Cushing, who was in severe distress. Despite her own wretchedness, Mary could not help but feel sorry for her. Between her hysterical hiccoughs and wails, words eventually began to come through. She was so very sorry. She never intended to upset dear Sir Nicholas. She held Miss Smith in the highest esteem. She did not know what had come over her.

Mary sensed the elderly lady's genuine terror. With each second that passed, even as she issued soothing words to poor Miss Cushing, Mary became increasingly—and entirely irrationally— angry with Sir Nicholas.

Once the housekeeper had arrived with hartshorn and the ladies had led Miss Cushing gently to the sofa in the next room, Mary slipped out. Her anger, born of hurt and frustration, and shock, was all-consuming. Marching directly to the library, she flung open the door and stamped inside.

He was at the window, his back to her. On hearing her enter he turned, his expression one of surprise. 'Mary! Miss Smith! What—?'

'How could you? How could you do such a thing to Miss Cushing?'

His mouth fell open in shock. 'I was defending you, Miss Smith, as you may have noticed.'

'I do not require your assistance and I did not ask for it!' She marched up to him, wishing for a moment that he was not quite so much taller than her. 'Miss Cushing is crushed by your unkind

words and is even now lying down and being offered hartshorn. Have you no thought for her?'

'Miss Cushing,' he replied slowly, 'has been
vexing everyone in this household for many
weeks. Including you!'

'And what has that to do with the matter? Yes,
she can be irritating, and illogical, and small-
minded. She should not have said what she did.
But she is *poor*, sir. She has nothing except Mrs
Fenhurst's favour and the hope of remaining useful to her mistress. Can you not see what that must
be like for her?'

She almost saw him withdraw behind a
haughty mask. He was suddenly every inch the
Baronet. Never had she seen him like this. His lip
curled. 'If she truly wishes to remain in service to
my sister, she would do better to behave in a reasonable manner, avoiding pestering everyone with
her empty chatter and her unwelcome opinions.'

Helplessly, knowing she had lost control of her
temper, Mary continued to press him. 'And why
should her opinions be less welcome than those
of any other person? Is she of less value simply
because she is a governess? Are servants not *people*?'

He gave a puzzled shrug. 'I had not taken you
for a revolutionary, Miss Smith. It is the duty of
servants and employees to be of use. That is why

they have employment. Yet fear not, my sister will not abandon Miss Cushion in her later years.'

Mary shook her head, allowing rage at this evidence of arrogance to fuel her hurtful words. 'You simply refuse to understand. The woman's name is Miss *Cushing*, not Cushion. I had thought your misnaming of her a humorous curiosity. Now I see it as a sign of your callous unconcern for her.' She stabbed an angry finger into his chest. 'I see you, Sir Nicholas, and I do not like what I see!'

Now he was truly listening. Pale and grim, he bit out, 'We have had this conversation before, I believe.' He straightened, goading her. 'Tell me more. What is it you see?'

Lost to all sense, she told him. 'I see selfishness. Indolence. Unconcern for the needs of others. Tell me, what is your sister's opinion of me?'

He opened his mouth, then closed it again, seemingly unwilling to voice it.

Mary nodded grimly. 'Let me answer that question myself. She does not like me. She does not like the attention you once gave me. It was *her* enmity driving Miss Cushing's words. Miss Cushing is nothing more than a vessel for your sister's desire to be rid of me. Instead of attacking a defenceless elderly lady, you would have done better to discuss it with your sister.'

Now he looked incensed. 'I did in fact discuss you with my sister not an hour ago!'

Now it was her turn to be taken aback. 'You did? And what was the outcome?'

'I said that if she were to let you go I would forget you within a half-hour!' he revealed angrily. 'Now tell me, Miss Smith, why was a Bow Street Runner in my house this day?'

Mary drew herself up to her full, limited height. 'That,' she declared, 'is my own business and no concern of yours!'

'Anything that occurs within these walls is my business!'

'Then why do you act with such indifference regarding the truly important matters?' Driven by a need to make him see, she continued, 'You are so absorbed by your books, and your own comfort, that you do not see the troubles of those around you. How can anyone think of asking you for assistance when you are so removed from others? Your nieces and nephews crave your attention, but you are too lazy to bother with them, apart from Beatrice. Your sister seeks your good opinion. You could guide her, instead of sneering and making it clear that you barely tolerate anyone except me and Bramber! Well, at this moment I can barely tolerate you, sir!'

Turning on her heel and ignoring the hot tears that spilled down her cheeks, she ran from the library, seeking the refuge of her chamber upstairs. Once inside, she slammed the door with a mighty crash, hoping it could be heard downstairs in the library. 'Insufferable man!'

She raged up and down for what seemed like an hour, noticing him ride out and off through the woods. Flinging curses at his back, she watched him until he was gone, then slid to the floor beside the window, finally giving way to despair.

All was lost. Sir Nicholas did not care for her. She had shown him too much brutal honesty. Mrs Fenhurst wanted her gone. Sir Nicholas would forget her within a half-hour. The Bow Street Runner was determined to see Papa convicted. The magistrate would not help. She had no money, no hope and, soon, she would have no position and nowhere to live.

Never could she remember feeling such despair.

No one came to her, for she had no one who cared.

She cried on the floor, her back leaning against the wall, her mind dwelling on every hurt, every problem she now must bear. After a long, long time, a quiet emptiness came over her. Nothing mattered. All was already lost. There was no point in any of it. And so, when one of the housemaids called her to the salon to see Mrs Fenhurst, she washed her face, then went downstairs with a strange detached feeling of calm.

Vaguely, she half-heard Mrs Fenhurst speak of

Miss Cushing's distress and how difficult it was for her to have another governess in the same household. There was something about the party being over and the remaining engagements all in place. There was her intention to allow the children to have a break from their studies for the remainder of their stay in Norfolk.

'Feel free to take whatever you need in your bandboxes,' she said. 'Once you have a new position we can send your trunks on to you.'

'Of course,' Mary replied neutrally.

What is she saying?

'The stage to London will pass through Fakenham tomorrow afternoon, so one of the grooms can take you there in the morning,' Mrs Fenhurst added, then frowned. 'Are you quite well, Miss Smith?'

'Yes, I am well,' Mary lied. 'Quite, quite well.'

Mrs Fenhurst rose, crossed to the side table and returned with some money. 'It is not as much as you might have earned if you had remained for the entire duration,' she said, 'but it is more than enough for the stage to London.'

Mary took it wordlessly and turned to go.

'Miss Smith!' She turned around. 'I wish you well.'

Mary did not reply.

Chapter Twenty-One

Nicholas could not remember ever feeling so angry, or so hurt. Anger predominated at first. How dared she speak to him in such a way? How *dared* she? Particularly when he had only been trying to assist her.

Why, she knew well how absurd Miss Cushing was! How irritating and limited and petty. It was all very well for the pious Miss Smith to criticise him, but she, too, had enjoyed sharing humorous glances at some of Miss Cushing's absurdities. He rode at full gallop through the riverside meadow, heedless of the cold wind, nursing his just complaints.

Servants were servants. Why on earth was she so angry about Miss Cushing—or any other servant, for that matter? Everyone had their place in society—including servants. Including governesses.

The charge that he did not see to his nieces and nephews—outrageous! Why, together he and

Mary had engaged with Beatrice and worked with her to help with her Greek. Indeed, the younger ones had even had an art lesson in his own library.

On this last point he was forced to concede that his motives had not been the purest on that occasion. Indeed, he admitted with, he thought, admirable honesty that his purpose had been to spend time with Mary, nothing more. The way she had looked at him then! How they had caressed each other only with their eyes, her merest touch as intense as anything he had ever felt. Confusingly, amid the anger, his desire for her remained undimmed.

How she had changed his existence from order to disorder, from calm to storm-like! And to think he had thought it an improvement. Truly, at this moment he did not welcome it. Not one bit. He wished, in fact that she had never—

He interrupted the thought.

Perhaps not.

Remembering the ordered emptiness of his old life, he could not at this moment be sure what exactly he believed.

As the anger began to subside, soothed by self-righteous justifications, the hurt he felt underneath became more apparent. If he had been truly innocent of all the charges Mary had laid before him, he might have been unmanned by her sharp tongue and angry disdain. As it was, even though he knew himself to be not as evil as she had painted him, still it hurt.

He had, he acknowledged, come to depend on her. On her sunny smile and her quick mind and her pert challenges. She was determined to improve him. He had known it since the day she had first spoken plainly with him. Ever since, he had come to read her expressions. He now knew when she approved or disapproved of something he had said or done and, in truth, it was changing him.

Unlike today, when she had quite lost her temper with him, her earlier hints had been more in the way of holding up a mirror so that he might see himself more clearly. And it had been influencing him. These past weeks, he had been surprised to discover within himself something of a conscience.

Where previously he would never have considered the needs of his valet, or Bramber, or the night-footman, he now occasionally inconvenienced himself in order to make their lives a little easier. Telling the night-footman to go to bed if he himself would be staying up late. Undressing early and then dismissing his valet at eleven instead of having the man wait up half the night. Telling Bramber to dance with young ladies at the ball last night.

He gave a wry grimace at the last thought. Bramber had clearly noticed his particular interest in Mary, for they had had a guarded conversation about the matter this morning—Bramber jesting with him about the waltz and how fine Miss Smith had looked. To his relief, there had again been no hint of any particular feeling for Miss Smith from Bramber.

In turn, Sir Nicholas had teased his secretary about his prolonged attendance on Miss Reeve last night, following the waltz. Bramber's ears had become decidedly pink—he had clearly enjoyed Miss Reeve's company a great deal. Sir Nicholas could not help but smile at the memory, his smile fading again as he recalled anew Mary's verbal destruction of his character.

Very well! Turning his horse, he began the journey back home with determination. He would call for her as soon as he had changed his clothes and he would put before her his defence. No doubt she would test him, with her headstrong passion and her sharp words, but this time he would not be knocked sideways. He had the magnanimity to acknowledge the kernel of truth in her assertions, but she would surely acknowledge that she had falsely accused him in return. After that…

After that, who knows?

He still had not had time or space to consider the extraordinary events in the woods this morning, nor his brief thoughts of marriage. Should he really consider marrying a woman who thought ill of him? He shook his head. He could not countenance that she would truly believe him to be so heinous, so irredeemable.

First things first.

Full of indignation, and avoiding with determination some of the more confusing thoughts and feelings agitating within him, he made his way home.

Vaguely, Mary was aware that she was somehow possessed of a wave of vigour. Driven by the fear of further humiliation when it became known in the house that she had been turned off, she stuffed some clothes and her hairbrush into a bandbox. Placing Mrs Fenhurst's money into her reticule, she quickly donned her bonnet, black cloak and kid half-boots. The rest she left behind.

Slipping down the back stairs, she managed to evade detection and soon found herself outside. However, she was not yet safe from interested eyes. Keeping to the gravel path outside the house, she walked the long way around, so as to avoid the salon, where the ladies would be seated, and the library, where Sir Nicholas would probably be if he had returned.

Once at the gate, she took the road to Walsingham. Somewhere inside, there was regret that she would never see Beatrice again, or the younger children, but she pushed it away. At this moment she had no clear purpose, beyond the need to visit Papa one last time.

Thoughts of the stage to London were meaningless. How could she go to London and not be near Papa? Besides, where could she go in the city? Mrs Gray's registry office was lost to her. That lady was known for placing unusual staff and had made it abundantly clear that she was taking a chance by offering Mary this position as governess.

Mary had promised to remain in Stiffkey Hall until Easter. She had failed in her purpose of behaving as a governess ought. She had become romantically engaged with her employer. She had earned the mistrust of the children's mother. She had behaved abominably towards Sir Nicholas, allowing her anger to make her say things that she did not even mean.

She had broken her vow.

As she trudged along the lanes towards Walsingham, despair enveloped her like a giant, heavy shroud. The more she thought about how badly she had behaved, the more numb she became. Her situation was entirely of her own making.

My fault, she recited, as she trudged along the road. *My fault. My own foolish fault.*

Dusk was coming and a cold wind had sprung up. Mary thought about gathering her cloak around her, but did not bother doing so. Her body was not her own. Indeed, she felt strangely distant, as though she were watching herself move along the road.

Finally, she reached Walsingham village. The light was fading and yellow candles were glowing in the windows of the dwellings and alehouses as she passed. Inside, people were no doubt gathered with their families, or settled before a fire in the alehouse, with the company of friends. Gathering herself for one last deed, she rearranged her features into what she hoped was a suitably neutral expression and stepped into the Bridewell.

To her surprise, a different guard sat behind the table in the guardroom. This man was thin, dark-haired and closed-faced.

He looked up. 'Yes?'

'I—I was expecting Mr Gedge.'

'He's been called away.'

'I am in the habit of visiting the prisoners, and reading to them from the B-Bible,' she managed.

'Gedge told me about you, miss. But we have only two prisoners here now,' he said flatly, 'and they are locked up for the night. No more visitors until tomorrow.'

If it were possible, Mary's dead heart turned a shade colder, as dread made itself known. 'Which two?' she managed, her voice tight with fear. 'And where have the others gone?'

'We have a father and son, accused of burglary, awaiting Sir Harold Gurney's session next month.'

His words made no sense. *Where is Papa?*

'As to the other two,' he continued, 'one died of fever yesterday and another was taken from here this very afternoon.'

The room began to spin alarmingly. 'Died?' Her voice sounded small, and very, very far away. 'What was the name of the man who died?'

'Smith, I think.' He frowned. 'No, he is the traitor. It was the poacher what died.'

It was already too late. Blackness overwhelmed Mary and she slumped to the floor.

Sir Nicholas checked his appearance in the cheval mirror. By the time he had arrived home and called his valet, it had been too late to change and call for Miss Smith. Dinner was only a half-hour away, his ride having taken much longer than he had realised.

So he had submitted to his valet's ministrations and now stood in his own chamber in full evening wear, feeling unaccountably nervous. Descending for dinner in his own house had taken on the proportions of a nightmare.

First, his sister. She would be brimful of resentment at his treatment of her favourite earlier. He would be made to pay for his outburst. He sighed. The girls should not have witnessed his temper, either. He hoped Miss Beatrice would not now fear him or, worse, think less of him.

He bowed his head. Miss Smith's words, though hotly spoken, had enough truth in them to shame him. Instead of being a model of gentlemanliness, he had been boorish, inconsiderate and curmudgeonly towards Miss Cushing.

Next, Miss Cushing herself. No more would he pretend to mispronounce her name. Miss Smith, herself a governess, had finally opened his eyes to the insecurity of those who served him, or served the family. Miss Cushing had no independent income. In her advancing years the woman's only possibility of avoiding abject poverty was to remain in his sister's employ. Of course Miss Cushing would do everything in her power to keep her place in the family.

Reflecting now, he realised that his sister knew quite well that Miss Cushing had neither the skills nor the vigour to manage three children and two debutantes.

I must have a quiet word with Susan, he thought. Miss Cushing should be designated 'companion' rather than 'governess' from now on.

That would create an opportunity for his sister to recruit a competent governess. Perhaps—

No. There had already been too much friction. It could not be Miss Smith. Yet, unless she was working for the Fenhursts, he might not have cause to ever see her again once their visit ended. He closed his eyes against the thought. *Never?* Impossible.

Finally, there was Miss Smith herself. Meeting in the salon before dinner was less than ideal. He would have done better to have private speech with her beforehand.

A thought occurred to him. Perhaps she would be first down and he might enjoy a brief moment with her before the others arrived. Instantly he turned and, moving swiftly, went downstairs.

Entering the salon, he saw a solitary lady seated by the fire, but it was not Miss Smith.

'Miss Cushing!' He hurried towards her. 'Please accept my sincere apologies for my abominable behaviour earlier. I had no right to abuse you as I did. My words were not just harsh, they were unpardonable.'

'Oh, sir, it is I who am sorry. I know myself to be a burden and lacking in competence.' Her voice trembled. 'I have told Mrs Fenhurst she should be rid of me.'

His heart turned over at her genuine distress. 'Well, I shall certainly advise her against doing so. Miss Cushing, I must be honest with you. You have in truth outgrown your work as governess...'

She looked stricken, so he hurried on. 'I mean to say that, in my view, you are now a member of the family.'

Tears sprang into her eyes. 'Oh, Sir Nicholas, I am overcome. What a wonderful...' She fished for her handkerchief. 'But I cannot conceive of such a thing...'

'Well, he is quite right, of course, and I should have seen it long before!' It was Mrs Fenhurst, observing from the doorway, Beatrice and Amabel behind her. She glided forwards, her chin at a haughty angle as she addressed Sir Nicholas. 'I have not forgiven you, Brother, for your cruelty today, but I will own that was well said.'

She turned to Miss Cushing. 'My dear Agnes, will you live with us as my companion and friend from now on? For indeed you are part of this family and I see you as if you were our actual cousin.'

Miss Cushing lost all restraint at this point and the ladies bustled around her with handkerchiefs and kisses until she was able to smile through her tears. Unlike earlier, when such a display of emotion had only served to irritate him, on this occasion Sir Nicholas felt himself to be profoundly moved. It was not often that one had the opportunity to witness a transformation in a person's life circumstances.

With his newfound insight into the insecurity of a governess's situation he had to own that doing good things for others could perhaps give one a sense of purpose—understanding that one's own place in the world included a requirement to assist others where possible.

That is why Mary diligently visits the poor.

The thought rocked him. Strange that, in one short day, so many profound insights were coming to him. He seated himself on the nearest sofa, his mind racing as he pieced it all together. Thunderstruck, he now recalled another detail from his earlier conversation. It was Miss Smith's strange assertion that, in essence, a poor governess like Miss Cushing was just as valuable as he, a gentleman.

He had been raised by indulgent parents to understand that someday he would be master of Stiffkey Hall, its lands and properties, and that he, somehow, was more worthy, more important than everyone else in the district. Until today, he had not questioned the matter.

The gong sounded for dinner, interrupting his thoughts. 'But where is Miss Smith?' asked Beatrice, her brow furrowed.

No one could answer, and they all traipsed through to dinner, where they were joined by Bramber. The footmen began serving and still Miss Smith did not appear.

Sir Nicholas, believing he knew the reason for her absence, felt decidedly uncomfortable. He could only be relieved that, when one of the girls repeated her surprise at Miss Smith's nonappearance, his sister replied nonchalantly that she had probably decided to eat in her chamber. That ended the conversation, to his great relief.

A silence followed as they all reflected on the drama enacted at nuncheon and the mortification Miss Smith must have felt. It was perfectly reasonable for Mary to plead a headache and to avoid company this evening.

They might also know, of course, about the scene that followed, when she and I argued long and loudly.

That might have had more to do with the matter than his own rude behaviour at nuncheon.

He intercepted a frown passing between two of the footmen—something he would not have noticed before today, he was sure. The servants saw and heard everything. Strangely, now that he saw the servants as individuals, they had lost something of their invisibility. *They certainly know what took place between me and Miss Smith.* They knew why she was eating alone in her chamber, instead of with the family.

The conclusion was inevitable. *She does not wish to see any of us tonight. She does not wish to see me.*

Pain stabbed through his chest. The food on his plate was suddenly unappetising.

Somehow, he endured the endless chatter of the others, the presentation of dish after dish of well-cooked food that he could not bring himself to eat. It was not right that Mary was not here. Her empty chair troubled him. She should be here.

Chapter Twenty-Two

A revolting stench comprising ale, bad breath and tobacco was the first sensation. Then, a voice. 'Wake up, miss!' This was followed by a series of shocking expletives.

Someone is very cross, Mary deduced, opening her eyes.

'Thank the Lord!' The new guard was leaning over her, his expression now panicked rather than surly. She seemed to be lying on the floor.

The Bridewell. *Papa!*

'Who died?' she managed to ask. 'Tell me again. Which prisoner died?'

The guard had seized her elbow and was even now levering her into a sitting position. The room continued to spin alarmingly.

'Such a fright you gave me! I thought you were fallen down dead. I do not hold with people dying in the guardroom and neither would Sir Harold Gurney!'

She ignored this, gripping his arm. '*Who* died?' she repeated forcefully.

'The poacher!' he replied, equally forcefully. 'Though why it should matter to a prison visitor, I do not know.' He frowned. 'Perhaps—did you know the man?'

'I did not,' she replied truthfully. 'I met him when I began my visits. I am sorry to hear of his death.'

The guard pulled out a chair and helped her up on to it. 'A word of advice, miss. If you faint every time a prisoner dies, you may not have the stomach for this work.' He was eyeing her dubiously. 'Would you like something?' He shifted his weight from one foot to the other, clearly uncertain what he could do for her. 'All I have is ale, but you are welcome to it!' His surliness was gone. Her distress had revealed the good heart he hid beneath the frown.

Everywhere there is goodness, if one can only see it.

'I thank you for your kindness, but I shall be well shortly.' In reality her heart was still pounding furiously and she felt decidedly weak. 'Tell me about the traitor,' she added, as if simply making conversation. As if fainting in a Bridewell was an everyday occurrence. As if she was not experiencing the worst—and longest—day of her life. 'Where has he gone?'

'Ah, well.' The guard's eyes lit up. 'There's a

tale in that. Because it is such a serious charge, the prisoner has been taken to London. He did not even have to wait for Sir Harold Gurney's Quarter-Day Session. An actual Bow Street Runner took the man this very day!'

He obviously expected this to create a dramatic effect. 'You shock me! A Bow Street Runner! Here?' Mr Potter must have come directly from Stiffkey Hall to take possession of his prisoner.

This seemed to satisfy the guard, for he nodded, excitement gleaming in his dark eyes. 'To think we have had such a notorious prisoner here, in Walsingham, miss! He will probably hang,' he added lustily. 'Or be transported.' He touched her arm, sudden concern returning to his expression. 'Miss, are you feeling unwell? Please do not swoon again.'

She had felt herself sway on the hard wooden chair. 'No, no,' she lied, gripping the edges of the seat with both hands. Hanging! Transportation! Somehow, she had thought it would not come to this, that Sir Harold could be made to see reason and let Papa go free before the distant London judges gained control over him.

The guard clearly did not believe her, and insisted she remain where she was until he was certain she had recovered from her fainting fit. He gave her great detail on her father's supposed crimes and on the Bow Street Runner's travel plans. 'The prisoner will be in Newgate by Monday, where he will languish until they see fit to try him.'

Newgate. The very word struck fear into Mary's heart. Newgate, a place so full of disease that very many prisoners failed to survive long enough for a trial. If a prisoner could die of fever in somewhere relatively clean, like this Bridewell, then what chance did poor Papa have in Newgate?

In the end, Mary could linger no longer. Thanking the guard and assuring him she had fully recovered, she took her leave. Exiting the Bridewell, she hefted her bandbox and stepped out into the cold, dark night.

Finally, the seemingly endless dinner was completed and the ladies rose to return to the salon, leaving Sir Nicholas and Bramber to their port. At the last instant Sir Nicholas's sister hesitated, informing the others that she would follow them in a few moments. Pointedly, she waited until the footmen had also departed before speaking. 'I should inform you, Brother, of something that happened earlier.' She was still stiff with him, he noted. At this, Bramber left the room, leaving them to converse.

'I am all ears,' he assured his sister neutrally as the door closed behind his secretary.

'I spoke to Miss Smith this afternoon,' she said, 'and informed her that I intend to release the children from their studies for the remainder of our stay here. I also highlighted that the invitations have all gone out for the remaining soirées.' She took a breath. 'I therefore told her I would have no further need of her services and that she was released from her contract.'

He froze. 'You did *what*?'

She raised an eyebrow. 'My dear Nicky, you made it plain earlier that you would not care if I let her go.'

His fingers were gripping his wine glass so tightly he was in danger of breaking it. 'A theoretical conversation, as well you know. You had no right to speak to one of my employees about such a matter without discussing it with me first.'

She snorted. 'After the way you spoke to Miss Cushing earlier—a woman in *my* employ—you have no right to quibble on such a matter. Besides, why should it matter? You only hired her to assist with my children.'

On this parting sally, she sailed out, head held high. A moment later the footmen, who had plainly been awaiting her exit, re-entered the dining room to continue to clear away the dishes. They were met with a string of expletives so colourful that their normal implacable expressions were severely compromised. They hesitated just inside the room, clearly unsure whether to stay or go.

Sir Nicholas turned to the man on his left. 'James!' he said.

The footman gulped, his eyes widening. 'Yes, sir?'

'Your name is James, is it not?'

'It is, sir.'

'I am glad of it.' Unaccountably pleased that he had remembered the man's name correctly, he asked 'Did Miss Smith eat in her chamber this evening?'

James froze, and the hairs on the back of Sir Nicholas's neck stood to attention. 'You should ask the housekeeper about that, sir,' he offered after a moment, his gaze shifting away.

This is not good.

'Very well. Send her to me instantly.'

The man vanished with alacrity and the other footman departed with some of the dishes. Neither man returned.

Instead, Mrs Kett appeared, her demeanour a mix of concern and defiance. 'You wished to see me, sir?'

Sir Nicholas was rapidly losing patience. 'Where is Miss Smith?'

'Gone, sir!'

'Gone? What do you mean, gone?'

She glared at him. 'She left here this afternoon, with naught but a bandbox, after Mrs Fenhurst turned her off.' Mrs Kett folded her arms. 'And if I may say so, sir, the staff are not happy about it. Miss Smith is well-liked in this house and we do not like to see one of our own treated like this!'

He put his head in his hands briefly, unable to fully take in the enormity of his sister's folly. 'Where did she go?' he croaked.

Mrs Kett shook her head. 'No one knows for sure. One of the grooms seen her going down the drive with a bandbox and she has not returned.'

'But it is dark outside!' he said stupidly. His brain was refusing to function.

Mary!

'Tell my sister I wish to speak with her at her earliest convenience,' he said through gritted teeth.

'Very good, sir!' With a toss of her head, Mrs Kett departed.

Gone? Gone where? Nicholas could not think. Why would Susan have done such a thing? It was bad enough that his sister had dismissed Mary, knowing full well the governess's contract was with him, not her. But to turn her off immediately? He could not fathom the cruelty of it.

It could not be true. Perhaps she had sent her somewhere. Perhaps Mary was delivering something, or visiting someone in need. He desperately hoped his sister would have some answers. But why then had she not told him before if she had known that Miss Smith was gone?

'Now what?' His sister had returned and was looking most put out.

'I am informed that Miss Smith has left the house with nothing but a bandbox because you turned her off immediately!'

'Nonsense!'

Relief flooded through him. 'I knew there must be some mistake. Where, then, is she?'

'I have not got the faintest idea. She is none of my concern.'

He eyed her angrily. 'You do not feel any sense of responsibility towards her? None at all?'

His sister looked puzzled. 'Why should I? She is little more than a servant.'

'And you have no responsibility, no feelings of concern for any of your servants?'

She looked at him blankly. 'I have not got the faintest idea what you are talking about, Nicky. Concern for servants? Why?'

In her tone he recalled his parents. They had seen servants as unimportant—little more than a commodity. This was how he and Susan had been raised. He also recognised himself. His former self, at least. The person he had been before Mary.

'Yet today,' he noted, 'you told Miss Cushing she was family, a companion.'

She waved this away. 'Ah, but that is different. Miss Cushing is gently-bred and has been with us so long that she is like family. In truth, I have come to depend on her.'

'But what if you did not depend on her? Is she of less worth?'

She laughed. 'Obviously. Her worth is her usefulness, no more and no less. She has been useful to me for many years, so I owe her a debt. Otherwise, I have no need to feel responsible for her. Lord, Nicky, what has come over you?'

'A severe case of conscience,' he replied unsmilingly. 'Now, what did you say to Miss Smith?'

'I paid her—you will naturally reimburse me—and told her that we would arrange for her to go to Fakenham on the morrow, so that she might take the stage to London. If the foolish girl has walked out tonight, that is none of my doing.'

His jaw tightened. 'How was she?'

'I did not particularly notice.' His sister tilted her head to one side. 'Let me recall… She was strangely quiet, now I come to think of it. Almost as if she did not care.' She shrugged. 'Miss Smith will no doubt write to us once she is settled and we can arrange to send on her trunks. But why should you trouble yourself over this?' Her eyes narrowed. 'Is this to do with your ogling the girl?'

He winced. 'Susan, there are moments when you truly offend me. Now, go, before I say something rash.'

Her eyes widened, but she stepped away.

Nicholas rose and reached for the bell, pacing the floor until a housemaid arrived. 'Tell the groom to saddle my horse,' he ordered, 'and send my valet to my chamber instantly!'

Chapter Twenty-Three

On leaving the Bridewell, Mary had instinctively taken the Fakenham road, as if she were returning to Stiffkey Hall. Yet that home was gone, just as surely as if it had burned to the ground. Even now, Sir Nicholas and the ladies would be seated in the salon after a hearty dinner, enjoying the fire and the comfort of family.

With her headstrong candour, she had removed herself from their circle forever. What she had said to Sir Nicholas had been unforgivable. His sister clearly detested her. Miss Cushing had been distressed by her very presence there. Only the children and, she thought, the staff might miss her a little. Mr Bramber. Mrs Kett. Jarvis, the butler. Cook.

She walked on in the darkness, moving slowly as there was little light tonight. Heavy cloud obscured the moon and the stillness of the night made her feel as though she were the only creature in the world. That sensation then changed abruptly. As she approached the crossroads with the road to Great Snoring, she suddenly heard the jingle and clop of an approaching horse.

Instantly terrified, she dived into a gap in the hedgerow, crouching down and covering herself with her cloak as best she could. Who could be out riding after dark? Holding the hood of her cloak to one side, she peeped out. The traveller had a single lantern to help him find his way and, as the horse trotted closer she recognised the rider. It was Sir Nicholas himself, his features harshly lit from below. As the horse reached the place where she was hiding, it sidled a little and he spoke. 'Easy now. Good lad.'

An instant later and he had passed her. Her eyes followed in desperation as he disappeared into the darkness. He was so dear to her and she had broken what had been between them. It felt as though a hole had cracked open in her chest. A sound, half-wail, half-groan erupted from her and finally she gave way to tears. Crouching in the hedgerow, frozen, alone and lonely, with no solace and no hope, she cried. She had felt it earlier and now the knowledge hit her with renewed force. All was lost.

Nicholas accepted a glass of port from Mr Easton. It was of slightly better quality than the one he had enjoyed a half-hour ago, in another vicarage—the home of Mr Fuller. Miss Lutton, the housekeeper in the Houghton St Giles vicarage had not invited him in beyond the hallway— her employer, Mr Smith, being still away.

All three had reacted with varying degrees of confusion and puzzlement when he had asked after the whereabouts of his governess. Miss Lutton had seemed deeply concerned, while the two vicars had been more bewildered that he would put himself out so for a governess.

'Depend upon it,' Mr Easton was saying now, 'she will have a beau in the district. These young girls,' he almost sneered, 'have no moral substance. They think only of fashion and fornication.'

'Miss Smith,' Nicholas replied coldly, 'is the most virtuous person of my acquaintance. She has no beau and her disappearance is of grave concern to all at Stiffkey Hall.'

I am her beau, he was thinking. *I and no other.*

On leaving home, he had been desperately trying to work out where Miss Smith might have gone. As the daughter of a clergyman herself, it stood to reason that she might have sought refuge in one of the three local vicarages. The only other people she might know in the district were his own tenant farmers, for she often visited them when they were in need. He had called there first, but no, none of them had seen Miss Smith for a few days. He had then called at the vicarages in Houghton, Great Snoring and Walsingham before admitting defeat. He had no ideas left.

Turning for home, he could not rid himself of the desperate hope that she might have returned in his absence.

Bramber, who had been informed of the situation, met him at the doorway, his expression sombre. 'You did not find her?'

'No,' Nicholas replied curtly. It was now almost midnight. 'You should not have waited up.'

Bramber snorted. 'I like her, too, you know!' He sent Nicholas a rueful glance. 'But not, perhaps, in the way that you do.'

Nicholas put a hand to his head, glad there was no one to witness their conversation. 'I have made a mull of it, Bramber. She is gone and I do not know where she may be.'

Bramber put a hand on his arm. 'She will have sought shelter in a farmhouse or barn, perhaps. She cannot have gone far. We shall find her tomorrow for certain.'

Nicholas shook his head. 'It is imperative that we do. I cannot—I am lost without her.'

Bramber nodded, his expression one of concern. 'I know.'

Silence stretched between them. 'Bramber,'

Nicholas said, 'I have not always been kind to you. Know that you are a friend to me, not simply a secretary.'

Bramber nodded tightly, seemingly unable to speak.

It was true, Nicholas knew. Here before him he had had a friend all along. He had simply not recognised it until now. And as for Mary, why had he not seen before how dear to him she was?

'Now, you must rest.' Bramber's voice croaked a little. 'I shall call your valet to come to you. Fear not, we can begin to search again at first light.'

Nicholas eyed him bleakly. 'You are right, of course. I just wish there was something... It is my fault that she has gone and now she is alone out there somewhere...' His voice tailed away. There was nothing more to be done, except wait for daylight.

Chapter Twenty-Four

Was it possible to cry cold tears? Mary was still sobbing what felt like an age later. She had left her hiding place in the hedgerow once she was sure he had truly gone and had trudged slowly down the roads and lanes, despair having taken hold of her. At what must have been near midnight, she passed the gateway to Stiffkey Hall, her feet having taken her there without conscious thought.

As she passed by the gates, the clouds had finally begun to discharge their heavy load. It seemed fitting. Now rivulets of rain rolled relentlessly down her face, mingling with her tears so that it felt as though she was crying a stream, a river, a flood. A dog barked in a lonely farmhouse as she passed and she hurried on, knowing she needed to avoid all contact with people while she was in this state.

After a long, long time, her tears dried. Not because her despair was eased, but because her spirit

was now so crushed, so empty, that it seemed
there were no tears left inside her. The rain continued endlessly, soaking her through to the skin.
Her boots had long since become saturated and
each step she took was accompanied by a painful
squelch as they blistered her frozen feet.

Finally, a hint of thought penetrated her stupor, the fear of being discovered lending her renewed vigour. They might come looking for her,
and she must not be found. At this point she had
quite forgotten who 'they' were and why it was
so vital that she remain hidden, but she knew now
where she must go.

Hopelessly, she turned towards Houghton
St Giles.

The embers were dying, yet still Nicholas remained downstairs. How could he take to his own
bed when he knew not if Mary was safe? Only he
knew how harshly they had spoken to each other,
how cruel his words to her must have been. For
her to be turned off on the same day must have
sent her into despair. *That* was why Susan had
said Mary had acted as if she did not care. It had
to be.

His thoughts returned to their argument. They
had both been angry, each with the other. He
now saw an honesty in their dealings with each
other—honesty that he did not believe he had ever

experienced before. He had hurt Miss Cushing and without good reason. Mary cared enough for him to chastise him for it. Yes, she had expressed herself with great force, but that was undoubtedly due to her passion to improve him.

Listlessly, he poured himself a glass of brandy. It was too late for insight!

She is gone.

Summoning the last of her strength, Mary knocked on the vicarage door. It was well past midnight, the rain had finally stopped, and her body was racked with shivering. When Miss Lutton opened the door, Mary saw that her father's housekeeper was in her nightgown and nightcap, a candle in her hand and a fearful expression on her face.

'I am sorry,' she said, 'for taking you from your bed. I—I need your assistance, for I have nowhere else to go.'

Miss Lutton's eyes grew large. 'Oh, you poor dear. Come inside!' She took Mary's arm and guided her in, exclaiming at Mary's state. 'Have you been outside in the rain all this time? My word, what a calamity!' She fussed and chattered, but before long she had provided Mary with hot tea, helped her out of her wet clothes and lit the fire in Papa's spare bedroom. After what seemed like a long time Mary began to feel its warmth. She still could not speak, her body was still shivering ferociously, but she understood that she yet lived and would sometime—be warm again.

Miss Lutton fussed around her and Mary's soul was soothed a little by the woman's warmth and caring. Somewhere deep in her mind were bad things that must not be looked at. For now, though, her physical discomforts were so great that they were drowning out the anguished voices inside. When Miss Lutton bade her lie down in the bed, she did so obediently. All was lost, and nothing mattered.

Nicholas had never experienced a night so long. When dawn finally broke, he rose from his bed with a sense of relief, having barely slept. Each time oblivion had overcome him, he had awakened with a start, fear coursing through him at the thought of Mary, lost and alone.

In the hazy delirium of half-sleep, her words had haunted him. *'I see you, Sir Nicholas, and I do not like what I see.'*

He clenched his hands into fists and walked to the window, the wooden floor morning-cold under his bare feet. Pulling back the curtains, he scanned the gardens, the trees, the morning sky. The rain had ceased and dawn was sending purplish hope across the horizon. Not even the woodland creatures were astir. Was Mary in those woods somewhere—injured, perhaps?

A lone crow cawed, its tone somehow mocking. *She does not even like me, while I—I—*

He refused to complete the thought. Every accusation she had laid before him had been damning. At the time, full of outrage, he had wanted only to defend himself. Now, regret was his shadow.

He rang for his valet. Quite where he was supposed to begin his search, he simply did not know.

Mary's second dress had been aired before the fire and when Mary donned it the warmth of the soft fabric against her skin felt somehow consoling. In her haste Mary had instinctively packed the darkest and plainest of her gowns—a plain grey wool walking dress that was serviceable and comfortable, with nothing of adornment or beauty about it. A gown for sadness.

It fits my temper, she thought as she went downstairs. *And my future.*

It was, in essence, a half-mourning gown. Half-mourning. Half-alive, half-grieving. Fully broken.

Now the housekeeper was offering breakfast, but Mary felt sick even at the smell of it. Miss Lutton, seeing her response, took it away, biding her to go to the parlour and drink the tisane she had made. Mary did so, and brushed and pinned up her hair at the same time. Such small measures gave her an illusory sense of ordinariness, of an everyday habit sustained. A dreamlike quality pervaded the room. Papa's books. A warm fire. Hairpins. Nothing of this was real.

A little later, Miss Lutton joined Mary in the parlour, an air of decisiveness about her. 'I shall not pry, miss, but I should tell you that Sir Nicholas Denny was here last night, seeking news of your whereabouts.'

Mary almost dropped her tisane. 'Oh, no! He must not find me!'

Her true alarm must have been apparent, for Miss Lutton's expression turned grim. 'Lord, miss!' She nodded. 'Very well.' She began untying her apron. 'I know your father to be a good, decent man as has been wronged and I trust you are cut from the same cloth. If something has occurred to distress you, I do not need to know what it is. I shall mention to no one that you are here.' Folding her apron, she sat it on Papa's desk. 'I shall have to go out now, as is my habit, to buy provisions for the day. Is there anything in particular you would like to eat?'

'No, nothing. Thank you.' Miss Lutton tutted at this, but said nothing.

After a few minutes Mary heard the back door close, and a moment later she spied Miss Lutton, in cloak and bonnet, leaving through the front gate. The same creaking gate she had come through some hours ago. The same gate Sir Nicholas had come through last night.

Looking for her.

Why? Memories came flooding back. Sir Nicholas's sister had made it plain that she had the power to dismiss Mary. Why, she had even paid her! Sir Nicholas himself had stated that he would forget her once she was gone.

The memory sent pain needling through her. Of course he did. As a governess, despite her efforts with the children, Mary had brought nothing but vexation. She had been an inconvenience. Headstrong. Plain-speaking. Critical of her employer.

I do not like what I see.

Had she really said such a cruel thing? An agony of mortification washed over her. She had called him selfish. Indolent. Had accused him of being unconcerned with other people's needs. Harsh words, spoken in anger. When would she ever learn to bite her tongue?

An innate sense of fairness led her to recognise that she had been entirely unjust. Yes, Sir Nicholas had been used to pleasing only himself. But she had also seen him offer numerous kindnesses to others, including herself. She put her head in her hands. Circumstance had led to Papa's misfortune. Her own was entirely of her own making.

She tried to consider events from Sir Nicholas's

perspective. He had been drawn to her—but then, she had heard many ladies warn that some gentlemen would indulge thcir fancy with any willing maid. Sir Nicholas was clearly driven by the same desires—Mary felt a now-familiar heat go through her at the recollection of their abandoned behaviour in the woods.

Yet he was enough of a gentleman to recognise that she was not a suitable target for dalliance. *I am your employer and you are in my care, and this cannot be right,* he had said. Because he was a gentleman. Because he had a sense of morality and enough self-control to overcome his body's urgings. Tears pricked her eyes.

A true gentleman. *And to think how I abused him!*

She recalled anew how vehemently she had attacked him after his comments to Miss Cushing, how shocked he had looked at the time. She had given him no real opportunity to speak, and besides, he would have needed time to properly hear and understand her cruel words.

He had ensured she was dismissed, yet had come seeking her afterwards. Why?

The conclusion was inescapable. He wished to defend himself. To tell her, in turn, how she had misjudged him. To tell her what he truly thought of her.

Fear and distress coursed through her. It was,

of course, no more than she deserved. Yet she was too much the coward to withstand his displeasure, broken as she was. Justice dictated that Sir Nicholas should have his chance to speak—as Papa surely would in a London courtroom. Weakness on her part meant that she could not give him that opportunity. Not yet, at least.

Fairness meant she ought to. Cowardice meant hiding here until she was stronger.

The gate squeaked, causing her heart to jump. She glanced to the window. Thankfully, it was not Sir Nicholas, but a stocky dark-haired man in breeches and a plain black coat who looked as though he might be a messenger or tradesman. Sure enough, he came to the back door, not the front, and knocked loudly.

Mary bit her lip. What to do? While she did not wish anyone to know she was here, the man might already have seen her. She glanced around distractedly, her eye falling on Miss Lutton's apron. She jumped up and donned the apron as she walked through the house to find where the back door must be. Taking a breath, she opened the door.

His eyes swept over her, noting the plain dress and apron.

I am a housemaid, she thought silently. *Naught but a simple housemaid.*

Thankfully, the man came to the right conclusion. 'Is your master at home?' he demanded.

'No, sir,' replied Mary, with what she hoped was suitable deference. She gave no further information.

He tutted and fished under his coat, withdrawing a sealed parchment. 'When he returns, you may pass him this.'

'Yes, sir. And your name, sir?' It would be normal to take the name of such a person.

'Never mind my name. Just pass on the message.'

Something in his manner was not quite right. Caught up in her own situation, it had taken a moment for Mary to sense it. She glanced down at the letter in her hand. The parchment was of good quality, the penmanship clear. The only writing on the outside were the words *Vicar, near Walsingham, Norfolk*. Instantly her mind ran to a conclusion that seemed impossible.

Desperate to hide from the messenger the thoughts that were now tumbling through her fevered brain, instead she feigned disinterest. 'Very well, sir.'

Vicar, near Walsingham. Vicar, near Walsingham.

Hiding in the hallway until she heard the creaking gate signalling the messenger had truly left, Mary tiptoed back into the study, her heart racing. Sure enough, the man was now mounting a piebald horse that he had tethered outside the vicarage. As she watched, he trotted away, passing Miss Lutton who was now returning, a basket on her arm.

Mary opened the front door. 'Miss Lutton! Come quickly!'

A look of alarm crossed the housekeeper's face. 'What is it, miss?'

'That man, riding away. Have you seen him before?'

The housekeeper set down her basket on the hall tiles and began untying her bonnet as Mary closed the front door. 'Yes, I have. He came with a package for your father—oh, it must be two months ago.' She paused, reflecting. 'It was the day we had snow, for I recall commenting to him about it. That means he came in early January.' She frowned, belatedly working out why Mary was so interested in the man. 'Is this to do with your father and the accusations against him? Could it be he who brought the—' her voice dipped '—the secret papers?'

'I do not know. But we must consider the possibility.' Briefly, Mary detailed her conversation with the man. Was it possible this was the error that had condemned Papa? 'Look at the direction. It is vague in the extreme!'

Miss Lutton studied the package. 'Vicar, near Walsingham... I see what you mean. That could be any one of three men—your father, Mr Easton in Great Snoring, or even Mr Fuller in Walsingham itself, for the vicarage is on the outskirts of the village. If the messenger is not a local man, he may not know of the other vicarages.' She frowned. 'But that would mean that the true traitor is definitely a man of the cloth!'

Mary took her hand. 'I know, Miss Lutton. It seems impossible. And yet, surely we must at least consider it?'

'Of course we must!' She nodded firmly, yet her air of bewilderment persisted. 'But, Miss Smith, what should we do? Is there a man who might assist us in knowing what to do for the best?'

'A man? Why do we need a man?' Fleetingly, Mary thought of Sir Nicholas. If only they had still been friends... Shaking herself, she replied brightly to Miss Lutton, 'We must read it ourselves, of course!' Mary led the way to the parlour. 'The Bow Street Runner told me they had been following the messenger and saw him deliver the first papers here. That was why Papa was taken. I saw no one else outside just now, so perhaps this time he has delivered his letter undetected.'

Miss Lutton looked concerned. 'This entire situation is shocking! And to think we might open

Mr Smith's personal letter!' She nodded firmly. 'Yet we must. You are right, miss.'

Mary laughed nervously. 'If it is simply a sermon or a letter about Dante's masterpiece, we shall know we are being fanciful. I am not in the habit of interfering with my papa's private correspondence, but these are not usual times.'

Selecting a sharp letter opener from Papa's desk, Mary broke the seal, taking care to preserve it as much as possible. She studied the wax imprint carefully. It was of poor quality and not a pattern she recognised. There seemed to be a dog or wolf in the centre, with something indistinct on the left side.

With great care, Mary unfolded the leaves and spread them out on the desk. It seemed to be mostly lists, with titles such as *Cadiz* and *Food Supplies*. Remembering her conversation with Papa in his cell, Mary realised that this was more secret information.

Her heart pounding, she glanced at Miss Lutton. 'This is information from the War Office, I think. Information that Napoleon would pay a great deal for.'

Miss Lutton put a hand to her bosom. 'Lord! Spying! It is true, then!'

Mary was only half-listening. 'Look, instructions for the traitor!' She read aloud the handwritten note she had found on the back of one of the lists. '"My dear Vicar, I hope this finds you well and that you received the first package without mishap. My contact has not yet received the first package and I am assuming that something occurred to prevent you from passing it on the first time..."' Mary looked at Miss Lutton. 'So the spy does not know that Papa has been taken to gaol!'

Returning to the note, she read on.

'"This time I require you to follow different instructions. You will take both packages to Erpingham Gate on Tuesday next, the twenty-sixth, and there leave them hidden, in the alcove below and to the left of Sir Thomas. As originally agreed, once this second package has been transferred you will receive your payment. Not before."' She took a breath. 'There is no signature.'

Her hands, she realised, were trembling. *If I can figure out who the true villain is, I can perhaps even show Papa to be innocent.*

'Well!' Miss Lutton was transfixed. 'Well!' she repeated. 'Such nefarious activities amid Christian men! I was never so shocked.' She blinked, seemingly incapable of comprehending the complexities of the situation. 'I have brought some good meat, miss, for you must eat something!' She bustled off, muttering about spies and wickedness.

Mary watched her go, her mind racing. Why involve the nameless vicar at all—whichever vicar it was? Surely the messenger himself could have been charged with placing the package at—she rechecked the note—Erpingham Gate, wherever that was. A village, perhaps? Or an actual gate?

She sat down by the fire again, trying to understand the reasons, but her mind seemed incapable of operating. It was hardly to be wondered at, she supposed. She had left her bed in Stiffkey Hall yesterday morning, after the ball. She had slept briefly, last night, but it felt as though a month had passed since she had been truly at rest.

First there had been the encounter in the window yesterday morning, where Sir Nicholas had looked at her in such a way...then the meeting in the woods, where she had been lost to all reason. Her memories unfolded like a play. Miss Cushing. Her harsh words to Sir Nicholas. Mrs Fenhurst ending her contract. Papa who might have died of fever. Papa who was on his way to Newgate. Despair. Walking for hours last night in the rain... She had snatched a little sleep in Papa's guest room, yet still her mind was foggy and unclear.

The heat of the fire and the comfort of the armchair was her undoing. Her eyelids fluttered closed.

Nicholas made his way through the woods slowly and carefully, his head continually turning left, then right. What if she was nearby and he failed to see her? A few yards away to his left,

James the footman walked. To his right, Bramber. Two grooms flanked them on either side. This was their third and final pass through, with all of the small wooded area now having been searched. The other two farmers, along with their sons and labourers, were systematically checking every barn within four miles. Jarvis, the butler, was out with one of the farmers, checking all of the local roads in daylight, while the other footman— Seth— waited at the house under strict orders to come immediately to find Sir Nicholas if Miss Smith should arrive or be discovered.

Where are you, Mary?

In daylight, some of his fears seemed fanciful, yet Nicholas could not shake his concern. He, and no one else, knew of all the trials Mary had faced yesterday—including her near-seduction in this very woodland.

I should not have done it, he told himself for the hundredth time. *She, an innocent, gently-bred female, and I, little better than a beast.*

She had been stung by his rejection then and he, also bereft and longing, had been unable to find gentle words to explain why they had had to cease. He recalled the furious pride in her eyes as she had whirled away from him, that absurd gold cloak swirling, and he smiled sadly at the memory.

'What next, sir?' Bramber's question brought

him back to the present. They had reached the edge of the woodland. Ahead was the great empty field leading to the river, to their right the road that led to the house.

'Call me Denny,' he murmured abstractedly. From now on he was determined to afford Bramber all the privileges of friendship, while continuing to pay him well.

All is changed, now.

'We return to the house and hope she is safe.' He gathered the men around him and thanked them for their efforts, before trudging home in silence, Bramber by his side.

Chapter Twenty-Five

Mary awoke with a start, surprised to find herself curled up in an armchair. Then memories flooded back, and with them anxiousness.

What time is it?

Her head lifted to view the clock on the mantel. Three o'clock.

Oh, no! She had slept for hours.

Jumping up, she hurried to find Miss Lutton, her mind racing.

Papa is bound for Newgate, but I have proof that might save him.

Miss Lutton was in the kitchen, stirring a pot of delicious stew. Despite her urgency, Mary's stomach growled with hunger. When had she last eaten? She could not remember. Nuncheon yesterday, perhaps.

'Ah, there you are, miss!' Miss Lutton gave a welcoming smile. 'I brought you some food earlier but thought it best to let you sleep. Now, sit down and have some of my lamb stew. You'll like it, I promise.'

The stew, and the freshly baked bread that accompanied it, turned out to be quite the most delicious food Mary had ever tasted, sitting at a scrubbed wooden table, on a plain chair, in a kitchen. It brought her back to childhood memories, and a cherished feeling of being safe.

Her mind now clear for the first time, Mary thanked Miss Lutton, then, banishing Sir Nicholas from her mind, turned to matters at hand. 'Where does Sir Harold Gurney live, Miss Lutton?'

'The magistrate? He lives about fifteen miles from here, near Dereham.' Miss Lutton frowned. 'Are you thinking to bring the letter to him?'

'I am, in the hope he might take it to London to speak on Papa's behalf. It will be dark soon and fifteen miles is much too far to walk tonight. I shall have to leave at first light tomorrow and walk through the day, which is not ideal. Such a pity he did not live closer.'

'What about…?' Miss Lutton bit her lip. 'I do not wish to know what passed between you and Sir Nicholas, but can you not call on him to assist?'

Mary shook her head. 'Sadly, that is impossible. I am the last person he would wish to aid.'

Miss Lutton thought for a moment. 'In that case…young Arthur!'

'Excuse me?'

'The haberdasher's boy, Arthur. He is about seventeen now, and his da—Mr Todd, that is—sometimes sends him to Fakenham or even as far as Holt to pick up deliveries. He might be willing to take you to Sir Harold, if you pay him.' She flushed. 'I have a little money put by. It is not much, but you are welcome to it, miss.'

Mary placed her hand on Miss Lutton's. 'Thank you, but there is no need. I, too, have some money.'

Though not very much.

'Very well. Can you ask him today?' She halted. 'But, no, he might mention it to someone and they might tell someone from Stiffkey Hall, and then...'

The thought of Sir Nicholas coming here to berate her was too much.

I remain a coward, she admitted.

'I shall tell him that it is I who needs to travel to Dereham. Then when he comes in the morning, you can take my place.'

Another deception. Now Miss Lutton was being poisoned and having to be untruthful—and all because of Mary's own actions. Mary shook her head. 'No, there is no need for you to deceive him. Just say that someone staying with you has need of it.'

If Sir Nicholas comes here, I shall simply have to endure it.

Miss Lutton agreed and set off for the village centre again. Mary, feeling decidedly strange, washed her dishes, shook out her other dress which had dried beside the kitchen fire, then returned to Papa's study.

She spread out the papers again, but could make no more sense of them than she had before. Her mind could not focus and her heart was sore. It was bad enough that she was so worried for Papa, but that aside, leaving Stiffkey Hall in disgrace was surely one of the worst days of her short life.

It was not simply her failure to behave as a governess ought, although the notion stung. It was her restless mind speculating on how the children would speak of her abrupt departure. How Miss Cushing might react. The things Mrs Fenhurst might say about her. Sir Nicholas's sister had a strong need to be right and, since she had been the one to let Mary go, she would undoubtedly be justifying it to anyone who would listen.

Briefly, Mary allowed herself to remember various moments when Sir Nicholas, amused or irritated by his sister's latest vacuous statement, or some nonsense from Miss Cushing, would make an ironic remark that only Mary—and sometimes Bramber—would comprehend. Now and again, when Mrs Fenhurst or Miss Cushing was being particularly absurd, his eyes would meet Mary's and they would share a moment of perfect under-standing. There had been no cruelty in it, despite the accusations she had thrown at him.

Mary closed her eyes hard against the tears that had sprung up. 'Lord,' she said aloud, 'I am becoming a watering pot! How tiresome!'

Her sensible tone cracked as the brokenness within her rose up again. *That would be my heart, I believe.*

The realisation was overwhelming. Her *heart* was affected. Not just her pride. It was too much to consider. Desperately, she pushed the notion away.

Arthur was red-haired, broad-shouldered and tall for seventeen and, he assured Mary, he was well able to handle his father's cart and the plod-ding horse that was currently standing stoically in the dawn light outside the vicarage.

Mary had not met him before and was glad to understand he did not know of her recent con-nection to Stiffkey Hall. It would make the situ-ation less complicated. She had already tucked the secret papers into her reticule and Miss Lut-ton had given her some bread, cheese and sliced meat, all wrapped in a clean muslin cloth, to eat on the way.

Mary had not slept well, despite her exhaus-tion and despite truly appreciating Miss Lutton's welcoming her in without question. When dawn finally appeared, glowing coldly, Mary had been relieved.

Miss Lutton fussed and chattered as Mary climbed up into the cart and gave young Arthur some detailed last-minute instructions about keeping his passenger safe and stopping to shelter should it rain, as she remained unconvinced that Miss Smith would not take a chill.

Arthur bore this with equanimity, seemingly used to adults continually giving him instructions. He requested that Mary call him by his given name since, he said, being addressed as 'young Mr Todd' was not something which he took any pleasure from in life.

They set off, Mary tying her bonnet with deliberation and trying not to show fear as they passed through the village. Thankfully, at this early hour no one was around. Mary had deliberately asked to set off soon after dawn, partly because it would take most of the day to travel to Dereham and back, but also because she knew the servants would be busy in Stiffkey Hall at this time, while the family would still be abed for another couple of hours yet.

Still, there was a tingling along her spine as she constantly worried about any sound that might indicate someone was following them. Thankfully, Arthur had no curiosity about her or her purpose in visiting Sir Harold, having clearly assumed she was related to Miss Lutton. Mary did not challenge this.

It was not until they reached Fakenham that she began to settle a little and think more about her forthcoming conversation with Sir Harold and less about the chance that Sir Nicholas might find her.

And so it was that Mary entirely failed to notice Sally, the Stiffkey Hall scullery maid, who had been given time off yesterday evening to visit her ailing mother in Pudding Norton. Sally was returning to work in her uncle's cart, the two vehicles passing each other at the Hempton Road junction, and it was only afterwards that Sally realised that it had been none other than Miss Smith the governess sitting bold as brass with a man in the middle of the main road from Fakenham to Dereham. She had barely seen the man, but had the impression he was young and well-proportioned.

'Well, I never!' Sally sniffed. 'To think that the whole house was in an uproar, the master thinking something terrible had happened, and all the time she was eloping with a young man!'

Her uncle was gratifyingly interested and they spent the rest of the journey to Stiffkey Hall discussing the matter. It was not long before Sally had formed the opinion that Cook ought to know the truth about the governess. 'Stands to reason,' agreed Sally's uncle. 'If they know she is safe, they can forget about her.' By the time they had reached Stiffkey Hall, Sally had convinced herself of Miss Smith's shocking depravity and a number of embellishments had been unconsciously added to Sally's account.

Oblivious to the scullery maid's recognition of her, Mary continued on her journey. Arthur was a pleasant lad, Mary realised, eager to please and grateful to be earning a small sum for the day's work, for his papa had agreed he could keep the entire amount for himself, rather than handing it in to the household.

'It will be the first time,' Arthur confessed shyly, 'that I shall have earned money of my own.'

Mary, glad of this reminder that she could play a happy role in another person's story, encouraged him to talk about what he might do with the money. She had to stifle a small smile when he revealed he planned to buy a new hat—a dashing dark beaver, in fact, he being deeply unsatisfied with the boyish cap he was forced to wear.

In the midst of sorrow and unease, there are always moments of harmony, if we can but see them.

Mary hugged the thought to herself. Just yesterday morning, in rain-drenched despair, who would have thought that she would now be on her way to see the magistrate, hope concealed within her reticule? Sir Nicholas was lost to her, but Papa could yet be saved. And only she could save him.

The knocking came again, this time more loudly. It reverberated through Nicholas's brandy-aching skull, penetrating the oblivion that he had been seeking as the night ticked slowly by. The sound persisted, forcing him to open his eyes.

'Stop that infernal racket!' he roared, realising as he did so that he was in his library, cold cinders in the grate and an empty bottle by his side. Daylight was slicing through a gap in the curtains, hurting his eyes. His neck ached from sleeping in the chair and—

Mary! Memory flooded through him and, with it, the same sense of loss that had haunted him since her departure.

'I apologise, sir, but I need to speak with you. The matter is urgent.' It was Bramber.

Have they found her?

'Come in!'

The door opened, admitting a nervous-looking Bramber.

'Well, spit it out, then!' All pretence of politesse was gone. Nicholas felt exposed, bloodied, vulnerable.

She is gone and I am nothing.

'Miss Smith has been sighted. Possibly.'

Nicholas sat up straighter, gripping the arms of the chair tightly. 'Is she—?'

Please do not tell me she is dead.

'Sally—the scullery maid—swears she saw Miss Smith today. Less than an hour ago, in fact.'

'What? Where?' He could barely take it in.

'Just south of Fakenham, on the Dereham road. She was travelling in a cart with a young gentleman. They were reportedly being…intimate with one another, which seems unlikely.' Bramber's tone was flat.

Nicholas caught his breath. *She is alive!*

Then the second part of Bramber's information hit him like a punch to the gut.

Intimate.

He closed his eyes, as pain lanced through him, cold and knife-like.

No. Of course it cannot be true.

'A cart, you say? They will be no match for my curricle.' He jumped up. 'Tell the stables to prepare the horses and send my valet to my chamber!'

He strode from the library, barely registering Bramber's 'Yes, sir'.

In the corridor he saw his sister. 'Ah, there you are, Nicky.' She tutted. 'You look a sight! When are you going to start being sensible again? This unseemly focus on a governess is beneath you, you know.'

'Susan,' he bit out, 'remove yourself from my

sight this instant, or I shall be forced to say things that both of us will wish unsaid.'

Her eyes widened. Paling, she stepped aside, her usual serene self-regard briefly shaken. 'I—of course, Brother. I did not mean to cause offence.'

'No,' he agreed, passing her without breaking stride. 'You never do.'

Just beyond East Bilney, the sky began to darken, and the wind to pick up. 'Looks like rain,' Arthur commented and something about the glowering sky made Mary shiver a little.

'Let us continue faster, then,' she replied. The wooden cart seat was decidedly uncomfortable and she wriggled, trying to find a way of easing her discomfort. Suddenly, she felt strangely unsettled, as though some nameless threat was upon her. She resisted drumming her fingers in frustration as Arthur drove a little faster, but yet with care.

He seemed to have sensed her impatience, however, for he glanced sideways at her, muttering, 'My da always makes me drive carefully. Better to be sure than to be sorry is what he says.'

'A wise man,' she commented, while inwardly repeating, *Hurry! Hurry!*

The cart rumbled on, inexorably, following the road to Dereham.

Chapter Twenty-Six

Sir Nicholas Denny, when he was inclined to do so, was known as a man who could have true mastery of his horses. His black-and-red curricle was top-of-the-trees, costing a tidy fortune from Messrs Frame and Barlow at Tattersall's itself. As a young man, he had won numerous races with his friends and it was rumoured he had once flown from London to Brighton in just four hours. More recently, he had had neither the time nor the inclination to race his horses and used his curricle merely for pleasure jaunts around his own neighbourhood.

Today was different. His matched bays pranced and sidled, sensing his mood, and he was happy to let them have their heads once he had passed beyond his own gates. Those who saw him pass watched with awe at his handling of the ribbons, for he could wheel around a corner with tremendous accuracy and skill, and pass a lumbering cart within a hairsbreadth.

The horses ate up the yards with ease, while their master drew upon all his skill, all his dormant power. Nicholas, grim-faced, continued on resolutely, his mind remaining entirely focused on finding his fugitive and her companion.

The village of Beetley was small, with a solid medieval church on the main thoroughfare. It was a pretty place, Mary supposed as they passed through, and yet she barely noticed it. Dereham was now only about three miles away and her apprehension was acute.

The nameless dread that had been following her for the past few miles had now taken over her thoughts entirely. She could not for the life of her understand why she was feeling such fear.

Perhaps it was because so many terrible things had already occurred that her heart refused to believe that she could simply arrive at Sir Harold Gurney's house and he would then instantly agree to free Papa. Or perhaps, having lived for so long with fear and mistrust, she was now frightened even when there was no sensible reason for feeling so. Yet, when she heard the jingle and rumble of an approaching carriage behind them, she instantly became even more uneasy.

She was right to do so. The increase in noise indicated that the approaching carriage was travelling at quite some speed. She turned to look back, but could see nothing, as they had just come around a bend. Another twist in the narrow road was ahead but, sensibly, Arthur was already pulling the cart towards one side of the road. 'Easy now,' he said reassuringly. Mary was unsure if he was speaking to his horse, or to her.

In a thunder of hooves and heavy wheels, the pursuing carriage was suddenly upon them. Mary, twisting, had time only to see that it was being pulled by two greys and was a high-perch phaeton, of the kind she'd used to see regularly in London, before it collided with them, knocking the cart sideways. She felt herself fly through the air towards the hedgerow, understood there was about to be an impact, then the world went black and she knew no more.

Beetley. Nearly there. Nicholas knew that, assuming Miss Smith's destination was the town of Dereham itself, he needed to catch her on this road. Otherwise a frustrating search of Dereham lay ahead.

What if they were travelling on further, to Norwich or beyond? Or perhaps taking the other road from Dereham, if they were bound for Bury St Edmunds, Cambridge, or even London?

It depends, he conceded, on their purpose.

Intimate.

What if she had taken up with some man as her

only option? So, marriage, perhaps? A special licence from a London bishop? Surely Miss Smith would not be so lost to all reason that she would run away with a young man *without* promise of marriage? And how on earth could she have found a man so swiftly?

His hands gripped the ribbons tightly, causing the horses to slow a little. Deliberately, he softened his grip, yet the emotions remained. On the surface, anger and wounded pride. Beneath, only pain.

Why? Why had she done this? Oh, he knew how low she must have felt when she had been turned off that day. He also knew how women who were truly destitute often had very little choice about how best to survive. But had she actually turned to this unknown man? He couldn't imagine so.

He shuddered at the thought of her being voluntarily intimate with the man, shuddered even more at the possibility that she had not submitted willingly. Oh, she might have been compliant of necessity, but every instinct in him was crying out that, whatever the evidence, Mary remained a person of good character.

He recalled her vehement defence of Miss Cushing, herself a vulnerable woman with limited choices…and yet Bramber's account had been clear. Mary had been engaged in intimacies with this man, according to the scullery maid. The thought slew him, as pain greater than any he could ever recall blinded his mind and prevented him from reaching any rational conclusions. Yet his heart remained convinced of her innocence.

Leaving the village, he managed the curricle around a particularly nasty bend, then pulled up as he saw the aftermath of an accident ahead. To his right, a gaudy phaeton lay on its side, an axle clearly broken. A groom was attempting to settle two terrified horses, while a gentleman who looked a little the worse for wear sat on the verge. To his left, a farm cart had been knocked into the ditch, although it looked intact. As his carriage, slowing, approached the cart he realised there was someone there, in the grass by the side of the road. A young red-haired man, and he was gazing down at a lady, holding her in his arms.

Mary! Without clear thought, Nicholas halted the carriage, wrapped up the reins and jumped down. 'What on earth are you—?' He broke off, as it became clear to him that the woman was strangely still. *No!* His heart lurched.

He rushed forward, noting absently that the man with her was extremely young and that he looked terrified.

As well you should be, he thought grimly, trying to tell himself inwardly that Mary was not dead. She could not possibly be dead.

'She ended up in the hedgerow, sir—I've only

just lifted her out. And now she will not awaken.'
The youth's red hair accentuated the paleness of
his complexion as he eyed Nicholas.

This was the man Mary had been intimate
with? Why, he looked barely eighteen!

*Oh, why did you not trust me, Mary? It need
not have come to this.*

He knelt down beside them. The youth was cra-
dling Mary protectively, her head lolling in the
crook of his right arm. The sight was highly offen-
sive to Nicholas, but at this moment he had more
pressing concerns. Leaning down close to Mary,
he felt the faintest of breaths caress his cheek.

She is alive!

There were some small cuts to her cheeks,
but no visible serious wounds. Gently, he ran his
hands along her arms, checking for injuries.

'No broken arm,' he muttered, then, with as
much detachment as he could muster, he checked
her legs through her woollen dress. 'Apologies,
Miss Smith. I am your only doctor in this moment.'

The youth had noted Nicholas's use of Mary's
name. 'Then you know her!'

'I do and I am wondering why she is here with
you.'

The youth looked bewildered. 'You will have
to ask her yourself, sir.'

This was reassuring. If this young man had
been her beau, then surely they were bound for a

specific destination, agreed between the two of them. Why would the youth not say so?

He went to question the young man again, but just then, Mary stirred. One hand moved towards her face and then her eyelids fluttered open. Nicholas could not help it. He put himself directly in her line of vision, determined to ensure that her first sight would not be the youth's face, but his.

'Which prisoner died? Who was it?' she murmured sleepily. Her eyes then focused on his. 'You are not the prison guard,' she announced firmly. 'You are Sir Nicholas.'

Prison guard? What on earth was she talking about?

She is raving. She must have hurt her head.

'I am,' he confirmed, his voice cracking slightly.

'Last time, it was the guard—and he turned out to be kind.' She glanced around. 'Wait. Where am I? And why are you here?' She espied her companion. 'Arthur!' A dull flush suffused her face and neck. 'Oh!'

'Quite,' replied Nicholas, leaning back as she struggled to sit up. Her face was pale and she swayed a little, even in sitting, but she did not swoon. The youth, having assisted her, now shuffled back from her so that they were no longer touching. It looked as though the lad had only been assisting her while she was unconscious. At least, Nicholas desperately hoped that was the case.

Part of his mind was still functioning. She had called the young man 'Arthur', he noted, yet only once, during that episode in the woods, had she referred to him as anything other than the formal 'Sir Nicholas'.

Because she was your employee, he reminded himself.

She had been his hireling, not his social equal. And he had never given her permission for a more informal form of address. Of course she and her friend would address each other by their given names. A pang went through him as he realised she would never again call him 'Nicky'.

She sat for a moment, looking from one to the other. 'The accident!' She frowned. 'That carriage was travelling dangerously fast!' She wriggled, pressed her stomach and touched her face. 'I appear to be largely uninjured,' she confirmed, 'though my head aches. But—' she eyed Nicholas '—why are you here?'

'I am here,' he replied grimly, 'because there are matters I wish to discuss with you.'

Her gaze shifted sideways. 'I know,' she replied quietly.

His heart sank.

So does that mean it is true? Is this lad her beau? No, I cannot believe it.

'But,' she continued, 'not yet. I must again be cowardly, and delay this reckoning for a little longer. In the meantime I must visit Sir Harold—immediately!'

'Sir Harold?' This was completely unexpected. 'Why on earth would you wish to do that?'

She ignored this. 'Arthur, please may we continue? I *must* speak to Sir Harold today.'

Again, Arthur.

'What is your name, boy?' Nicholas knew he was being arrogant, but the thought of this boy being intimate with Mary was too much to bear.

'Arthur…' He gulped. 'Arthur Todd.'

'Todd?' Sir Nicholas frowned. 'Are you, then, related to Mr Todd of Houghton St Giles? The haberdasher?'

'I am his son, sir.' Nicholas now recognised the lad.

I did not know she was friends with the Todds. Why are they in her confidence, yet I am not?

'So is that where you have been?' He fired the words towards Mary. 'While my entire household was searching for you, you were plotting with the haberdasher's son!' No doubt the boy was enamoured of her. She was, of course, bewitching. But what was her plan? And why was she so intent on visiting Sir Harold? Nothing made sense.

Mary was still frowning. 'Plotting?' Her brows lifted. 'Have you, then, heard about my papa?' She placed a hand on Nicholas's arm. 'I assure you, Sir Nicholas, there is no plot. It has all been a mistake!'

He snorted, too confused and hurt to believe her earnest tone and wide-eyed expression. 'A mistake. Really?' His raised brow and ironic tone indicated what he thought of that. He should have been the one she turned to. Not—not Arthur Todd!

The reference to her papa was confusing. Had her papa washed his hands of her? Where, indeed, was her papa? The situation, he realised, was becoming more confused by the minute. He did not like it. Not one bit.

'I might have known you would not believe me,' she said softly. 'I had suspected it, wondered if I might have trusted you. Now I know I was right to keep my own counsel.'

Arthur had wandered away to assess the rear left cart wheel, which was currently lodged in the ditch. 'It is not damaged, only stuck,' he called to Miss Smith. 'It will take at least a half-hour to get the cart back on the road again,' he offered, 'and I shall need assistance.'

She stood, brushing grass and other debris from her skirts. She was clearly unaware of the numerous twigs in her hair. Nicholas, his dander up, did not enlighten her. His mind was racing, trying to figure out why on earth Miss Smith had taken up with the Todd family so soon after leaving Stiffkey Hall. It did not make sense. None of it made sense.

'Be on your way, sir. We have no need of you.'
Her tone was dismissive and, contrarily, when he
had had every intention of leaving them there, he
now decided on a different course of action.

'Miss Smith,' he said, his tone honeyed, 'I shall
convey you, if you wish it, to Sir Harold Gurney's
residence. Young Todd here may seek the assistance of yon gentleman and his groom—' He indicated the broken-down carriage a few yards away.
'Indeed, they will undoubtedly require assistance
to get to the nearest village for help.'

Mary opened her mouth to respond, then
seemed to think better of it. After a pause, she
looked at him haughtily. 'Much as I desire to give
you a sound trimming, I am a rational being and
I can see that your suggestion has merit. It will
get me there a lot more quickly than if I wait for
Arthur.' She stepped towards her young man. 'Arthur, I think you should assist that gentleman,
even though his dangerous way of driving caused
the accident. He should pay you for your assistance.' She smiled and patted Arthur's arm. 'Who
knows, you may have *two* new hats!'

With this obscure comment, she picked up the
reticule which was lying on the ground, checked
inside it, then walked towards Nicholas's curricle.
'Well, hand me up, then,' she commanded tartly.
'I cannot climb all the way up there by myself!'

Feeling strangely put out, Nicholas walked

across to obey her. Quite how she had turned the tables on him, he was unsure. He was the one who had been castigated, his character blackened by her blistering assessment of him. He was the one who had gone searching after her like a lovesick fool, thinking her dead in the woods, only to find her with the son of the respectable Mr Todd. A youth who yet lived with his parents in the village.

No. Something was not right here. He had no idea where Miss Smith had spent the past two nights, but her approach to young Arthur Todd, despite the pat on the arm, was not at all loverlike. Dismissing the tale by the scullery maid that she had been 'intimate' with her companion, he now had to figure out what was actually happening.

He frowned as he handed her up into the carriage. Why did she have such a pressing need to visit Sir Harold Gurney? As far as he was aware, she had met Sir Harold precisely once, on the night of the musicale. The night they had kissed under the stars. A different pain lanced through him. This time, there was nothing of anger in it. It was made entirely of loss and sadness.

Wordlessly, he climbed up beside her.

Chapter Twenty-Seven

Mary stared straight ahead, hoping Sir Nicholas would not speak to her. Despite her confident charade just now, she still felt crushed inside. After everything she had endured, to now discover that her instincts had been right and that he was not to be trusted, was difficult to accept. Deep inside, she had hoped for some sort of miracle, where she could find again the connection to Sir Nicholas that she had sensed at different points during her time at the Hall.

It was not to be. He, like everyone else, would judge Papa and her and find them both guilty. He had just accused her of plotting. Did he honestly believe she was capable of treason? The thought hurt her immeasurably, but she could not give into weakness right now. Papa still relied on her.

If this was the response of Sir Nicholas who, she had thought, had seen something of her true character, how then could she hope for clemency from Sir Harold, who had already assumed Papa to be guilty?

She clutched her precious reticule close, wondering if he would even be interested in this second secret letter. Was there a form of words that might attract the magistrate's interest? Should she show him the letter first, or tell the story initially? Perhaps it might be better to—

'Do you intend to remain silent throughout this journey, Miss Smith?' Sir Nicholas's tone dripped with mockery. She closed her eyes briefly as she felt his words arrow through her, then gathered herself.

'We might speak of the climate, I suppose,' she offered, with seeming equanimity. 'The weather is strikingly wet for this time of year, is it not?' Her hands shook in her lap. She pressed them tightly together in case he should notice.

His jaw tightened. 'I do not wish to speak of the weather.' He stared grimly ahead and she was conscious of having scored a hit. There was no pleasure in it.

How sad that such a promising friendship had come to this! How sad that he would never know of her true regard for him. Tears started in her eyes and she closed them tightly. They must not fall! She sensed him turn towards her, his arm brushing against her shoulder as he turned. Opening her eyes immediately, she stared directly ahead, refusing to acknowledge him. After a moment, he turned his attention back to the road.

If he heard her sniff a moment later, he did not acknowledge it and, when she fished in the reticule for her handkerchief, he politely ignored it. Heartbreak had reared up inside her, threatening to overwhelm her once more. Having stopped the waterfall of grief that had overcome her that first night away from Stiffkey Hall, she sensed it was now threatening to break through again. Terrifyingly, she recognised that if she broke again, she had no way of knowing if she could find any sense of control.

Desperately, she focused her mind on distractions. Her own nails, digging in to her palms. Her poor sore feet, still blistered from her night of walking. The soothing rumble of the curricle as it travelled along the road. The sight of the horses, as near perfect twins as she had seen. Birds soaring in the huge sky above them. Her breathing steadied a little.

The sun glinted through the clouds, illuminating the landscape beneath, soothing her soul and helping her turn her attention away from her troubles.

There are greater things than my own difficulties.

Determinedly, she ignored the man beside her as best she could, and concentrated only on breathing, not crying and not feeling anything.

Beside her, she heard him sigh. 'Very well, Miss Smith. Please will you tell me why we are visiting Sir Harold Gurney.'

She eyed him warily. Should she tell him?

He will discover the truth soon enough.

Her shoulders slumped. 'My father was arrested.' Her tone was flat. 'He is falsely accused of treason.'

He gaped at her. 'What? *Treason!* When did this happen?'

'Before I came to Norfolk. I have been visiting him in the Bridewell.' She took a breath. 'You have met him, before this happened. He is the Houghton vicar.'

'Reverend Smith!' His voice was tight, his expression shocked.

'Yes. But I assure you he is entirely innocent!' She eyed him warily, hope warring with dread inside her.

Will he believe me?

Nicholas was astounded. Whatever it was he had thought Mary might say, this had not ever crossed his mind. His mind was awhirl. Her father, a traitor? And she had known since before coming to Stiffkey Hall. All this time and she had never said anything?

Instantly he felt a wave of ire at the person or persons who had done this to the gentle scholar he remembered. If Mary's father had been imprisoned wrongly, then everything must be done to ensure he was released.

Wait. A lifetime of caution, of not acting on others' behalf, pulled him back. Instead of allowing his gut to rule him, he should apply logic. Treason was no small matter.

If Mr Smith was guilty—and he must consider the possibility—then Mary was either denying the truth to herself, or she was dishonest. *No.* That he could not believe.

If it had been the case then she, too, might be taken up and imprisoned by Sir Harold. Considering her demeanour as she had spoken just now, he did not believe this possibility had occurred to her. Or perhaps it had, but she was too brave to show it.

His thoughts were awhirl, and nothing made sense. *Stop.* This was not a conundrum to figure out with his clever mind. This, he realised, was a moment to look into his heart.

So, sitting there in his curricle, his heart thumping and his mind in turmoil, finally he asked himself the core question. *Is Mary false, or true?*

Instantly he was overwhelmed by memories, swirling around in a whirlpool of emotion. Mary working hard to help young David overcome his suspicion of maths, encouraging Beatrice to believe in her own capabilities, taking the younger ones outside to run and play. Mary deceiving the children's mother about those very same 'lessons'.

Mary, who visited prisoners, perhaps not because she was a good person, but because her own father was among them. A man who might well be a traitor. Mary, who also visited the poor, tended the sick and criticised him for not doing more.

Mary, who had been accused of being 'intimate' with the young man in the cart. Who had patted Arthur's arm as though he were one of her young charges.

Mary, who had been shockingly intimate with himself in the woods, causing him to reconsider the very course of his life.

A sudden thought occurred to him. If she *were* truthful, and her father was indeed the respected and innocent Mr Smith, then he might marry her without objections even from his sister! Not that he would ever allow Susan to determine such an important choice. It was only...

His heart bouncing in his chest at the thought that complete happiness was a possible outcome, Nicholas forced himself to consider again Mary's known deceptions.

His voice catching a little, he spoke directly to her. 'You did not mention anything of this before. For weeks you have been living in Stiffkey Hall, visiting your father and not being fully open with anyone about your true purpose in taking up employment in my household.'

Her shoulders sagged. 'I know. I did not

know if anyone could be trusted. If you could be trusted.' Her face was pale, her hands trembling.

She had allowed their friendship to develop, yet not once had she entrusted him with the truth about her father. That stung and suggested again that deception came easily to her. And yet...he recalled sensing at times she was troubled, yet she would not speak.

How could she?

His heart lurched as he recalled her words to him earlier. 'I wondered if I might have trusted you,' she had said. 'Now I know I was right to keep my own counsel.'

From her perspective, that was entirely justified, he owned. Until now, he had spent his life as a scholar, not engaging viscerally with his companions and the wider world, unaware of whatever troubles they might have. Mary had challenged him to become a better person. Here, then, was his greatest test.

His decision was made. He brought the curricle to a stop.

Mary held her breath as he halted the carriage. Once he had tied up the reins, he turned to her. Strangely, she had a sense that time was holding still, that this moment would define everything that was to come.

'Mary,' he said and his use of her given name

made her heartbeat skip, 'I have no way of knowing whether your father is or is not a traitor, but I do know *you*.' He gazed intently at her. 'I believe you.' His words were uttered with fierce intensity. 'And I will help you in whatever way I can.'

Relief rushed through her. Her throat was tight, but she managed to force the words out. 'That is possibly the most beautiful thing anyone has ever said to me!' Overwhelmed, she reached for him, enveloping him in a tight hug.

Seemingly surprised, it took him a moment to respond, but when he did, and his arms came around her, Mary had the strongest sense of safety that she had felt since the nightmare had begun. They clung to each other, not speaking, as the world waited and even the wind held its breath.

After what seemed like forever, they separated enough to smile slowly at each other. Neither of them moved for a kiss, as this was not the right moment to indulge in the passion between them. That could wait. Instead they smiled and kept their hands entangled, as they discussed the enormity of the challenge before them.

'Sir Harold is notoriously judgmental,' Nicholas offered, his brow creased.

'That was my impression, too.' She shook her head. 'Actually, it remains vital that I see him as soon as possible. I have some evidence which I believe will help poor Papa.'

He grinned. 'Let us go then!' He untied the reins, and clicked his tongue. Once the curricle was underway, he sent her a sideways glance. 'Fear not, Mary. I stand with you.'

The glow this sent through her gave her cause to hope that maybe, just maybe, she could persuade Sir Harold. Taking her hand, Nicholas tucked it into the crook of his arm, and there it rested until the curricle turned into a gateway and up a private drive. 'Sir Harold's residence,' he murmured, 'as requested, Miss Smith.' He slowed the horses, then came to a stop outside the front door.

The house was large and impressive, with a portico in the classical style and wings either side of the main building. It had all of Sir Harold's glowering bluster, without the elegant homeliness of Stiffkey Hall. The comparison sent a pang through her. Would she ever see Stiffkey Hall again? So much now depended on Sir Harold.

Mary waited for Sir Nicholas to hand her down, part of her savouring his hand in hers, however briefly.

Landing lightly on the gravel, she managed to avoid visibly wincing as her kid boots rubbed against her torn heels. The door was opening and a groom had arrived to take charge of the horses. Straightening her shoulders, Mary walked forwards, Sir Nicholas by her side.

Chapter Twenty-Eight

Sir Harold was currently dressing for dinner, they were informed. The butler led them upstairs to a pleasant parlour, procured refreshments and offered them both the use of the retiring rooms. Mary could not think of eating or drinking, as her throat was tight with anxiety. Wary of the silence between herself and Sir Nicholas, she asked the housemaid if she could possibly freshen up.

Following the girl to a small retiring room, she was able to use the chamber pot and wash her face and hands. Shockingly, she discovered numerous twigs and bits of leaves on her dress and in her hair, and the housemaid obliged by helping her brush down her clothes and redo her hair.

'There you are, miss,' the girl said with a smile. 'You look beautiful.'

Her kind words helped, although all Mary could see was the scratches on her face and the paleness of her skin. She shrugged. 'At least I do not look as disreputable as I did a few moments ago. There was an accident on the road, you see, and I was flung into a hedge.'

'Lord, miss, how terrible!' The maid's horrified look surprised Mary. By this point she had almost forgotten the accident, more important matters claiming her attention.

'Yes, I suppose it was,' she replied, 'although no one was badly hurt.'

'Thank the Lord for that!'

A knock on the door signalled that the footman had come to fetch Mary back, with the news that Sir Harold was now in the parlour. Mary's heart thudded in her chest as she returned to the parlour.

This is the moment. Do not fail.

'She will tell you herself.' Sir Nicholas was saying as the footman opened the door for Mary. Both men turned to look at her, the brief silence confirming that she had been the topic of their conversation. Drawing upon all her courage, Mary exchanged pleasantries with Sir Harold, then took her seat.

'I am sure you must be wondering why I wished to see you, Sir Harold,' she said, then took a breath, conscious of the intent gaze of both men. 'It is because I have information to share with you as Justice of the Peace.'

Sir Harold frowned. 'Eh? What's that? But you

are only a slip of a girl, and gently-bred at that. How could you possibly have such information?'

Mary's heart sank. *Already he dismisses me, for my age and my sex.*

'I assure you, Sir Harold, that this is important. I have intercepted a letter containing what I believe to be information about our armies on the Peninsula, along with details of stores and artillery. It is, I believe, the second such letter to appear in the county in recent weeks.'

Sir Harold was suddenly all attention. 'Indeed?' His eyes narrowed. 'You told me you have visited the Walsingham prisoners recently. Have you, perhaps, been given this letter by one of them?'

'No!' Mary immediately saw his assumption. 'Indeed, that prisoner—the one who is being held because of the first letter—is, I believe, entirely innocent.'

Sir Harold curled his lip. 'Now then, young lady, you can leave the conclusions to the men who have responsibility for such things. Just tell me the story of how you came by the letter, give it to me and we shall have done.'

'I am perfectly capable of reaching conclusions myself,' she retorted, 'since I have a good brain and an ability to make deductions!'

'Of course, my dear.' Sir Harold smiled soothingly, making Mary's hackles rise further. 'Now, give me the papers and tell me how you came by them.'

'No.' The single word dropped like a stone in a well, the shocking defiance of it clear to all.

There was a silence. Sir Harold's eyebrows rose. Beside him, Sir Nicholas shifted in his chair. Both men were still staring at her intently. Sir Harold looked outraged, while Sir Nicholas's gaze held admiration and pride.

'Not until you listen to me.' Mary's voice trembled a little, but she would not, *could* not allow them to browbeat her into compliance. Here was a moment when her rebellious nature was, for once, helpful. Or so she hoped.

Sir Harold, as if Mary was not even present, turned to Sir Nicholas. 'She gives her opinion very forcefully, this girl.' His words echoed what Mrs Fenhurst had said about her. And Miss Plumpton.

Sir Nicholas, his expression a mask of geniality, kept his eyes on Mary. 'I wish to hear what she has to say. Partly because she does indeed have a good brain.'

Sir Harold lifted his eyes to heaven, then sighed. 'Very well. Get on with it.'

Haltingly, for she knew already that Sir Harold was not truly listening, Mary began by stating that she had been lately residing with Miss Sarah Lutton at the Houghton St Giles vicarage.

Sir Nicholas nodded resignedly at this revelation, and lifted a hand as if to say *Of course! I should have realised!*

She flashed a brief smile in his direction. *We have so much to talk about.*

Putting this distraction aside, she focused on telling her tale. She spoke of the messenger with the piebald horse, who was not a local man, and how the package had been addressed with such vagueness. 'You may not be aware, Sir Harold, that there are *three* vicarages that may be described as being near Walsingham.'

He waved this away, his air of disinterestedness causing Mary's heart to sink further. 'But twice now, these letters have come to the Houghton vicarage,' he said dismissingly. 'That is proof enough for me.'

'Indeed, it is not proof! It is only proof that the messenger does not know the area. Surely justice must be certain that the right man has been accused? It seems preposterous that any vicar could be involved in this, but there are *three* men, not just one, who might be the traitor.' Her hands were clasping and unclasping a fold of her skirt. Desperately, she forced them to lie still. 'Surely it is your task to ensure that an innocent man is not unfairly imprisoned?'

He remained unmoved, so after a moment's pause, she moved on to her next point. 'I am not sure why, but this vicar—whichever of the three—is asked to pass the papers on to someone else. Why would the source not send his messenger directly to that person?'

Sir Harold patted her hand. 'My dear, you do not understand how these villains think. They do not trust even each other and so each man is only a connection to the next, with no way of tracing back to the original traitor. They use cheap generic seals, disguise their handwriting as best they can and use hired messengers for some links in their evil chain. Messengers like a certain man with a piebald horse, who has been watched these many months. They do not intend to arrest him until the full chain has been revealed. Unfortunately, they moved too quickly to imprison the corrupt vicar.' Mary closed her eyes briefly at this damning description of Papa. 'Still, if there is a new letter, we might use it to discover who was to be next in the chain.'

Ignoring his air of condescension, Mary continued, hoping that his sense of self-satisfaction might be assuaged a little by having an opportunity to instruct her. Carefully, she hinted at her plan. 'There is certainly an opportunity here to sniff out the true traitor, for the papers also include instructions about where they must be delivered.'

'Indeed?' Sir Harold was suddenly more alert. 'And where might that be?'

'The package is to be brought to a place called Erpingham Gate on Tuesday, and left in an alcove "below and to the left of Sir Thomas"—though I do not know where that is, or who this Sir Thomas may be. A grave, perhaps, in a village called Erpingham Gate?'

The two men looked at each other. 'Erpingham Gate!' declared Sir Harold. 'An ideal place to hide some papers and for another to collect them there.'

'It is one of the gates to Norwich Cathedral,' explained Sir Nicholas, his eyes alight. 'At the top is a statue of Sir Thomas Erpingham.'

'Ah,' breathed Mary. 'I should imagine there are crowds there. A person may leave or collect a package without being particularly noticed, I think?'

'Unless,' declared Sir Harold, 'someone is waiting and watching, ready to catch a traitor. We may find the next link in this evil network!'

'To catch *two* traitors, perhaps,' corrected Sir Nicholas. 'The man who collects them and also the man who brings them there.'

Mary squared her shoulders. 'I should also inform you, Sir Harold, that Mr Smith, the man falsely accused, is my father.'

Sir Harold slapped his knee. 'I might have known it! Relatives often go to extraordinary lengths to have villains set free.' He wagged a stern finger at her. 'Young lady, your lies are exposed. We cannot take anything you say with any credibility whatsoever. Oh, I have seen this many, many times.'

'But, no! I have told only the truth!' Mary's voice was shrill, as fear iced through her.

Sir Harold was not listening. He turned to Sir Nicholas. 'So there you have it, my friend. The whole thing is likely a pack of lies. Now we must attempt to deduce if there even was a second letter, or whether this woman has created a false paper to deceive me further!'

Mary looked at him in horror. He thought her an out-and-out liar!

Sir Nicholas maintained an enigmatic expression. 'I believe, Sir Harold,' he said slowly, 'that there is a solution here—a way to establish if Miss Smith is telling the truth.'

Mary looked at him, feeling desperation threatening to overcome her.

What is he planning?

Whatever it was, she would trust him.

Chapter Twenty-Nine

Nicholas thought for a moment. The situation was fraught with danger. Sir Harold had clearly already made his mind up and it would take all of Nicholas's ingenuity to rescue the situation. He decided to take a cautious approach.

'Miss Smith,' he said, regarding her evenly without, he hoped, any sign of his regard for her. 'You suggest that one of the other vicars may be the unknown traitor. It is difficult to imagine that either Mr Fuller or Mr Easton could be capable of such treachery.'

'I know. And yet the possibility exists.' She sat there, wringing her hands together, yet determined to be heard. 'It must be considered, before an innocent man is judged.'

He turned to his host. 'Sir Harold,' he said, 'I have been wrestling with this, trying to discover if there is proof as to whether Miss Smith is truthful or not. Despite my own instincts on the matter, and yours, I have concluded that we cannot at this moment divine it objectively. I therefore suggest we assume for the present that she speaks the truth and we use the information she has to entrap both the person who delivers the papers to the Gate and the person who collects them—if such individuals exist.' His tone was brisk and businesslike. 'In three days we shall know for certain.' He glanced at Mary and his heart lurched at the hope shining in her eyes.

Sir Harold remained unconvinced. 'It goes against everything I know to do this. In all my years as a magistrate I have never yet found an innocent person to be falsely accused, yet many times I have found family members willing to perjure themselves for a prisoner. Why should I follow your plan?'

Sir Nicholas eyed him levelly. It was time to reveal something of his heart. 'You have not had the benefit of an acquaintance with Miss Smith, having met her, I think, only once before. I, on the other hand, have come to a deeper acquaintance with her these past two months. I know her to be essentially honest, although willing to practice timely deceit in a small way and only to aid others. I have also,' he continued, avoiding Mary's eye, 'seen her belittled and slighted by someone whom she later defended, showing more generosity than I myself would be capable of. In short, I believe her to be honest and good-hearted, and shall continue to do so until she is proved otherwise.'

He heard Mary gasp. Unable to help himself, he looked at her and their eyes locked. In that moment, he felt himself to be both entirely lost, yet entirely content.

Mary's heart was soaring. He truly believed her! To have such support was more than she could have ever wanted. Sir Harold, unconvinced and yet unable to make a strong counter-argument, reluctantly agreed to Nicholas's proposal.

Mary passed the papers to Sir Harold and sat silently as the two men read them, then laid their plans. Nicholas would charge Bramber with creating two similar, but false packages, one to be delivered to each of the other local vicars by Fred, his recently-hired London groom. Neither vicar would know the man and it was important they were not alerted to any connection with Nicholas, or Sir Harold.

Nicholas himself would spend Tuesday in Norwich, along with his trusted secretary, awaiting the possible delivery and collection of the papers. He would, he said, ensure that Miss Smith remained at all times within the house and grounds of Stiffkey Hall.

She stiffened at this, anticipating the humiliation of being once again in the company of Mrs Fenhurst and Miss Cushing. Having left, she would find it difficult to turn back. Still, it was no more than she deserved, she supposed. She should have known to trust Nicholas sooner. It was not lost on her that, at a time when he had every reason to take revenge on her, he had instead shown a generosity of spirit unlike anything she had ever known. Her heart swelled with love for him.

She stilled, catching the scent of her own feelings. Love? *Love?*

Well, of course you love him, you stupid girl!

How could she not, when he was the most handsome, the most well-built, the cleverest, and now the most generous young man she had ever known? In truth, she had loved him for weeks. She simply had not seen it until now.

She feasted her eyes on him, uncaring what he and Sir Harold might think. She loved him and he would help free Papa, and she cared not what the future held. Now, this moment, was enough.

The trip back to Stiffkey Hall was strange and beautiful, all at once. They conversed on many topics, including Arthur, who had been hired as Mary's driver for the day, and Miss Lutton, who had looked after Mary in her distress. Both apologised, each to the other, for the angry words they had exchanged after nuncheon the other day.

Nicholas informed Mary that Miss Cushing's security had been agreed and she was happy to hear it.

Reluctant to allow the journey to pass too quickly, Nicholas kept the horses to a walk. After Beetley he took her hand and she allowed hers to rest there. In their guarded speech, they began assembling again those gossamer-thin connections that had been so harshly sundered these past few days. They each disclosed the assumptions they had made about the other and laughed at their own foolishness.

There were yet no kisses, as they warily and carefully rebuilt the foundations of the friendship that had become so essential to both of them. 'If only you had felt able to confide in me!' he said ruefully as they passed through Fakenham.'

'Oh, I wanted to. I knew you to be a man of integrity. Yet too much was at stake. With some more time, I suspect I would have told you the whole. But then Miss Cushing, and your sister, and the Bow Street Runner...everything was upon me at once, and I knew not what to do.'

He squeezed her hand. 'My poor Mary!' he said roughly. 'Never again will you carry such burdens alone. This I promise you.' His gaze pinned hers, and she nodded mutely, before leaning her head against his shoulder. Letting go of her hand, he instead snaked his arm around her.

She cuddled close and closed her eyes, feeling safe. Feeling loved.

Nicholas had politely but firmly declined Sir Harold's invitation for them both to stay for dinner, stating that he preferred to leave for home before darkness fell. Now, as they neared Stiffkey Hall, the evening star, Venus herself, appeared in the western sky as if guiding them home.

Nearly there. For the first time since Nicholas's defence of her, Mary began to feel nervous. As they turned into the drive, he must have sensed it, for he smiled at her, saying, 'Have courage, little one. After all you have been through, my sister is no match for you.'

A lump formed in her throat at his kind words and the warmth behind them. She sent him a misty smile, the remade connection between them a balm to her recent wounds. They both knew that next Tuesday would mark a closing-point, but neither spoke of it.

He handed her down from the curricle, then kept her hands in his for a moment. 'I still stand with you, Mary,' he murmured. 'Now, let us face her together!' He winked, which made her laugh.

And so, Mary was able to respond to Mrs Fenhurst's displeasure and Miss Cushing's disapproval with polite equanimity. She had been, she explained, staying with Miss Lutton in Houghton

St Giles, but Sir Nicholas had persuaded her to return to Stiffkey Hall.

'This time, Sister,' he informed Mrs Fenhurst, 'Miss Smith is our guest rather than my employee. She is free to enjoy her visit and be at her leisure.' He turned and bowed deeply to Mary, the honour in the gesture apparent to all present. 'Your room awaits you, Miss Smith—unless you would prefer a larger chamber in the family wing?'

'Oh, no!' Mary felt herself blush. 'My own room is delightful!'

'Excellent!' he declared, rubbing his hands together. 'Susan, be sure to inform Cook that Miss Smith has returned and I shall expect dinner just as soon as we have both changed.' They left the parlour together, separating at the top of the upper stairs with a joyous shared smile.

Nicholas had sent a groom to Miss Lutton with a message, and had invited her to visit Miss Smith the next morning. She arrived bright and early, bristling with protectiveness. Mary, who had chosen to wear a primrose-yellow muslin, as it matched her mood, greeted her with a sunny smile and a fierce hug.

Miss Lutton naturally wished to hear of everything that had occurred and to check that Miss Smith was content to once again be residing in Stiffkey Hall.

'Oh, yes!' Mary confirmed. 'Indeed, I regret not telling Sir Nicholas the truth sooner as you suggested, for he has been extremely fair.' She explained the plan to Miss Lutton, who declared herself to be 'fair impressed' and hopeful that it would lead to Mr Smith being released at last.

Her words revived that eternal knot in Mary's chest. Not until she saw it done could she believe that all would be well with Papa. After Miss Lutton departed, Mary joined Nicholas and Bramber in the library.

Bramber was already writing the false lists, complete with a slightly amended copy of the covering note—one which suggested that this was the first, not the second package. Neither of the two local vicars had ever, he was sure, seen his handwriting.

During their conversation Mary sensed a change in the connection between Nicholas and his secretary. There was some easiness there that she had not before seen and which allowed Nicholas to tease Bramber about Miss Reeve, whom he happened to have encountered in the village that very day. Bramber took this in a good-natured way, but Mary had no doubt of his particular interest in the shy Miss Reeve.

They will do very well together, I think.

The notes were done and Bramber departed to instruct Fred the groom on the discreet task.

Mary and Nicholas, alone together, grinned like children. Leaning across the table—the very one where the children had worked on their art what seemed like a hundred years ago—Nicholas reached for Mary's hand. She gave it, her body leaping to life as his thumb gently caressed her palm. 'Tuesday,' he said softly.

'Tuesday,' she agreed. It felt like a vow.

Tuesday came, and Nicholas and Bramber set off for Norwich. They took the curricle, Nicholas vowing to return as quickly as he could. As far as the rest of the household was concerned, he was away on matters of business. He raised a hand to Mary in farewell and she, proud and anxious all at once, returned the gesture.

It was quite the longest day of Mary's life. She filled the time playing with the children, reading with Beatrice, and enjoying tea and politeness with Mrs Fenhurst. That lady had still not forgiven Mary for thwarting her attempt to be rid of her, yet, buoyed by Nicholas's evident regard, Mary was well able to weather the occasional barbs.

In the early evening, with the temperature dropping and her impatience rising, Mary donned her cloak and went walking in the woods and along the river. So much had happened since she had had that first, shocking letter from Miss Lutton. That day, her life had changed for ever. Today, regardless, it would change again. A thousand things could go wrong with the trap they had set. The vicar—whichever of the two was the traitor—might not act on the note, thinking better of it. What would that mean for Papa? The papers might not be collected afterwards. This was less important from Papa's standpoint, but Mary did hope that the next villain in the chain would be captured.

Crucially, would Sir Harold agree to have Papa released, based on today's events? Or would he instead declare Mary to have been guilty of perjury?

Mary shuddered. *At least I have Nicholas.*

He had made it clear in these past days that he believed her. Even now, when he was gone from her side, Mary felt—nay, she *knew* that he stood with her. She had to have faith that all would be well.

As she walked briskly back through the darkening woods, her ears pricked up. Was that the sound of a carriage? She broke into a run. Sure enough, it was the curricle.

Breathlessly, she reached the edge of the gardens just as Nicholas brought the curricle to a halt. Throwing the laces to Bramber, he jumped down, running towards Mary. She, too, kept running, their shared haste eating up the yards between them. They collided fiercely, arms immediately enveloping each other in a desperate embrace. He kissed her neck, her ear, her cheek, before searching for her mouth. Neither cared that they could be seen from the house. Neither cared for anything in that moment, except for their desperate need for each other.

The kiss lasted just moments, both knowing they also needed to speak. They leaned back enough to look into each other's eyes, bodies still aligned at the hip, arms still entwined. 'It worked!' he declared with delight. 'We have the traitors and your father is to be freed!'

Abruptly, the strength seemed to disappear from Mary's legs. Her knees felt like water and she sagged in shocked relief. He held her, murmuring reassurances. 'Sir Harold has already sent a message to the Runners to release your father, along with instructions for him to be brought to Sir Harold's own town house. You are invited to travel to London tomorrow, as Sir Harold's guest.' He grinned. 'He sends fulsome apologies for doubting you, my love.'

He called me his love!

In her joy, she was all generosity. 'It was not unreasonable for him to doubt me. I just hope that Papa is yet well, and that he has not succumbed to prison fever. I—thank you for having faith in me.'

He kissed her again, this time gently. 'How could I not, my darling?' He nuzzled her cheek. 'I shall accompany you to London in the morning. I have an urgent desire to meet your papa, for more reasons than one.'

His intentions could not have been clearer. Mary's heart felt as though it were flying, soaring through the sky as if Venus herself could be reached. She swooped on his mouth and lost herself again in his kiss.

Epilogue

Mr Smith, lately recovered from illness, presided over the wedding of his daughter, Mary, and Sir Nicholas Denny, Baronet, in the simple village church of Houghton St Giles. There, before the villagers, farmers, Stiffkey Hall staff and all the local gentry, the bride and groom exchanged their vows, pledging their love and loyalty to each other.

The bride looked delightful in an elegant gown of pale blue silk, adorned with intricate silver flowers, and had a garland of flowers in her hair. Sir Nicholas wore dark breeches, a dazzling white shirt and cravat, and a well-cut black jacket over a richly-embroidered waistcoat. He carried a top hat in one hand and kept a firm hold of his bride's hand with the other.

Miss Lutton, previously the vicar's housekeeper, cried tears of happiness and afterwards she was the first person whom the bride embraced. Miss Lutton's recent betrothal to Mr Smith was now openly discussed in the village. She had, with the bride, lovingly nursed the vicar back to full health following an illness that had struck him down while he had been away from home. The villagers, who had known and admired Miss Lutton for years, firmly approved of both weddings. Mr Smith and his daughter were, it was universally agreed, good, kind and deserving people.

Word had also reached Houghton of the shocking news that Mr Fuller, vicar of Walsingham parish, had been arrested, with rumours that he was accused of treason. Sir Harold Gurney had been honoured by the Prince Regent himself for helping to uncover a network of spies and was basking in the well-deserved praise he was receiving. He congratulated the happy couple most heartily, wishing them a long life, happiness and a brood of fine, healthy children.

As they walked along the herb-strewn path outside the church towards their carriage, the sun broke through the clouds, sending a warm light over the bride and groom. They would complete the short journey to Stiffkey Hall for their wedding breakfast and next week they would leave for an extended honeymoon in the north and Scotland. Sir Nicholas handed his bride up into the carriage before climbing in beside her. They eyed each other, grateful for this first moment to have private speech together since they had kissed goodnight at the vicarage gate the night before.

'Good day, Lady Denny,' he murmured. 'Never have I seen you look so beautiful.'

She felt a glow of happiness radiate through her. 'Good day, Husband,' she returned. 'I must say I had never thought to have such a handsome man place a wedding ring on my finger. Indeed, there was a time when I believed I should never marry.'

He grinned, his eyes caressing her face. 'I love you, my Mary. Have I told you that before?'

'A hundred times in these past weeks, yet I never tire of hearing it,' she replied softly. 'I love you, too, Nicky.'

His eyes darkened, a heated promise in them. 'Tonight, finally, we can be together as we have wished to be.'

'I cannot wait!' She dimpled at him, squeezing his hand tightly.

A cheer from the crowd alerted them to the fact that the carriage was now moving. As they waved to their friends and neighbours, Mary's eye was caught by the sight of young Arthur Todd. He was saluting them with pride, a huge grin on his face, as he lifted a fine new beaver hat.

* * * * *

MILLS & BOON

Coming next month

THE VISCOUNT'S UNCONVENTIONAL LADY
Virginia Heath

'Are you not a fan of art, Lord Eastwood?'

'I am not a fan of disruption or invasion, Miss Brookes.'

Out of the corner of her eye she could see he had folded his arms. It made him look arrogant and ever so slightly intimidating because the stance emphasised both his height and breadth. There was muscle on those bones which suggested he did—or had done—much more than sit behind a desk and waste his life with idle pursuits. It irritated her immensely that she noticed all those things, and worse, wholeheartedly approved of them, and that irritation leaked into her tone.

'Because of your *important* work?'

'England is at war with Napoleon and America simultaneously, Miss Brookes. There is much to do and not enough hours in the day to do it.' It was the longest sentence he had uttered thus far and by his expression he wasn't happy to have strung so many words together solely for her entertainment. Those expressive green eyes were irritated. It was obvious he held her and her work in little esteem.

'I am curious, my lord... How does one fight a war abroad from the comfort of one's armchair in Mayfair? Aren't you a tad withdrawn from the action to be of any *real* use?' She slanted him a glance and was pleased to see her well-aimed barb had made his eyes narrow, while something hot and dangerously human swirled molten within them.

'Armies march on their stomachs and cannot fight without bullets. It is one of my responsibilities to ensure they receive the necessary supplies to do their jobs properly.'

'I suppose that makes you a strategist, Lord Eastwood.'

'It does.' His handsome features rearranged themselves back to severely put upon rather than defensive. 'Two things which require order and quiet, Miss Brookes.'

'Well, unless you have the sudden urge to strategise here in this ballroom, I think you can be assured of both, sir. Is your private study close by?' Because hell would have to freeze over before she ventured near that part of the house.

'Unfortunately, it is just along the hall. We are to be neighbours, Miss Brookes.' Faith stifled a smile. She couldn't help it. He was as stodgy as a treacle pudding and more self-important than any man she had ever met. If it weren't for his eyes, which spoiled his attempts at calm inscrutability completely, she would have assumed him entirely emotionless and stiff. But those eyes were anything but.

They were dangerously compelling.

Continue reading
THE VISCOUNT'S UNCONVENTIONAL LADY
Virginia Heath

Available next month
www.millsandboon.co.uk

COMING SOON!

We really hope you enjoyed reading this book.
If you're looking for more romance, be sure to
head to the shops when new books are
available on

Thursday 21st January

To see which titles are coming soon, please visit
millsandboon.co.uk/nextmonth